THE LUDLOW LADIES' Society

Ann O'Loughlin

BLACK & WHITE PUBLISHING

First published 2017
by Black & White Publishing Ltd
29 Ocean Drive, Edinburgh EH6 6JL

1 3 5 7 9 10 8 6 4 2   17 18 19 20

ISBN: 978 1 78530 127 8

Typeset by Iolaire, Newtonmore
Printed and bound by Nørhaven, Denmark

To John, Roshan and Zia

Acknowledgements

I stitched a memory quilt once. I was just a teenager, and my mother, a dressmaker, to keep me busy, suggested a patchwork quilt using the bits and pieces of fabric she had stored over the years from all the clothes she had made, many of them for me. It soon became a labour of love and over a shared passion for sewing we talked and laughed, making precious memories.

My mother Anne passed away two years ago, just as my first novel was published, but her influence is enduring. She was my greatest champion and she would be especially proud that her sewing and our patchwork quilt were the inspiration behind *The Ludlow Ladies' Society*.

This is my third novel, and one thing I have learned on this writing journey is once you type those magic words The End, it really is just the beginning of a new and exciting phase.

But even before I got to the end, my agent Jenny Brown of Jenny Brown Associates was there with her words of encouragement to get me over the finish line. Thank you Jenny! There beside Jenny was the home team, my wonderful husband, John, and our children, Roshan and Zia. Without their love and unstinting support, it would not be possible to stay on the writing road.

I am also very lucky to have a dynamic team at Black & White Publishing. A huge thank you to my editor, Karyn Millar, word wrangler extraordinaire. Thanks Karyn for your hard work and excellent eye for detail. Thank you to the whole team at B&W,

especially Managing Director Campbell Brown, Publishing Director Alison McBride, Rights Manager Janne Moller, Digital Director Thomas Ross, Daiden O'Regan and Chris Kydd.

Thanks too to Henry Steadman for yet another wonderful cover.

A special thanks to all the readers who have stayed on this writing journey with me. I hope, like *The Ballroom Café* and *The Judge's Wife*, you enjoy the story of the Ludlow Ladies' Society.

To new readers who happen on this book, welcome, and enjoy your time at Ludlow Hall.

Ann

1

Rosdaniel, Co. Wicklow, Spring 2013

His words pounded inside her head.

Understand. Forgive.

Each word throbbing, festering in her brain.

Understand. Forgive.

The air was cool crisp, the town quiet. Briskly, she walked down the main street, her head low, her hands punched into her pockets, her step heavy, matching the monotonous beat of his words.

The dog curled up in the doorway of Bugler's chemist kicked off a slow scratch, all the time his eyes on her back. The owner of Darcy's Delight Café, lifting a delivery box of bread and rolls from the doorstep, nodded, but she did not respond. Stepping inside, he leaned against the glass of the window, observing her as she scurried faster towards the end of the street and the turn-off for Ballyheigue.

She was not sure if she was going the right way, but she kept her pace.

An old lady at the bus stop beside the bridge, a knitted hat pulled low around her ears, a large shopping bag in her hand, eyed the stranger up and down, making Connie accelerate her step.

Understand. Forgive.

Bawling words hammering through her head.

At the bottom of the hill, as she crossed the narrow bridge, she faltered, the strength of her determination ebbing away, leaving a dark cloud of uncertainty pressing down on her heart. Distracted, she plucked a leaf from a dusty buddleia spreading across her path, kneading the damp grey greenness between her fingers, digging into it. Agitated, she let the torn leaf fall over the side, floating to the stream below, caught up in the gurgling water.

She pushed forward, her head sinking in concentration, crossing to the opposite side of the road, where the path disappeared under a froth of grass. The bus for Dublin boomed towards her, forcing her to step into the soft, damp earth on the bank. Hot fumes billowed around her coat as the double-decker charged past. Feeling unsure, she stopped.

A blackbird crashed through the briars, letting out a throaty warning call. On a high tree, a magpie sat studying Connie as she took out her phone, checking the time: 8.30 a.m. The time everything changed ... Her heart raced in recollection, sweat seeped out of her. Every day she felt the gouge of the pain, as raw as when it was first delivered, the intensity of loss strangling her, the frail beauty of an early morning forever tarnished. Slipping her phone into her pocket, she forced herself to push on.

It mattered little she was in a strange place. Home: a comfortable four-letter word for most, yet it was her no-man's-land, where only pain and loss were neighbours.

Loss, once rooted, never dies, pain flares and swells at its own bidding. Letting her head burrow deep into the soft fur collar of her maroon coat, her thoughts swirling, she walked faster, as if somehow she could escape the emptiness which chased her relentlessly, wrenching her back down, smothering her.

At the bend in the road, she weakened again, regretting her decision to leave her car in the town. She could see the gate, paint peeling from it, huge scrapes of rust along the spikes at the top. Both sides of the gate were pulled across, a chunky chain laced between them, a padlock discoloured with rust pinched in near the handle. Household rubbish, neatly tied in plastic bags, was clumped in one corner, as if somebody thought by being neat they were exonerated from littering.

A half attempt had been made to block up the stile in the stone wall with black, dampened boards wedged tight. Yanking fiercely, feeling it give a little, she kicked the bottom of the largest board with her foot, making it surrender. Gripping harder, she managed to free it enough so it slipped out, leaving a narrow gap for her to get through. Squeezing through the stile, she stood on the pillow-moss centre of the long avenue, dithering on the final part of her journey. Her phone rang, making her jump.

"Connie, I was afraid you were dead. Where are you?"

She did not answer.

"Jesus, you haven't gone to that place, have you?"

"I had to, Amy, I have to find out."

"What is there to find out?"

"I don't know."

"I will come over, you can't be there on your own."

Connie, even through her tears, smiled to think of her sister crossing the Atlantic.

"I have to do it on my own, Amy."

"Are you mad?"

"Alone, not alone, what does it matter?"

"Connie?"

"Talk soon."

Pressing the red button before Amy could respond, she paced up the avenue past the disintegrating old wooden posts where there had once been gates, the copse of hazel trees creaking in the light breeze, the bank of rhododendron majestic, pink in bloom, a small red azalea fighting to be seen nearby. Faltering, she stopped to stare at a patch of daffodils, their gentle movement in the breeze a reminder of a more tranquil time.

Understand. Forgive.

A chill snaked inside her, anger swelled up to her heart, a raging loneliness whirled through her. How could she ever understand or forgive?

She walked faster, not noticing the tulips gently bending in the breeze, bunches of ferns flaking water over her shoes, the man walking towards her. He was practically on top of her before she saw him.

"Mrs Carter? I am Roger Greene. Your attorney said to meet you here. My firm has had the estate up for sale for quite some time."

She allowed him to take her hand.

"May I extend sympathy on behalf of myself and all the employees at Hayes and Greene on your loss."

She did not answer.

Finding it awkward, he continued. "I didn't expect you to be walking."

Lightly she pulled her hand from him. "I am taking it off the market." Her voice was husky low, but firm.

The young auctioneer, about to brush fluff from his jacket sleeve, stopped, staring at her. "The market is starting to pick up. Just give it a few months, I will have a very good offer on the table."

"I am not selling Ludlow Hall, Mr Greene."

She made to walk past him; he stepped to the side.

"You could make a pretty penny."

"It is no longer for sale, Mr Greene."

His face reddened and he began to stammer. "Whatever you say." Kicking out at the river of clover and grass in the centre of the driveway, he studied a cloud of insects as they rose up. "You might reconsider. Ludlow is a lot to take on."

"I won't."

"What will you do with it? It has been closed up for years."

"I don't know. Open the windows, let the light in."

"It is going to need more than that. There is a lifetime's work in the old place. The previous owners did their best, but a place like this eats money, with little to show for it."

As she pressed past him, he handed her a bunch of keys.

"The big key is for the front door, but you will have to go in

4

the back. The electricity still works, so that is a start. We will send out a final statement of account."

She took the keys and waved to indicate she had heard him, shooting up the path, anxious to turn the corner. Pushing past the pink rhododendron, she let it slap against her, spewing droplets of water over her shoulders.

The words screeched inside her brain again.

She wanted to shout to the sky, to this house bathed in the watery sunshine of a late spring day, that she would never understand, could never forgive.

Ludlow Hall: forlorn, each window boarded up, the front door hemmed in with damp, dirty plywood. Old geranium pots lining the four front steps spilled over with weeds, a stone seat in front of the house was stained and pocked with moss. She stood, taking it all in. Two storeys over a basement, a worn sadness about the place, as if the house had read and copied her heart. Anger swelled up inside her.

His words hammered louder in her head.

She wanted to bolt after the young auctioneer, throw back the keys and tell him to take the first bid that came in on the place. But she didn't, feeling somehow compelled towards, drawn to a house kept secret from her for so long. Gingerly, she stepped across the gravel, shifting her weight, so that the stones only softly crunched her arrival. Making for the back of the house, she noticed the hoarding on a part of the side bay window had slipped, hanging half off, as if somebody had once tried to break in and squat but thought better of it. Walking to the window, she eased her hands on the sill, pressing her head against the filthy glass to look in.

The dark shapes of thick old-fashioned furniture she could make out in the dim light. Two armchairs either side of the fireplace as if the occupants had only recently left the room and a mug on a small side table reinforced her feeling of calling too late. She saw a book left turned over on its pages, indicative of either a hasty leaving or the intention for an early return.

A tinge of trepidation crept through Connie. She ducked quickly away, lest the ghosts of the past detect her intrusion. Clutching the keys tight, she took long strides, stepping quickly around the back of the house. The cobbled yard was riddled with weeds, her foot skittering more than once. The old stables were shut up, huge cobwebs glinting in the sunshine, an old mop and bucket thrown to one side of the back door, paint peeling off in strips, as if the sun had burned its way through, blistering and curling it up.

Pushing the mop handle out of her way, a cloud of ants spread out in all directions, making her dance from one foot to the other. She was about to turn the key in the lock when a man called out to her.

"Excuse me, miss. This is private property. Can I help you?"

Startled, Connie jumped back.

He spoke again, a little louder this time.

"May I ask what is your business here?"

He walked slowly towards her. She fiddled with the key.

"I might ask you the same. I am the owner of this property."

Her voice was firm, but soft. He stopped to take her in: the faded jeans, the runners bright white because they had only ever walked a city street, her coat fitted and well cut, looking out of place.

"Mrs Carter?" He fumbled with his pocket, not sure what to say. "We were all so sorry to hear of Mr Carter's death." He reached out and took her hand. "I am Michael Conway. I look after the gardens, keep them tidy for Mr Carter."

"I saw the rhododendron on the way in."

"I will have to cut it back after it finishes flowering." He stopped for a moment, concentrating on nudging a dandelion in bloom in the fertile grike between two cobblestones. "I have not known what exactly to do since Mr Carter passed. I just tipped about, waiting to hear." His words spewed out too quickly, as if trying to fill the awkwardness crouching between them.

Jiggling with the key, Connie spoke softly. "I am going to live here."

"You are taking the place on?" His voice boomed, reflecting his surprise.

"I don't see why not, Mr Conway."

Recovering his composure, he placed his hands on the stone back wall of the house. "It will take a bit to get it ready to live in again, but I suppose it could be done."

"I want to stay here tonight."

He was not sure if she was joking, and when he realised she was not, he threw his hands in the air.

"I have nowhere else to stay."

"That place is as cold as Siberia, seeping damp. The hoarding will have to come down for starters. You might want to reconsider your plans."

Her face crumpled, making him soften towards her.

"I could get a few men to take down the boards, but this is an old house. It is no place for a woman on her own, not until you have done a bit to it at least." He rubbed his hands together, and she thought he seemed to like being her only source of information. "There is a small bed and breakfast on the other side of the town. Maybe Mrs Gorman will give you a good rate for a long-staying guest."

She nodded, and he thought he should leave, but he dithered, pushing with his foot a discoloured ice-cream wrapper caught up in the blown dust around the back door.

"Are you by any chance going ahead with the plans for development?"

"What plans?"

"Mr Carter only ever wanted to build on the land."

"You need buckets of money for that. I do not have such resources."

"Very few do, these days." Afraid he had overstepped the mark, he reached out and lightly touched Connie's arm. "Don't go in here now. I can get a few lads over tomorrow to help take down the shuttering. At least then you will be able to see where you are going."

She hesitated.

"It should only take us a couple of hours. Would that do you?"

She nodded and, seeing tiredness sweep across her face, he offered to give her a lift to the guesthouse.

"I might walk around the gardens a bit first, make my way there later."

He left her with directions, and said the hoarding should be down by noon the next day.

Connie watched him as he made his way down the back lane, where he had parked his car. She waited for him to be gone, for the stillness of this place to envelop her. Reaching into her pocket, she felt for the small sticky note, so handled, so fingered, it was no longer gummed along the top.

Touching the contours of the tiny stick-on hearts, two of them, pink, she traced the words "Love You Mommy".

It was the note from the before, her crutch in the after. Tears coursed down her cheeks.

How could she ever understand or forgive?

Squeezing her eyes shut, she wanted to scream, to kick the walls of this great house, to break down the door and tear through the rooms seeking out answers. Ludlow Hall, whether she liked it or not, was both her past and her future.

She had done enough for now. Slowly she turned away from the old house, setting off down the front driveway, letting the rhododendron slap against her and the long straggles of grass thrown over the sides of the avenue deposit sprays of water across her feet.

2

Eve Brannigan got up early to sit by the window and thread her needle. Picking up the red taffeta skirt, she began to stitch the wide hem slowly and deftly, so that none of the thread showed on the outside. The fabric rustled as she shifted it across her lap, making her smile and want to dance across the floor, to show it off more.

It was a plain skirt with a slight gather at the waist and two side pockets. Mary McGuane would hardly do it justice with her thick waist, but such things she knew she could never say out loud. The red colour was too bright for a heavy woman. No doubt Mary McGuane would wear a hideous bling top with it when she attended the rugby club dance. She could have run along the hem with her machine for all her customer would know, but Eve was particular and determined that any garment which passed through her hands was one she could be proud of. Stopping to rethread the needle twice before she got to the end, she got up and stood at the ironing board to press the skirt with a warm iron, ready for collection.

When the doorbell sounded, Eve first checked her hair in the mirror before swinging back to open the front door to Mary McGuane.

"Bang on the button," she said, showing the woman into her front room, away from the sewing machine and the floor riddled with loose threads. She took the taffeta skirt from the back of the armchair. "A beautiful colour. It will suit you just fine. What are you wearing with it?"

"I brought it with me. Would you like to see it?"

Eve nodded, hoping the silly woman might just hold it up to her, but instead Mary McGuane pulled off her hoodie, showing a white bra gone grey, fastened too tight, her skin bulging over the sides. Taking out a sequinned black top, she pulled it on, at the same time stepping into the skirt, leaving on her tracksuit bottoms underneath. She stood back, moving over to the full-length mirror that Eve had asked Michael Conway's son Richie to fix to the wall by the window.

"The belle of the ball, that is what you will be. Such a lovely top and perfect with the skirt."

"I was in Gorey and saw it in that fancy boutique. I took a chance. Wasn't I right?" She swayed around the room, the taffeta whooshing across the carpet. "I was wondering, Mrs Brannigan, is there any fabric left over? Maybe we could make a little rosette to pin to the bodice?"

"I am not sure I would be able to fashion such a fancy thing, Mary."

"Sure, what is it, only curling up the fabric to look nice."

"There might be a bit more to it than that."

Mary McGuane straightened up and Eve worried she might find it hard to get the money out of her if she did not acquiesce to the request.

"Hold on there, I might be able to find a small bit of the red among the scraps."

She padded into the kitchen, cursing Mary McGuane and her fancy ideas. A full metre she had left over. Whoever sold that fabric had seen the dentist's wife coming, telling her she needed five metres for a long skirt. Pulling out the taffeta, she snipped a quarter of a metre in two big, uneven patches so it looked as if she only had scraps left over. She brought them back to the front room.

"These are the biggest pieces I could find. We might be able to twist them into something."

Mary McGuane snatched the taffeta from her. "I was in

Clerys in Dublin yesterday and I saw this lovely rosette." She began to fumble with the fabric. "It looked so simple, why can't I do it?" Scrunching the fabric, she balled it tight. Eve reached across and took it from her.

"First, we will cut out some circles, and maybe if we stitch them together, they will form a flower of sorts."

Mary McGuane impatiently looked at her watch. "Can you do it now? I have to go to Arklow to get my hair done, along with my nails and make-up. I will never get back out here again."

A frustration rose up in Eve, making her want to pelt the fabric at Mary McGuane, but she smiled, leading the other woman to the armchair by the window.

"You take a seat. I will run this up on the machine and then we can try our hands at the rosette."

Mary McGuane made to follow Eve to the little sewing section at the back. "I will keep you company while you work."

Eve guffawed out loud. "You won't, you will only be a distraction. Sit down there and wait for me, like a good girl."

Surprised, Mary McGuane did as she was bid.

Eve made sure to close the door of the front parlour behind her on the way to the sewing room. Neatly, she cut out eight circles from the taffeta. She sewed one all the way around, quickly pressing the machine pedal, making sure to leave enough of a gap to turn the fabric right side out. She did the same with the next group of circles, until she had four completed. Gathering them up and opening the parlour door, she paused as Mary McGuane picked up an ornament on the mantelpiece, turning it upside down to examine it.

"That is a nice piece of china, you have a good eye," she said as she stepped into the room, making Mary McGuane jump back in embarrassment.

"It is so beautiful, I hope you don't mind. Is it from Ludlow Hall?" she asked, her voice shaking a little.

"It is from a different time all right. I will just get this corsage together for you."

11

Sitting in her armchair, she pinched one circle in the middle, taking it in her hand, so it looked like the fragile petals of a flower. She did the same with another circle, tacking them together at the bottom, and continued with the remaining circles until she had formed a full red bloom. Reaching into her sewing box, she picked out a safety pin.

"Just a few stitches and it will be ready."

"Mrs Brannigan, you are a wizard. What would we do without you?"

"I imagine, very well indeed." She ducked the needle around, in and out, securing the clasp of the safety pin, finishing with a double stitch, using her teeth to cut the thread. "That should do it." Walking over to Mary McGuane, she pinned the small corsage to her sparkly top.

"Better than anything I could ever get in Clerys."

Eve could not help but think a lot cheaper too, as she smiled tightly at her customer.

"What do I owe you?" Mary McGuane asked, making a big fuss about not wanting to make a fuss, while taking a scrunch of notes from her purse. "Charge me enough, Mrs Brannigan, you have done me a big favour," she bellowed, as if she had opened up the bank for free withdrawals.

"It is twenty euros for the skirt and a fiver for the corsage."

"Are you sure?"

Eve was tempted to say no, she bloody well was not, but she pretended to tidy away her needle and thread in her sewing basket as Mary McGuane stuffed a few notes behind the clock on the mantelpiece, before quickly changing back into her tracksuit.

As she made for the door, she turned to Eve. "I added a bit extra, because you always are so kind and patient with me, Mrs Brannigan."

"Thank you kindly, but really there was no need," Eve replied, taking a quick glance at the mantelpiece, where a twenty- and a ten-euro note were leaning against the wall.

12

Mary McGuane waved at her husband, who had been waiting for her all this time.

"Bert is the best in the world, I don't know what I would do without him."

She was going to say more, but she realised she had said too much already. In an attempt to hide her embarrassment, she babbled on about the weather before escaping across the road, where the car was already indicating out of its parking place.

Eve waved them gone, relief flooding through her. A silly, shallow woman, Mary McGuane was nevertheless very useful in providing extra fabric, which Eve squirrelled away in nice, neatly cut squares of different sizes for her patchwork. She had won first prize at the Wicklow Agricultural Show last year with a patchwork cushion made entirely from the McGuane fancy fabrics. If Mary McGuane found the cushion to be oddly familiar, she did not say anything outright, but might have hinted at it when she told Eve it was a piece dear to her heart.

Sitting down by the window, Eve reached for her button box. It was sad, she thought, that her life could be summed up in the contents of a rusted biscuit tin. That morning when she had been evicted from Ludlow Hall, her button box under her arm, they stopped her and asked her to open it. The young man doing the bank's dirty business took out a pen, pushing the buttons about. He did not say anything to her, but nodded to the security man to let her pass. She had clipped the cover back on, relieved she had taken Michael Conway's advice and moved her favourite family pieces and jewellery to his house several months before.

Ludlow Hall still held so much, but she had these special bits and pieces that defined all those decades at the Hall. When she moved into this house, on a terrace at the edge of the town and within spitting distance of Ludlow Hall, she was at first afraid to have the flotsam of her former life, silver, china, the odd piece of furniture, around her lest the bank bullies returned. But as the days and months passed, Eve realised the bank had no interest in her little life once it owned Ludlow Hall and its land. Within three months, the property and land were sold to the American Ed Carter for over the amount she owed, but any surplus was swallowed up by the bank's legal fees. These days, she tried not to dwell on those painful details, but she took down the Jacob's Afternoon Tea biscuit tin to sift through the buttons, which told her life story.

Swirling her hand through the box, the buttons caressed her. There were all sorts: sometimes she picked out a plain button clipped off a favourite item when it was well gone past its good wear or, like today, a precious button, a square one, from an outfit never forgotten. She remembered there were three on the red swing jacket she had worn that first night he brought her home to Ludlow Hall.

It was a beautiful suit, red fleck tweed, a longish straight skirt and a swing jacket with a wide collar. She had sewed it herself, not that she told Arnold of course; he was far too snobby for that sort of thing. He did not say he disapproved of the brash square buttons, but pointed out it must be very difficult to open them. "Silly man," she said, but somehow she never wore the suit after that day, feeling it might be too flashy for Mrs Brannigan of Ludlow Hall.

She sat back reflecting on that time, when the world was just the two of them and the Hall. When Arnold had brought her up the drive that first night, she thought she would never see a poor day. She certainly could not have imagined her life as it was now. The avenue was long and winding, and she had to get out twice to open and close the gates, swung across in place to keep the horses from wandering. When they pulled up outside Ludlow Hall, every light in the place was blazing.

"I told the housekeeper, Mrs Kelly, you were to be made welcome," he said, taking her hand, helping her from the car. She straightened her clothes and put her hand up to her hair to fix it, nervous about making the right impression.

Margaret Kelly had coffee and warm scones ready. A fire was

lit in the bedroom, a silk gown draped across a chair beside the bed. They had meant to start their married life staying on in London, but within days of the wedding Arnold was called home to Ludlow to manage the estate. His mother, Martha, would not hear any of Arnold's protests and simply informed him Ludlow Hall was his responsibility now, before leaving, retiring to Bath to live with her sister.

"After your father died, I stayed on here, kept it going. Now that you have decided to marry it is time to pick up the baton," she said firmly.

"I have a life in London; I have to travel to the States every few weeks."

"And you can do all that from Ludlow Hall. Your father was very good at juggling all the facets of his life. Ludlow Hall is your primary responsibility now."

She was on her way the next morning, leaving Arnold in no doubt but she expected him to settle into life in Rosdaniel. Arnold was sullen and quiet for a few days afterwards, refusing to answer even the basic questions which arose in the running of the estate. At one stage he took off to Dublin for three days, but when he came back Eve suggested they throw a party, inviting everybody from the village.

"Why would we do that?" Arnold asked.

"Silly man, they need to know you are running Ludlow Hall; a party is the perfect way to do it."

Two weeks later, when everybody in the locality was invited to Ludlow Hall, she shimmered in a dress she had specially made for the occasion. She did not tell her husband she had sewed it herself, as he would have frowned his disapproval, but she took extra pleasure when he admired the dress, a Vogue special design with a sweetheart neckline. She found the fabric at a drapery shop in Gorey, Margaret Kelly helping her carefully pin the tissue pattern in place before stitching the dress together on an old Singer sewing machine Margaret kept in the scullery. The neckline, highlighted with delicate old lace, she ripped from a favourite dress too old to get a public show. Soft pleats were nipped into a tight waist. Mrs Kelly made a flower in the same fabric for her hair and, after she curled up the sides, she clipped it in place at an angle, so it was the first thing her husband commented on.

"I think, my dear, you have brought a little bit of the city to the countryside," he said and she laughed, winking at Mrs Kelly as she arranged plates of food on the buffet table. A silver cauldron of beef stew was laid out, a small burner underneath at a low heat to keep it warm. Large plates with enough of a dip in the middle to hold in the stew were stocked high, with cloth napkins in a pile to the side. Arnold refused to open up the canteens of silver, so they brought in plain but shining stainless steel forks and knives, as well as small spoons for the dessert of rhubarb crumble and cream. Sherry, whiskey and stout were laid on, with orange squash and minerals for the pioneers.

Eve stood with her husband at the entrance to the huge dining room, greeting guests before they were ushered to the table and quickly moved on to the overspill sitting room beyond.

At one stage, Arnold leaned over and whispered in her ear, "You are the talk of the town, my dear, in the nicest possible way of course."

Arnold was formal and polite to everybody, but when Michael Conway approached he heartily shook his hand, thumping his old friend on the back as well.

"Michael and I understand each other well; he is one of life's true gentlemen. This man knows even more about the Ludlow estate than I do," he told Eve.

Michael Conway, shaking Eve's hand, noticed her looking over his shoulder.

"Arnold may not have said, but I lost my wife a few months back."

She thought his voice trembled.

"I am so sorry."

"An accident, a lorry doing deliveries from Arklow took

the bend at the bottom of the street too tight. Marion had no chance on the bicycle. We are only grateful she did not have little Richard sitting on the back."

Eve gasped.

"I am sorry, it is not the time or the place to talk about such things."

She caught his hand and squeezed it gently.

"Thank you for telling me."

Later, after the whole of Rosdaniel had all eaten their fill and oohed and aahed over the fine furnishings, and everybody had had a word with the new lady of the house, they tripped down the avenue home.

Arnold, glad to have the house back to normal, waltzed her across the sitting room in dance, expertly avoiding the two big armchairs jutting out at the fireplace and the couch which had been pushed back into the bay window for the day. Her skirt flowing, her head thrown back, she thought that with this man she was going to stay very happy.

An anger rose inside Eve. She shook her head fiercely to wipe away the memories. Pushing the button deep into the box, she pressed the lid back on, shoving the tin box onto the small shelf. It would stay there until she was brave enough another time to face the stories it contained.

There was little warmth in the past any more, no comfort in such reminiscences, so she went to her sewing place to scoop up the myriad threads from the floor.

3

Mrs Hetty Gorman twitched the net curtain lightly, to get a better look at her caller. Michael Conway had rung to tell her to expect a visitor, so she had her best room ready: a huge one at the top of the house, with a view over the fields away from the town.

He had also warned her to keep the talk simple. "She won't want to think of the town whispering behind her back; she hardly needs reminding of what happened," he said and Hetty felt slightly offended that he thought she might gossip.

She waited inside the window watching the newcomer, secure in the knowledge her lace nets were thick and of good enough quality that she could not be detected.

The woman stood by the plastic urn of young geraniums at the front and pressed the doorbell. Hetty waited a moment, so it did not appear she was so anxious for the custom. She took the visitor in. Tall, with a nice bone structure, she thought, but too slim. The hunched shoulders, dark circles under her eyes and the grey eating into her auburn hair made up a woman showing older than her years.

Hetty rolled her shoulders three times before pulling the front door back wide. "Good afternoon. Can I help you?"

"I am Connie. Michael Conway said to come by."

"You are looking for a room?"

Connie, slightly put off by the formality, dithered, not sure what to say, before mumbling that she wanted a room for the night.

"Only for the night?" Hetty Gorman looked put out, but she invited her guest upstairs. "I would not normally show a room so early in the day, it is only a few minutes past one, but I know you have come a long way. You are the new owner of Ludlow, aren't you?"

Connie nodded, but did not say anything.

Straightening her skirt with a nervous hand, Hetty stopped at the top landing, pushing the bedroom door open. "You will find it nice and quiet in this house, nobody to ask you your business," she said, immediately regretting her words when she saw a flash of alarm streak across Connie's face. "The sitting room is available every night, except Tuesdays: that is my women's group night. You are welcome to join us if you are at a loose end." Hetty knew she was gassing on, but she was nervous, afraid she would stray into the wrong territory. "The Ludlow Ladies' Society. It sounds fancy, but we love to chat, and we all adore the patchwork. I have to say we are pretty good at it. Our only limitation is the size of this place, otherwise we could go for those huge patchwork quilts ..."

"Ludlow?"

"Yes, Eve of Ludlow Hall started it when she moved to Rosdaniel; it has been going for donkey's years. When Ludlow Hall was sold off, we were out on our ears. It was the start of all our woes: with no proper place to meet, a lot of the women dropped out. These days we depend on the generosity of the remaining members to open their homes for the Society meetings. At this stage, everyone is getting fed up, but we are limping on. Kathryn, our chairwoman, does a nice newsletter-type thing – we can put you on the email list, keep you up to date on what is happening." Hetty giggled. "Kathryn often loses the run of herself. The emails are entertaining, if nothing else."

When Connie did not reply, Hetty led the way downstairs to the front room: small, with a flowery carpet, a cream leather suite taking up most of the space, along with a television.

"Sit down and I will make a cuppa. You are taking the room for tonight anyway." Worried she had said too much, Hetty scurried off to the kitchen.

Connie sat into the couch, listening to her host fussing in the kitchen, the rattle of china cups settling on to saucers, small spoons tinkling into place.

When Hetty came back in with a tray laden down with plates of biscuits and sweet cake, she seemed to have regained her composure. "I assumed you would have tea, but if I have got it wrong, I can easily make some coffee."

"Tea is fine."

Hetty poured, handing a china cup and saucer to her guest. "Do you think you will stay longer than one night?" she asked gently.

"I am hoping to move into Ludlow, and I am not sure how long that will take. Maybe after I get in to see the place tomorrow, I will have a better idea."

"Eve should be able to help you."

"Eve?"

"Mrs Brannigan. Mrs Ludlow as she is called around here. The Brannigans owned Ludlow Hall for generations." Hetty was afraid she had overstepped the mark. To hide her confusion she picked up the teapot and offered a refill.

Shaking her head, Connie set down her cup and saucer. "I must do a few things in town. Thank you for the tea."

Hetty grimaced, reaching into her pocket and taking out a set of keys. "You come and go as you please. Nobody around here is going to be asking you your business."

Connie pushed the keys into her pocket before slipping out into the hall.

Hetty, feeling flustered, poured herself another cup of tea and sat down at her computer to check her email.

Date: March 21, 2013
Subject: THE LUDLOW LADIES' SOCIETY

Ludlow ladies,

What are we going to do? If this great society of ours is to survive, we need to find premises.

We are most grateful to the kindness of Mrs Hetty Gorman, who has given over her cosy sitting room every Tuesday evening for the meetings of the Ludlow Ladies' Society.

Mrs Eve Brannigan has kindly offered her little sitting room for a few weeks after that, but frankly, ladies, unless we can find some more permanent arrangement, we are out on the street. Ladies, we cannot continue like this, depending on the kindness of our members. This year has to be the one when the Ludlow Ladies' Society finds a home to call its own. This is a most urgent matter and I want you all to investigate all possibilities. Surely somebody knows somebody who can offer us a permanent home. We are not asking for much: a big enough room for the ladies of the Society to sit and work, toilet facilities, and a little kitchenette or even a socket where we can plug in a kettle.

I have pestered the Town Committee about the use of the Town Hall again, which we all know is vacant on Tuesday and Wednesday nights. Chairman Jack Davoren is being particularly awkward and won't hear of it. He had the cheek to tell me we were too small to even be considered AND when we open up our group to all sections of the community, especially men, we may be considered. That is his twisted way of saying never!

What nonsense. What sane man would want to spend his evening with a group of women chatting and stitching. Honestly, if we were organising an orgy it would be easier to find some premises in this town.

Ladies, we shall overcome this by working together, so get your thinking caps on.

Kathryn Rodgers,
Chairwoman

★

Connie reversed quickly out of Hetty's driveway, continuing down the road a bit before pulling in to the side.

Was she nuts coming here, crazy to think she could take this place on? Maybe she should let the auctioneer sell off the estate, but then she might never get the answers to the questions constantly swirling across her brain, keeping her awake when everyone else slept. This house had been hers for two years now, but it was only recently she had decided to come here. Whether her decision was good or bad, only time would tell.

She had not even wanted to attend the reading of Ed's will after his death, but the attorney insisted.

"When can I have access to Ed's bank accounts, Charles? He has left me with so many bills."

"There is only one checking account, Connie."

"But there is the savings account."

"There is no savings account."

"Whatever it is called – the account with all the money from the Manhattan apartment sale. Ed set it up after he sold a small apartment his mother left him."

Charles Slowcum looked uncomfortable.

"He had a lot of development deals. He finally closed that account a while back, Connie."

Cold creeped up her back. Her knees were shaking, so she put her hands on her lap and pressed down on them.

"What do you mean?"

Charles Slowcum sighed deeply, as if he was about to explain something to a child.

"The last $2 million financed the purchase of that big property in Ireland."

"What the hell are you talking about?" Her mouth was dry, pain shooting up one side of her body. "He never closed any account."

"He did, Connie."

A ringing whirred in her ears, pain flared across her body, her knees jugged up and down.

"What does this mean, Charles?"

She stopped, the cold realisation freezing the words in her throat. Her heart was pounding, her nails digging into the palms of her hands.

"Is it all gone, Charles?"

He nodded his head, afraid to look her in the eye.

She stared out the window. Across the way, a woman was laughing, waving out an office window to the street below.

"What was he thinking? What did Ed know about Ireland?"

"I presumed you knew all about it, Connie."

"Ed shut me out."

Charles Slowcum threw his hands in the air. "I am sorry, Connie. Ed told me you guys were moving there but keeping it hush-hush until you were ready to tell everyone."

In the park, she could see the playground, the moms with their takeout coffees standing watching their kids, chatting, laughing and sharing gossip.

"At least the house in Ireland is yours and unencumbered."

"Unencumbered: a long and complicated word, just like my life. There are other things, Charles, that weigh down my daily existence."

Charles did not answer, but coughed to hide his embarrassment and continued to read out the will. Numb, she heard only words, the name Ludlow Hall. When he finished, Charles Slowcum sat back, his hands clasped across his ample stomach, his fingers fiddling with one of his shirt buttons.

"It has all been a dreadful business, Connie, but this is your chance to move on. Sell the monstrosity that is the Irish estate, live off the proceeds."

"Ed never said one word, never even hinted ..." She got up and walked to the window. "Down there on the sidewalk, he proposed to me, kneeling down. I thought it was so romantic. How could he do this to me?"

The attorney cleared his throat, waiting for her next question.

"What is this place in Ireland?"

"Ludlow Hall. About fifty kilometres from the capital city."

"Did Ed say why?"

Charles Slowcum abruptly closed the file in front of him and looked at Connie.

"Connie, please take this advice from a friend: you need to move on. The sale of this property could help you do that."

"Move on? Build a new life with what, Charles? He took everything I had, everything I loved, everything I held dear. The only thing left is this place in Ireland."

The attorney fidgeted with the corner of the file. "You have been through enough, Connie, it is time now to let it go. Sometimes we are only left with questions, because there are no answers."

Jumping up, she banged her knee against the desk, making it shake.

"Let it go? Let it go: what does that mean? It has a grip on me; I can never let it go. Now this! I never heard of this damn place until today."

Charles Slowcum drummed the table with his fingers.

"It need not be like this. You can get some money back. Not as much, but something."

Connie slumped back into the chair, her knees shaking. She pressed her hands on them, her bum pushing deeper into the cushion.

"What are you saying?"

"The property in Ireland is already up for sale. I spoke to the realtor over there and he is confident that if you slash the asking price he can get a sale, but I think you will be lucky if you get anything near what Ed paid for it. The country is only limping out of recession; property prices are still at an all-time low."

"Why did he do this?"

"Why any of it, Connie, we will never know. I did not see Ed again after he purchased that property."

"You never said anything to me."

"Why would I say anything? I thought you knew. I thought

in your own good time you would both announce your plans for the future." He stopped talking, realising his explanation sounded naive and stupid.

Pangs of pain blazed across her chest. She wanted to scream, to screech so loud, to wake the dead, so that he knew the pain she was in. Tears engulfed her body. She bent over, not caring that her attorney was sitting patiently, waiting for her to compose herself.

Charles Slowcum got up from his desk. He put his arm around her and she let him hold her, as she sobbed into his jacket lapels. After a few minutes, she pulled away.

"I am sorry, I should not be taking this out on you."

"Connie, there is no need to apologise. Very few have had to endure what you have."

"Have you told me everything, Charles?"

"Hand on heart, I have nothing else to tell."

"Why didn't Ed tell me?"

"I wish I could answer that one, Connie."

"Why didn't he involve me?"

Fisting Charles Slowcum's desk so he abruptly stood back, she shook her head from side to side.

"Are you telling me he owned this property and never told me? Why did he do it, Charles?"

"Did he have any connection with that side of the world?"

"Not that I know of. If he did, it would have been nothing but a made-up connection like all US presidents find at election time. But what do I know?"

Charles Slowcum did not answer, concentrating on straightening his tie.

"I must go there. I might live there." She only realised she had said it aloud when she saw Charles throw his hands in the air.

"Connie, what are you thinking? Are you crazy?"

"It is something to do."

"You won't know anybody there."

"That brings certain advantages."

"Are you seriously going to do this?"

She ignored his frustration, the thick frown edging into his big eyebrows. She heard herself say yes, she was content with her decision.

"What will you do?"

"I have no idea. I just want peace and quiet, away from the well-worn phrases of death."

"It is in a small town. You might find there is little there for you after a while."

She stood up and made for the door. "There is nothing left for me here, Charles. Amy wants me to go rest up somewhere, but I don't know. I can't think straight."

He followed her to the door. "If you need anything at any time, just call me."

She smiled at his sincerity, and that he thought anybody could offer her comfort. Like understanding, like forgiveness, comfort was never going to be her companion.

The bus for Dublin sweeping past made her jump. She started up her car again. She could remember the conversation with Charles so clearly, yet she could barely call up the following two years, when she got lost in a fog of grief and depression. All she could remember was the deep sadness pulling her down every day.

She found herself driving to Ludlow Hall. This time, she drove up the open back avenue to the kitchen door. It might not have any answers for her, and it made no sense, but Ludlow Hall was where she had to be.

Walking to the side of the house, she stepped through a rusted old gate into what must have once been a fine ornamental garden: four grass squares edged by a clipped low box hedge. A woman walking on one of the grassed squares nodded to her.

"You might as well enjoy the place. There is a new owner; I think it won't be long before we are all stopped coming in," she said, calling her two dogs, who romped across the grass barking.

"Shouldn't the dogs be on a leash?"

"Sure, there is nobody around these parts, what harm are they doing?" the woman said, giving Connie an odd look. She stooped down to pat the dogs, who were yelping and trying to jump up on her. "You are not from these parts?"

"Out of town."

The woman nodded her head, as if this meant something significant. "If you go through the far gate, there is a lovely yew walk down to the lake. Get it in now, before the new owner locks the lot of us out."

Connie thanked her and set off for the gate. Once she stepped through, a long, straight path lay ahead, the trees with branches arching over, creating a wide tunnel. The path was soft strewn with the fallen, faded flowers of rhododendron and cherry blossom. She stood and stared, the light dotting on the purple and pink blanket across the ground, her eyes sending soft messages to her heart, to slow down and take it in.

Why Ed had bought this place she did not know, but she knew one thing: she wanted to walk along, to feel the stillness and savour, for a moment, the fleeting peace it brought. Slowly, she made her way under the branches of the yew trees, feeling their protective cover, until they opened out at the end, where the water of the lake lapped gently, the rushes straggling along the side, the ducks in the middle detecting her presence, creating a fuss. A heron, disturbed, silently rose from the rushes, gliding across the water to the far end of the lake, its wings skimming the water in an acrobatic display, as if it wanted to be noticed.

This walk, this spot was why she was going to stay here: she knew that now. That she would have to share it with strangers who regarded the land as their own was something she would deal with in time.

Date: March 23, 2013
Subject: THE LUDLOW LADIES' SOCIETY

Ludlow ladies,

Just a quick update. As you all know, a number of ladies visited the local schools this week to show off our wonderful talent.

Eithne Hall arranged for us to visit Rosdaniel Primary and Secondary to bring the world of sewing to the students. Parents were very happy the tradition of sewing was brought back to the classroom.

We went to Rosdaniel Primary first, armed with needles and thread and small samples of patchwork. It all went very well until somewhere near the end. Everybody presumed, but nobody directly told us, we should not hand out needles and thread to the children. Although everything went well for so long, unfortunately one lad suffered a puncture injury to his thumb. Mrs Brannigan, who always carries all necessities in her handbag, attempted to placate the child and put a plaster on it for him. It was the tiniest pinprick! The teacher told us all we could do was put water on it. The poor lad sobbed for the rest of our time there. However, it became rather chaotic after one young lad (why is it always the boys?) stabbed another in the forearm with a needle.

That brought an abrupt end to our visit!

The visit to the secondary school and Transition Year went very well. We had no takers to do a bit of tacking, but the teenagers were good fun, taking selfies while wrapped in two patchwork quilts we brought along.

Thank you, Eithne, for organising the visits.

Unfortunately, Jack Davoren heard all about the fiasco at the primary school and is threatening to bring the matter up at the next Town Committee meeting. What a petty little man he is. He needs to be squashed like a snail.

Kathryn Rodgers,
Chairwoman

4

Eve walked down the street to Doyle Butcher's, where they were already clearing away the trays.

"Your usual piece of steak, Mrs Ludlow?"

The butcher, every Friday, set aside a small piece of round steak for Eve. He never let on it was about twice the size she ever asked for, and if she was aware of his generosity, she did not pass comment. Always, she peered over the counter grumbling, making him trim the little fat from around the sides, complaining he wanted her to build up too much muscle.

"I have lovely lamb coming in at the weekend for the roast. Will I keep one for you?"

She frowned. "I swore I would only ever eat lamb from the fields at Ludlow Hall. Nothing could measure up to it," she said, paying for her round steak, stuffing the small plastic bag, which was knotted at the neck, into her handbag.

Next on her list was Michael Conway's newsagent and grocers. Michael was watching out for her, killing time flicking dust from shelves that were not dusty. Whipping his cloth across glossy magazines, spanking the covers, an agitation rose inside him: whether he should tell Eve about the new owner of Ludlow Hall.

When Eve crossed in the door, she sensed his upset. His back was to her, and she took in the hunched shoulders, his tight grip of the teacloth as he swatted the spines of neatly stacked magazines.

"Can it be that bad, you have to take it out on *Horse & Hound*?" she giggled.

He swung around, his unease heightening when he heard the happy tinkle of her laugh. Hiding the teacloth, he stepped back in behind the counter.

"You are later than usual, you nearly missed me. I was about to lock up."

"I started mixing and matching all my fabric to see had I enough for a patchwork quilt. I lost track of time."

He straightened a stack of old newspapers, piled to the side. She could see he was nervous about something.

"Don't tell me you don't have Thursday's *Irish Times*, Michael. I love reading that property section, my little bit of escapism."

He laughed, reaching under the counter for the newspaper supplement. "Would I leave you without your favourite read of the week?"

"Michael, you are a star. I don't know what I would do but for your kindness."

"I remember when we used to deliver all the daily newspapers up to the Hall, bright and early, even before the rest of the shop was opened up."

"Poor Arnold liked the idea of keeping up with the news and thought he could only do so if he got three newspapers a day. It was the slant in the reporting which was often important, he said." She stopped and looked Michael Conway straight in the face. "You are trying very hard to hide something from me. What is eating you?"

It was always the same: she could sense his mood even before he knew it himself. He fidgeted, picking at the corner of the counter, where the Formica had split and the slivers of torn wood were visible.

"I will give you a lift home, if you give me a few minutes to lock up."

There was a slight shake to his voice. She did not argue, but

30

stood outside while he pulled out the cash drawer of the till and picked up his accounts book and keys. He handed them to her so he could pull down the shutter, letting it screech into place before he snapped a padlock on it.

Opening the passenger door, he took the heavy cash drawer from her and placed it on the back seat. She left him to the driving, enjoying the idea of a little spin, as he went around the long way, towards the Ballyheigue Road. So many times she had sat by Arnold when he took out the Rolls-Royce past the small town green and on to the square to buy an ice cream in Tierney's on a Friday afternoon. That they could have walked the distance never occurred to Arnold, even when their circumstances had drastically changed and there was barely enough petrol to put into the old car. Sometimes they had to scrape together the coins to buy two 99s.

"Michael, have you a delivery to make?"

He stared out the windscreen, indicating before turning in the entrance to Ludlow Hall. She did not at first notice the gates were open and swept back, a furrow from a previous car's incursion cutting through the moss on the avenue.

"What has happened?"

He slowed to a halt and turned off the engine.

Alarm swept through her. She felt her breath catch, so that he put his hand out and held hers. In all the years, she had not come inside the gate. No more than a half-mile down the road and she could not bear to visit.

"I am not sure how to tell you this, only to say it straight out. Ludlow Hall has a new owner, Eve, and she wants to live here." He cupped her hand tighter in his, fumbling in his trouser pocket for a handkerchief with the other. "You knew it would happen one day, Eve, especially since Carter died."

"Who is she?" Her mouth was dry, her voice croaky.

"Carter's widow."

Eve let the tears flow down her cheeks.

"The poor woman. I hope she finds what she is looking for at Ludlow Hall."

He told her as much as he knew, his words swirling about her, battering over her head. At one stage, he reached over, gently wiping away her tears with the hankie.

"I brought you out here in case you wanted to walk around the place. There is a lot of talk that she might close up the gardens and the land."

"She can do whatever she wants, if she owns it."

He squeezed her hand tighter. "You might like your own moment, see the house before it all changes."

"What good will it do?"

He did not answer, but got out and went around to the passenger side, opening the door. "We can take a stroll up the rest of the avenue, turn back whenever you give the word."

She thought she had never met anybody quite so considerate as Michael, as she allowed him to help her from the car.

She had not been back in four years, since that last day she walked down the avenue, but until now it had always been a comfort that the old house was here, all her furniture too. Maybe she had always harboured a hope that she could return to sit in these rooms. That was hardly going to happen now.

They walked and she linked her arm in his, because nobody was about and, once the road had veered to the left, nothing could be seen from the public road.

When they rounded the last bend, they stopped, the house spread out in front of them. The wood hoarding had darkened and dirtied in the intervening years, the house entombed without windows on the world.

"I am getting a few men to take down all those boards tomorrow, before she goes into the house."

Eve flinched to think of anybody else within the four walls of Ludlow Hall, but she pretended nothing to Michael.

Sensing her sadness, he pulled her to the left. "We can shoot past the front lawn, slip into the yew walk from the side, go to the lake."

She knew he was avoiding bringing her past the back of the

house and the old barn. She resisted, staying where she was.

"I have seen enough, Michael. My memories of the yew walk are beautiful; I don't need to see it to know the cherry blossom has danced across it, mixing with the bigger rhododendron blooms and petals. I have fine memories from there. Bring me home please, will you?"

There was a softness about her face but a determination in her eyes, so he did as he was bid.

When she got to her terraced house, she did not invite Michael in. He was not insulted, knowing she needed time to spend with the memories the short walk at Ludlow had revived.

Eve got to work on her supper straight away, taking down a deep frying pan and using a small splash of oil to brown the steak. Next, she chopped two shallots and threw mushrooms around the meat, letting them soften before she plopped water in to make a gravy. She sliced a few boiled potatoes from the night before into the gravy, leaving the stew to simmer, the meaty aroma filling up the room.

Reaching under the armchair, she pulled out a dark wooden box. How soon would it be before she had to sell off a piece? It was a tragedy that part of the Brannigan history could be cashed in to fill the oil tank for next winter. Slowly, she pulled out a small, plush burgundy velvet box and snapped it open. Rose gold, the necklace held a ruby dropping down to a single washed pearl.

For a moment, she was transported back: the excitement in the air, the anticipation of going out. Only six months married, they were invited to a dinner dance at the Gresham, Dublin. She was agitated, not sure if the dress she had picked in Gorey was grand enough. She brought three more home and paraded in front of the housekeeper and then her husband. Arnold liked the deep ruby-purple dress with the black lace at the bodice and the inside of the pleat, so that when she walked a froth of lace was kicked out. He was quite insistent and could not be persuaded on the blue silk dress, which was entirely more figure-hugging, with a padded neckline.

She remembered he became nervous, lest she not take on board his opinion. It was on the evening of the dinner dance, before they set off for Dublin, that she realised the reason for his anxiety. She was standing in the large hallway waiting for him, impatience rising in her that he was still not ready, when he came downstairs, his hands in his trousers pockets.

"Take your hands out of your pockets, it will ruin the line of your trousers," she snapped, a bit too severely.

He laughed, pulling a small velvet box from his pocket. "Darling, I have been waiting for the right moment to give you this. It belonged to my grandmother and I would like you to wear it tonight."

She opened the box, her hands shaking in excitement. "It is perfect."

He clipped it on her and kissed her neck. "This was the first gift of my grandfather to my grandmother. My father also gave it to my mother. It is my first gift of jewellery to you. I want you to wear it and treasure it and, in the future, even if times are hard, to keep it and hand it down to our son when he meets the woman he wants to marry."

She ran her finger along the ruby, moving down to lightly glance off the pearl.

She had promised Arnold so easily she would never let it go, but now, decades on, she was not so sure she could keep her promise. Her loyalty had been tested and replaced almost by a festering anger. He had opted out, thrown in the towel; put any name you like on it, but he had left her here to face everything alone.

Even if his death had wiped out the bank debt, she would still have been left alone, unable to keep Ludlow Hall going herself.

She sat down, picking at her steak and gravy stew, her appetite gone, a knot of worry expanding in her stomach. Eve snapped the velvet case shut and put it back in the wooden box, kicking it under the chair with her toe. Reaching for the kettle, she filled it under the tap and got her hot-water bottle ready. When the kettle whistled, she filled the bottle carefully before carrying it upstairs. Shoving it between the sheets, she undressed, switching off the light as she got into bed. Curling up in a ball, Eve let the tears rack through her body, knowing when she was spent she would fall into a dead sleep which brought no rejuvenation or rest.

She knew, too, she would wake up when it was still dark outside, to go over every detail of that day when Arnold made the decision to leave her.

It had been such a busy day: the huge trailer had come early and taken away the sheep. Arnold stood by the window of the landing, watching the sheepdog round up the animals for the last time, wheeling across the paddocks, doing his job as diligently as if it still mattered. She met the driver and thanked him for coming early, so those in the village might not notice. He nodded sympathetically at her, muttering he was sorry. When the truck trundled down the driveway out of sight, Arnold went to his study to sit and read.

She brought him a cup of tea and he seemed to perk up a bit, asking if the newspapers had arrived.

"I will call in to Michael's when I am out and about later."

"He is going to lose all his business if he does not deliver promptly in the morning," Arnold said, reaching for last Sunday's paper.

She had not the heart to tell him how, when they came back from Dublin, the day a judge in the High Court granted judgement of just over two million euros against them, Michael called her aside.

"Eve, I hate to bring this up, but the newspaper bill has not been paid for the last six months." He was frowning; she could see it pained him to tell her.

"He is supposed to pay you every week. I have given him the money myself."

"Arnold is under a lot of pressure, maybe there are other bills."

She knew by his voice he was not telling her everything. She didn't blame him.

"Give me the bill. I will pay it off bit by bit, over the coming weeks. Meanwhile, cancel the newspapers altogether."

"All of them, Eve?"

She hesitated for a moment. "What can I do? I don't know how I will tell him."

She never could tell Arnold and, to be fair to Michael Conway, each day when he had a newspaper left over, he swiped the masthead off and gave it to Eve.

If Arnold knew what was happening, he said nothing, bar a brief comment that Michael Conway had gone to the dogs if he thought customers would accept torn newspapers and magazines. When he complained bitterly the newspapers were not delivered any more, Eve humoured him so Arnold could pretend life was going on as normal.

That morning, it was Eve who walked the empty fields, mourning the loss of the Ludlow flock, closing the gates, old habits dying hard.

When the time came for her to meet the Ludlow Ladies' Society in the town for a quick meeting over tea in a café, she was glad to escape from Ludlow Hall. Before she left, she called in to Arnold, pushing a tray of soup and sliced bread on to his desk.

"I am going out for a bit. I should be back around 3.30 p.m."

"You have a good time, dear, you deserve it," he said, but he did not look up from his crossword. She was worried about him, but then she was always worried about him, these days. Stopping at the door, she called his name softly. When he looked up, she thought he was upset about something.

"Would you rather I stay?"

'No, dear, you grab any moment you can to enjoy yourself. Who knows what is ahead?"

She hesitated, but when he shook out his newspaper as if he was impatient to read it, she left.

At first she walked with a heavy step, but by the time she got to Rosdaniel her head had cleared. Kathryn Rodgers was in full swing when she arrived.

"I can't understand why they don't stock Earl Grey; they know it is the only tea I will drink."

"I doubt if there is much of a run in Rosdaniel for Earl Grey," Eithne Hall sniped.

"For God's sake, Earl Grey was being served around the world when Rosdaniel was only a few houses alongside a dirt track. If this café is to keep up, it would want to cop on to the ways of the world."

"Myself, I think I would prefer it if it served a few gin and tonics with a slice of lemon," Bernie Martin said, and the others laughed.

"I suppose I will have to make do with a black coffee," Kathryn said, annoyed.

'Now would that be Ethiopian, Indian, Colombian, Italian or French?" Dana Marshall interjected, and they all roared laughing.

Kathryn did not answer, but reached for a slice of coffee cake.

They were still giggling when Eve joined them at the long table at the café window.

"We are thinking of putting a picket on the café, because they don't stock Earl Grey," Eithne said.

"Are you willing Eve to walk up and down with a placard?" Dana asked.

'What is this nonsense? Tea is tea," Eve laughed.

"As much as I disagree with that statement, because tea is never just tea, I would like if we could get on to discussing the reason for this particular gathering of the Ludlow Ladies' Society: our entry to the country agricultural show," Kathryn said in her marbles-in-her-mouth voice.

Eve ordered a coffee to avoid any disturbance, but they all giggled when Kathryn asked for any ideas and Dana piped up:

"Tea cosies."

Later, humming a tune as she ambled up the driveway, Eve hastened her step as she moved past the empty fields where the sheep used to graze. Deliberately looking away, towards the copse of hazel trees and the bank of rhododendron at the bend, she picked up speed, anxious to get home. Stepping into the kitchen, she noticed the dog was not there to welcome her. Calling out to Arnold, she switched on the kettle and took down two mugs, shouting out did he want tea or coffee? When there was no answer, she made for his study, thinking maybe he had fallen asleep. He was not there. His soup left untouched on its tray, the butter on the bread congealing. She was not worried yet; she knew he hated the sliced white bread, complaining it was nothing, only factory-pressed. She headed upstairs to check the bedroom. Empty.

Fear studded through her. He hardly went out to walk the land; he avoided having anything to do with the farm these days. Her voice shaking, she shouted out his name, called the sheepdog. Nothing.

Bolting down the stairs, she almost tripped on the last step in her rush out to the yard, catapulting down the yew walk, its dark canopy a menace rather than a reassurance. At the lake, she stood, scanning the water as the ducks, disturbed, skittered across the surface.

Doubling back, she darted past the stables, where the last two horses stared at her confusion, their calm gaze compounding her panic.

She screamed Arnold's name as she raced to the barn. The door ajar made her hesitate. Her head throbbing, fear tightened across her heart. Poking at the door with her fist, it pushed back, creaking loudly. She saw the dog first, lying, his head blown off, warm blood seeping across the floor.

Arnold had his brown leather shoes on. He was suspended, hanging still over the hay that had been saved on a warm August day. Pain burst through her bones, buckling her knees.

A scream screeched through her, but there was no sound. She did not hear anything, only the pain of the words as they tore across her throat.

Arnold stayed still, suspended, the old chair from the cow byre next door tipped over, resting where he had kicked it in his final act.

5

There was a skitter about Rosdaniel. Word spread: Ludlow Hall was back on the map and Michael Conway was looking for help to get the hoarding off the windows. Four men volunteered to help, arriving shortly after nine, starting with the front door, easing the old timber from where it was wedged, sealed in with layers of dirt and black damp. Earwigs and beetles darted for cover as the wood was prised away to show the front door, its white paint dulled and streaked with dirt where water had seeped in and stained it during the winter storms.

Next, the ground-floor bay window at the side, light streaking across the room to every corner as the boards were lifted away. When the front drawing room windows were exposed, the workmen stood back and inspected the house.

Before they got the ladders to the upstairs windows, they stopped, poured tea into paper cups from a flask one of the wives had sent down, and stood around smoking cigarettes, all the time stamping their feet to keep out the cold.

"What does she want living in a place like this when she could flog it for a fortune?" one of them asked.

"An old place like this vacant for four years, it might as well be forever, it will be so damp," another piped up.

Michael Conway swung around, snapping. "It's none of your business. And aren't you getting a good clean day's work out of it," he said. The men, sensing his annoyance, stamped their cigarettes out on the ground and threw away the last of the tea from their cups before going back to work.

As the men concentrated on getting the top windows clear, Michael drove up to Eve's place. Tentatively, he knocked on the door.

"Eve, we are going ahead opening up Ludlow Hall for the American. I thought you should know." He was nervous, leaning against her door, fidgeting with his car keys.

"At least the new woman is not knocking the old place down... yet," she said.

"Will I tell her where to find you?"

"Did you say she is staying with Hetty?"

"I recommended Hetty's place to her."

"Well then, she probably knows more about me than I do myself. She will know where to find me. No doubt Kathryn Rodgers will also tell all in the Ludlow Ladies' Society emails."

He laughed lightly, bursting with admiration for this woman who, even now, could sum up Hetty and Kathryn so well. He stood by the door, but she did not invite him in. He was not insulted; he knew Eve too well for that.

"How does the old place look?"

"Like you never left it. The sun is out, though, catching all the dirt on the glass. She will have some job turning the place around."

"I don't think I will go down the town today, there will be too much talk."

"Hetty will make sure of that. If you want, I can run you down to Ludlow now for a quick look."

Her heart tugged, but she straightened up.

"There will be plenty of time for that. I have to finish altering a skirt for a woman in Arklow, that will keep me busy."

He turned away and she stood at the door to see him off, waiting until he was out of sight before moving back inside.

She knew Michael had called so she would be ready, in case anyone else came knocking with the news.

Michael was her first friend in Rosdaniel. Arnold and he had been friends since they were young boys: the boy from the village and the boy from Ludlow Hall. Michael never tried to keep up with Arnold, ploughing his own furrow. Maybe that was why they got along.

It was to Michael that Arnold went when he was deep in the financial quagmire, with no hope of repaying the bank loan. Michael gave him five thousand euros, there and then. Arnold had not the heart to tell him it would not even cover the monthly repayment.

"When you owe millions, thousands are mere coppers," he told Eve when he got home, and she had admonished him for not being more grateful. Straight away, she took the brown paper bag containing the money, leaving Arnold sitting staring out the window from his library chair.

She walked up to Michael's shop and handed back the bag.

"Take it, Michael, it is better in your hands than the greedy bank's. They are bringing us to court; five thousand or even one hundred thousand is not going to stop that. This is a lot of money, God knows, to any decent God-fearing person, but to a bank and the grasping bastards who work for it, it is just small change."

"I was only trying to help."

He told her to wait until Richie could take over at the front counter. She did, patting him on the back to thank him, before disappearing into the back, where Michael dipped a tea bag in a mug for her.

"The money was very much appreciated, Michael, but where we are now, we are beyond help." Her voice was shaky. He saw the wet of tears in her eyes, but she did not let herself sob.

"What happens next?"

"We go to the High Court and fight them and we will be in every newspaper in the country, that is what happens next. How do I ever forgive Arnold for this? I swear he only told me the extent of the trouble we are in about two weeks ago, I thought I had signed up for a €10,000 loan, to get the roof repaired, turns out it was almost €2 million. I don't know what he was thinking. He was an old fool with grand plans for development on a few acres at the far end of the estate, a man who never picked up a shovel a day in his life."

She hushed quickly, putting her hand up to her mouth to stop herself saying more of what she thought of her husband.

"I am here for you, Eve, for you both, you know that."

She left soon after, to go home and tell her husband what she had done.

When, almost a year later, she found Arnold hanging in the barn, just days after the High Court granted judgement against him for almost €2 million, it was to Michael Conway she turned first.

Afraid, she had fled the barn, past the old water trough, the horses, the bucket of scraps she, earlier in the day, had asked Arnold to throw for the hens. She rushed through the kitchen, where the kettle had boiled, the two mugs empty on the table.

Picking up the phone, she dialled Michael Conway's number. When he answered the phone, he sounded so carefree she thought of cutting him off, so as not to spoil his afternoon for him, but instead she uttered:

"You had better come. Arnold has killed himself."

She spoke quietly and he did not ask any questions. Back in the kitchen, she sat, her arms folded across her chest, waiting for Michael to arrive, the house silent, the air still.

Numb, she thought she should dial 999, but how would she tell them? She sat down, picking at the tablecloth, digging a hole in it. The crows broke into the eerie quiet, cawing out the news of Arnold's death. Slapping her hands over her ears to block the harshness, she did not hear the car when it pulled up. Michael, shouting out her name, ran into the kitchen, his face red, his eyes bulging.

She stared at him, but she could not say anything, only point in the direction of the barn. Shouting at her to ring an ambulance, he bolted across the yard. Hearing the urgency in his voice, she dialled 999 and her strength dissipated, the tears flowing so fast she could hardly give the address.

A loud, pain-filled baying filled the back yard, making Eve buckle in torment. When she ran to the barn, she saw Michael, tears coursing down his cheeks, holding Arnold's legs.

The ambulance raced up the avenue, the sirens blaring and flashing. Michael had to be pulled away from Arnold and ordered to look after Eve. Shaking, he took her away into the drawing room, pushing her gently into a velvet armchair by the fire before he pulled over the curtains. He sat beside her in the half dark of the room, the heavy stillness walling them in.

When Eve spoke, her voice was a hoarse whisper.

"What am I going to do now, Michael?"

"I don't know, but you will get through it."

Michael, who had lost his wife early in their marriage, knew what it was like to be the one left grieving.

"Do you think he suffered for long?"

He reached over and took her hand. "Best not to dwell too much on it."

She jumped up and he could see the black shape of her go to the window. One by one, she flung back the curtains.

"What am I supposed to do, sit in the dark because of what he did?"

"Out of respect, Eve, out of respect for the dead."

She swung around, her eyes clouded with fury. "What do you want me to do, Michael, shut myself away in the dark because of what he did? Respect does not come into it. If he had had respect, he would never have hanged himself but would have stood by me when they come to take our home."

Michael jumped up and made to put his hand on her arm. "Stop, Eve, before you say too much. It will only eat you up later." He tapped her shoulder like he was knocking at a door, and she responded, putting her hand in his and letting him guide her back to the armchair.

"I don't know if I can face the future on my own, Michael. What is to become of me?"

"You are not on your own. I am here," he said, turning to the door as a Garda knocked, politely asking if he could have a word.

When he came back in, the Garda behind him, Michael was wringing his hands.

"Garda Moran wants to ask a few questions, before they take Arnold's body away. Was there a note, something like that?"

She sat up, looking directly at the young Garda.

"If there was a note, a warning of some sorts, I would not have had to go through the pain of finding him on my own." The tears were coursing down her face, saturating the gathered silk on the collar of her good blouse.

Garda Moran, wary of her grief, quickly ran through what would happen next, before nodding to Michael and quietly leaving the drawing room.

"You can't stay here, come back to mine," Michael said, but she shook her head.

"I never have and I won't start today, feeding titbits to the gossips around here," she said.

"Eve."

She turned around fiercely. "This is my home. I am not giving it up now, not after the stupid man took his own life."

Michael knew better than to argue with her and quietly withdrew.

The memories made it hard for Eve to concentrate and, after an hour, she threw up the blue gabardine skirt she was altering. Her head thumping, she wanted to move away from the thoughts swirling about in her brain, so she sat down with her jewellery box. There were a lot of fine pieces thrown together, some wrapped around each other, but it was a small charm tucked away in a tiny velvet bag she was interested in. Letting the charm drop into the palm of her hand, she smiled to think of the day Michael gave it to her. She had only been in

44

Ludlow Hall a few months and Michael, just back from a trip to London, shyly handed her the little box.

"I saw this charm and I thought it would be nice for your charm bracelet. I hope you don't mind."

She thought it beautiful, a gold wishbone set with a pearl. She loved it even more when he told her why he bought it.

"I was thinking of all your dreams for Ludlow; the wishbone says may your wishes come true."

She knew then she had a friend in Michael, a friend who never asked her why she had not put the wishbone on the charm bracelet her husband had bought her only weeks before.

Neither did Michael ask if Arnold ever knew of the wishbone charm she cherished so much that she kept it apart, not including it among the garish charms Arnold insisted on bringing home every time he visited the United States.

Putting the charm back in the box, she decided to go to bed. Eve lay in the dark, listening. Rosdaniel was quiet, except for the dog three doors down, who barked continuously, guarding his patch. Arnold thought his debts would die with him and she would be left at Ludlow. The stupid man: how was he to know a court would decide otherwise, that she would be left a widow with the bank breathing down her neck for the millions still owing. If Michael had not stood by her, stood beside her in the Four Courts as a judge decided what was to become of Ludlow Hall, she would never have got through. Clenching her eyes shut, she pushed thoughts of Arnold and Ludlow Hall out of her mind. Instead, she counted backwards from one hundred, hoping sleep would soon take over.

6

Connie got up early, but did not go to Ludlow Hall. She sat inside the window of the attic bedroom, not able to see past the thick condensation clogging on the glass. Her phone was full of frantic texts from Amy, pleading with her to come home. What home did she have any more? There was no place in the States. And here, Ludlow was a big old house full of someone else's history.

Loss streaked through her, making her bend over, the pain clouding her, seeping into her brain, consuming every part of her.

She reached for her phone and texted her sister.

I am fine. Please give me time.

As rapid as a bullet from the chamber, her sister fired back a text.

Won't you even tell me where exactly you are?

I just need space. I am fine.

Amy, she knew, would overreact if she spoke too much the truth.

Would she tell her that even getting up each morning was difficult, that each day seemed interminable? That her loss was dragging her down at the heels, too huge to quantify? If this was the price of love, then she wanted not to have loved. It was grief tearing, pulling at her heart. She did not deserve it, but since when did only bad things happen to bad people? Two years had passed, the lost years when she could barely function, the years subsumed in a black fog.

Hearing a toilet flush and the whirr of a shower, she knew Hetty was up and about. Quickly, she snatched her jeans and jumper, pulling them on. She stepped into her shoes and grabbed her handbag.

Connie was halfway down the stairs when Hetty, wrapped in a purple fleece dressing gown, stepped out onto the landing.

"I am just about to do a nice full Irish breakfast for you."

"I have to go out, I won't be having breakfast. Thank you."

"But you can't start the day on nothing."

Hetty Gorman dithered, worried that her guest did not want to eat in her house. Connie, sensing her disquiet, took the last three steps of the stairs before turning to look at Hetty.

"I am sorry, Mrs Gorman, it must be the excitement or something, but I am not feeling too well. I just need to get some fresh air."

Hetty bristled, worrying if she should not have turned up the heat in the middle of the night.

"You know where I am if you feel hungry once the cold air has done its bit."

Connie made for the door, smiling at the older woman, whose brow was furrowed, her eyes full of disappointment.

"I think I shall be at Ludlow, until much later."

She drove to Ludlow Hall, parking under the expanse of an oak tree and halfway down the front driveway, so nobody could see her.

This house was all she had now, this place where nobody knew her, a comfort blanket against the good intentions of those who knew too much.

She strolled up the driveway, past the rhododendron, its leaves blotted with water from the heavy rain of the night before, past the old posts that had once held heavy iron gates across the avenue, and past the long swathes of paddock overgrown and uncut in three years, the high grass pounded down by the rain, making a thick cake of moss.

Skirting the corner, the dilapidated house, its best days long gone, made her gasp. The hoarding was down, and the windows looked like dull, shadowy forms of what they once were, reflecting an empty, lonely house. It was huge, a magnificent monstrosity in a small town. The building looked uncared for, as if it had been abandoned for more than four years.

Excitement bubbled up in her that she might be able to turn her life around here, but as quickly a hesitation sneaked through her, making her feel afraid. Spotting a bench in a clearing at the side of the avenue, she sat down, hidden among the trees.

A stone bird table, blotches of silver-grey moss in a garish pattern all over, stood tall in a maze of bindweed. The bowl was clogged with damp leaves, dark water edging to a scum.

Had Ed planned to move them here? She did not know. Molly would have loved this spot, sitting quietly, waiting for the birds to drop down to take nuts, grain and bread. For a fleeting moment, she felt the warmth of memories, soaring, then remembering the truth, crashing down, her heart bursting with pain.

Slumping over, all she could do was curl up in a ball on the seat and wait, like she had many times before, for the despondency to pass.

A robin flew down from the rhododendron branch to the bird table, perching on the rim, flicking at a fly trapped in the dank water. Cocking his head to one side, he watched Connie, scrunched small on the seat, before bobbing over her and flying away. A thrush hopped out of the undergrowth, snipping at the earth, but ducked back when Connie stirred.

She sat up, peeping through the foliage, straggles of daffodils wafting on the light breeze ruffling the land in front of the house.

The birdsong lifted high in the sky, flooding her with memories of that day.

The same crisp air, the flowers dipping their heads as she walked past them to the car that morning. Connie, her hair still damp, pulled her jacket around her, the cool nip in the air making her shiver. Mr Singh, out early, waved to her and she smiled.

Connie threw her kit bag on the passenger's seat and got into the car, her steel travel cup steaming on the dashboard beside her, a tiny sticky-note drawing Molly had made the night before half falling off, curling at the corners in the heat.

"Love you Mommy," scrawled in two different coloured markers, two pink glittery hearts stuck at one corner.

She must remember to drop into the mall and get some more glitter glue and puffy stickers to surprise her later. When she kissed her goodbye, Molly had not stirred, and when she had stuffed Cuddly Cat under the warm glow of the duvet, Molly hooked her arm contentedly around its neck, pushing deeper into her pink pillow. She heard Ed shifting around upstairs, but she continued out the door, calling goodbye softly as she went.

Connie had the car in reverse and was eyeing the mirrors to get out of the driveway when she realised she had forgotten her dance schedule for the day. Unwilling to go through the rigmarole of tiptoeing through the house, she shrugged her shoulders. She had most of the dance classes highlighted on her phone.

She drove around the long way, wanting to see the sunlight salsa across the sea, a chorus of gold surfing across the water. At one point she stopped the car and wound down the window, pulling in the fresh air, making her cheeks bristle with the chill of the bright morning. Hearing the sound of the water dragging the pebbles, she closed her eyes, letting herself drift into a half snooze.

When she got to the centre for her first lesson of the day, only three of her ten students were there. "So dancing in the morning is losing its lustre," she joked.

"Traffic is backed up, some accident," one man said as he entered the room, slightly out of breath.

"Let's warm up," she said, not noticing two men in suits with the building administrator loitering in the doorway.

The administrator nervously pointed at her. The dance students hung back. Sensing a shuffling behind her, she turned around. Startled, one of the men let his head flop down, pushing one of his hands in his pocket. The other man took a step forward.

"Connie Carter?"

The tone of his voice was urgent. Cold seeped up through the soles of her feet. She noticed that none of her students were warming up. One of them clicked the music off. The taller of the two men asked if they could go somewhere private. She nodded and led the way, her joints aching, her walk rigid, her brain flashing out danger signals.

The small office was cold, the light coming in the window watery grey, dancing in a pattern across the surface of the white table. Words swept past her in a whispered blur. She caught Ed's name.

"Did you talk to your husband this morning, Mrs Carter?"

When she did not answer, the detective gently touched her shoulder, pointing to a chair for her to sit down on.

"No, he was just about to get up when I was going out the door. I called goodbye."

"Sit down, Mrs Carter."

"I want to know what is going on. Why are you asking me about my husband?"

The short detective moved away to answer a call. The other man pulled out a tubular chair for her.

"We came across Ed's car. Was he going to take a trip today?"

"What do you mean?"

"Connie, Ed's car has been in an accident." The word seemed elongated on his tongue, tripping towards her, whipping her across the face.

50

"There is some mistake. I left my husband and daughter at home."

"You have a daughter?"

"Molly. Is Molly okay?"

Connie jumped up, barging past the detective to the door. Panic coursed through her, pain gushing up her body.

"Molly, where is she?" She was shouting, angry, afraid.

The tall detective reached out and put his arms on her shoulders. "Didn't you drop her at kindergarten?"

She flopped down, her voice a whisper, her throat tight. "She isn't in today, she has a dental check-up later. My God, what if he left her on her own? She's only five, anything could happen."

The short one left the room, and she heard him talk quickly into his phone. She saw her students gathering up their belongings to leave the studio, casting anxious glances towards the office as they went.

Her stomach felt sick, a pain was seeping up her arm, a chill creeping through her. She thought she was screaming, roaring at the tall detective, but it was only in her head. His lips were moving, but she did not hear his voice. He reached out and pushed her gently back in the chair.

Time ticked on. She waited. The detective in the room stayed silent. A woman walked in and left a glass of water on a table beside Connie, who braced herself for bad news when she saw the woman's sympathetic smile.

The short detective came back into the room, his face grey, his eyes blank, his fingers twiddling his phone, as if he was trying to pump up some courage. She took his face in and her body crumpled like a puppet, the strings cut. Tears coursed down her face, wetting her neck. Her head thumped.

"I must go to Molly. Where is she?"

The short detective put his hands out to stop her. She thought he shouted, but later realised he had not.

"Connie, is there family we can ring for you?"

"Ed, Molly…"

He put his two hands on her shoulders. "It is bad news, Connie. We found Molly in the house. She is dead, Connie."

The grey walls of the room spun around her, the light overhead flashing down spears of silver. In the corner, a discarded gym bag half open. The tall detective walked to the window and looked out, running his fingers through his hair. The short detective stood close, tapping her shoulder as if to comfort her. If he was talking, she could not hear him.

She could only hear Molly:

"Mommy. Mommy. Mommy."

She wanted to run to her, but could not; she stretched, but could not reach her. Molly was not there.

"Where was Molly?"

An older detective, his shirt barely tucked into his waistband, came into the room. He took her by the hand, winding her into a tight hug, and she leaned against him, this man in an ill-fitting suit.

"Let's get you away somewhere more private, before the TV crews start crowding round," he whispered. She let him lead her out of the room and the building. The security guard, wiping tears from his face, looked away as she approached. One of her students grabbed her hand and muttered something. Others looked at her, their eyes reflecting the pain in her heart, and she was glad she was being taken away.

Outside, the sun dazzled against the glass building, mocking her as she was guided on both sides to the police car. Reaching out, she grabbed the older detective by the collar.

"Why Molly? Who would do that to Molly?"

She sat in the rear, her head flung back. The car was pulling away when she shouted she did not have her travel mug. The driver braked hard. The older detective listened carefully to her garbled words before quickly getting out of the car and running across to the office building. Five minutes later, he emerged, gripping the travel mug, his thumb keeping the sticker in place as he marched quickly past a film crew setting up at the entrance.

The mug was still warm. She sat, tracing the childish writing. 'Love you Mommy.' Connie slowly pulled the note with the little shaky writing down her cheek, as if the innocence of that final expression of love could comfort her. If she died now, it could only be a good thing.

Opening her eyes, the sun was still shining around Ludlow Hall. A chaffinch flitted between the fuchsia bushes at the front. Deliberately, she turned away back down the avenue, not exactly sure any more where she was going.

Date: March 24, 2013
Subject: THE LUDLOW LADIES' SOCIETY

*****SPECIAL NOTICE*****

Ludlow ladies,

It is very important there is a full house for the next meeting of the Ludlow Ladies' Society.

I have, with great difficulty, managed to wrestle an invitation from the Rosdaniel Festival Committee for the Ludlow Ladies' Society to exhibit in the Town Hall as part of the upcoming festival.

Ladies, I am not supposed to reveal this to anyone, so please keep it under your hats. The first and second prizes at the Rosdaniel Festival exhibition will be included in a special event and exhibition in Glendalough to be visited by none other than the First Lady of the United States, Michelle Obama.

Ladies, I can say with certainty we want to be there, to have the great Michelle Obama throw her eye over our patchwork.

We are in luck too, ladies: Mr Davoren is not on the panel of judges. He is, however, an exhibitor and I am sure hoping to go to Glendalough.

Now is our time to kill two birds with one stone: crush Davoren and his dreams, and bring glory to the Ludlow Ladies' Society.

Ladies, we can do it. The first step is to attend the Tuesday meeting at Hetty Gorman's house. This is our IN, ladies, and not even Davoren can get in our way if we win a prize.

In other news, we note the new owner of Ludlow Hall is to take up residence. We in the Ludlow Ladies' Society wish the new owner well and think back with pride on our association with Ludlow Hall.

Kathryn Rodgers,
Chairwoman

7

When Hetty Gorman heard the knock, she thought it was Connie. Beaming her hostess smile, she swung back the front door. She tried to hide her disappointment when she saw Eve Brannigan.

"Eve, it is awfully early for you, are you all right?"

"I thought I would introduce myself to the woman who owns Ludlow Hall. Is she about?"

"She left early, did not even have breakfast. I think she has gone out to Ludlow."

"Never mind. It was just an idea."

Hetty stepped out to put her hand on Eve's arm. "Come in, have a cuppa."

"I am run off my feet, Hetty. I had better get back to the sewing machine." Turning on her heel, she mumbled a quick goodbye, hurrying towards the gate.

"Don't forget the Ludlow Ladies' Society. We have to decide what we are going to do for the Rosdaniel Festival."

Eve waved to indicate she had heard and scurried on towards the cemetery. It had been months since she had visited. Arnold had been dead four years, but she still had not put his name on the plaque of the Brannigan family tomb. Maybe one day, when she resented his leaving less, maybe one day she would be strong enough to read his name without cursing him for leaving her on her own. Maybe one day, too, she would acknowledge the death of baby James. Just three days old, his was the smallest coffin in the family crypt.

She stopped outside the Brannigan tomb. When she was a child she used to go to the local cemetery and peer in the lattice fretwork on the tomb doors. Now she stood back, never wanting to see the tiny coffin again.

James, the boy who could have saved Ludlow Hall, the boy who could have breathed life into the place, the boy with the thatch of black hair. Shutting her eyes, she could still smell him, hear the little catches of his throat, feel his perfect fingers, the little nails pulling at her.

Eight months after their marriage, she became pregnant. Arnold was a happy man.

"I have done my bit now for Ludlow," he said, and she was annoyed, telling him a baby was much more than an heir. "It is vital for Ludlow, that is the truth of it," he said, kissing her on the top of her head.

When he was born, James was limp like a doll. He fed, but he did not do it with any of the hungry gusto expected of a newborn. After a day he was taken from her, hooked up to a machine. She was not allowed in to him.

"Germs, you will only bring in germs," the ward sister said, and Eve did not argue. Arnold stayed at home in Ludlow Hall, waiting for news.

Eve felt the anger course through her now as she remembered watching his little body twitch and tremble and later become so still, before life finally ebbed away, a nurse standing waiting to record the time of death.

Eve walked across to the chapel to sit down. She did not believe in prayer: it had not helped her stop the life flowing from her son, it had not, in the absence of recovery, brought him an easy death.

She did not know as they unhooked the machine and sent his body to the mortuary that her life was also ending, though in hindsight, when Arnold refused to speak to her when she got back to Ludlow, that was the first sign. When they buried James, they did it quietly, with only Michael there to witness their grief. It was Michael who had walked beside her and tried to comfort her. Arnold walked ahead, carrying the coffin down the stone path to the crypt.

Eve thought she heard the priest in the little room to the side of the altar. She got up, quickly darting from the chapel, before he had a chance to call out to her.

Arnold was a polite husband, but never a lover after James died and while he treated Eve with respect, lavishing nice things on her, there was no doubt but he blamed her for the death of their little boy.

Even that last weekend away, when he brought her to The Shelbourne, she felt an unease in Arnold that she put down still to the death of James. They had last stayed in Dublin together towards the end of her pregnancy. He had brought her on a buying trip. They ordered the best of everything from Switzers and Brown Thomas on Grafton Street. Arnold insisted they buy enough clothes for both a boy and a girl. He laughed when she queried the prices and told her to hang the expense. After James passed away she could not bear the sight of his little clothes, never worn, so the fine outfits were sent to the children in the town most in need. For years to come in Rosdaniel, it seemed the poorest were often the best dressed. The only clothes she kept were those in her hospital case, because she never had the heart to unpack it.

Briskly, she walked out of the cemetery, turning right for the Ballyheigue Road. There was one spot where she could view Ludlow from the road without having to set a foot on the avenue. Her head down, she marched on like a woman on a mission, past the gate of Ludlow Hall, along by the boundary wall, where the stone shelf was still inset to hold the milk cans for the creamery. Where the bend swept off towards Ballyheigue, she climbed up on the embankment, pushing the briars out of her way, causing a blackbird, startled, to flit noisily past and dip across to the other side of the road. Pushing against the narrow branches of the hazel trees, they creaked as she leaned forward to view the Hall from across two fields. It stood now as she knew it would, its top windows glinting with gold as the glass flashed in the piercing morning light. Silently, she stood and took in the quiet buzz about the place, workmen busy with hammers to the side of the house. She had done this once before, just months after she had been evicted, crying as she watched the windows being boarded up, nails being hammered in, the house entombed.

Now at least the Hall had a chance to come alive once again, for the flowers to be tended and maybe for animals to graze the fields. It would no longer have the Brannigan name, but she did not care about that. She prayed the new owner would come to love it, as she still did.

She always felt she loved Ludlow more than anyone else. For Arnold, the burden of a certain inheritance weighed heavily on his shoulders and he preferred to slope off to Dublin and, later, the United States, whenever he could, rather than take part in what he regarded as the dull monotony of life at Ludlow Hall. He never did get over the fact that he had been forced to take over at Ludlow when he was living a high life in London. That was where she met him. She wondered, if they had stayed there, how life would have turned out. But then she would not know Ludlow Hall, and she loved the old place. Standing for a moment longer, she took the house in. It needed a new life, a new energy, and she felt a surge of excitement this might happen.

Climbing down the embankment, watchful she might slip, she thought of Arnold, how he, at various times over the years, had threatened to higher the wall, so that nosey parkers could not be eyeing life at Ludlow. She told him not to be so daft, what sort of a sad fool would bother to climb up to peek at the house anyway. She smiled to think of it now. The last time he had brought it up was as they drove off to The Shelbourne the weekend before he died.

"Don't you think we have bigger things to be worrying

about?" she said. He laughed, promising that, for the weekend, they were not going to think of Ludlow once.

Fumbling down the last bit of the slope, Eve was afraid she would slip. If she had known they were her last few days with Arnold, she would have preferred Ludlow above anywhere else. Instead, unbeknownst to her, he picked the Shelbourne hotel, where they sat in lavish surroundings among people who talked in high-pitched voices, when they should have stayed in the comfortable familiarity of Ludlow Hall.

Afterwards, she was angry too that Arnold had given her false hope, telling her it would soon be all over. He insisted he had come across some money in an old account and was determined they enjoy it. They stayed in a suite on the top floor, overlooking St Stephen's Green, and ordered room service, with Arnold choosing the most expensive whiskey. He was trying to put a distance between himself and their troubles, but who could blame him, she had thought. He might have been chattier and more attentive than usual, but there was nothing to indicate what was to come, that their lives would change so utterly.

Only weeks after he was buried, the credit card bill arrived and she understood then why her husband had been so generous. A strange last gift to her, she thought, as she informed the credit card company that Mr Arnold Brannigan was dead.

Eve wandered slowly home, making sure to be on the opposite side of the road to Ludlow Hall. As she passed the Hall gateway, she saw a woman in a strange car turn in and she surmised it must be the new owner, so she scurried along. In the town, she crossed over rather than pass Michael Conway's shop, as she wanted to make it home without talking to anybody, not even him.

Once inside her own door, she let her body slump. Falling into the armchair by the window, she wept hard tears for the lovely home she had lost and the little boy who had died without feeling the love of a mother's touch. James Brannigan was so loved, but he died without ever knowing it. She hated all the stupid rules in the hospital that prevented her holding her baby, whispering in his ear. She climbed the stairs to the bedroom and pulled out an old leather case with Arnold's initials printed in gold on the top.

Unbuckling the straps, silverfish darted about as she smartly lifted the case onto the bed and unclicked the clasps. The sweet baby smell drifted towards her, and tears surged again as she reached in for his little yellow blanket. Although not sure whether it was a boy or a girl, Arnold, in his excitement, had insisted on buying clothes for both. Yet these first clothes were yellow. There was going to be plenty of time later to get specific clothes. They did not know then that they would never get a chance to celebrate the birth of their son.

Dipping her head into the blanket, she let her tears moisten the soft wool. She caressed bootees she had knitted sitting by the drawing room fire at Ludlow Hall, never worn, ribbons for laces still tied in two bows. Abruptly, she stuffed the bootees back in the case and shut it. Pushing the case off the bed to the floor, she kicked it under as she pulled her hand across her eyes, cancelling the tears.

What had she left of James? Only baby clothes she was almost afraid to touch. In the wardrobe hung dresses and fine clothes of a past life at Ludlow Hall. Opening the wardrobe door, she pulled out a selection, the hangers creaking as she examined the fabric. They were taking up too much room. She should throw them out. Yet while her life at Ludlow Hall was over, she was reluctant to let go of the expensive dresses and jackets. It would be a pity to just throw them in the bin.

Kathryn Rodgers had a cousin in the States who had stitched a memory quilt to remember the good times. Maybe she could do the same, if there were enough different colours: a quilt to capture the good moments of Ludlow Hall. If the other ladies were up to it, maybe they could do the same, stitch memory quilts to remember lost loved ones.

Shaking her shoulders, she made her way downstairs and into

her little sewing place, where she picked up the skirt she was making for Teresa Rafferty, the teacher from Arklow. Deftly, she threaded a needle and began to tack big stitches down the side seam, before moving to the machine to sew a long straight line.

8

Connie let the workmen pile all the old hoarding to the side of the house and waited for them to pack up and leave, before even thinking of entering the building.

Michael Conway was the last to go, loitering at the bottom of the front steps.

"Can I drop into the shop tomorrow to settle up?" she asked, and he moved from one foot to another, embarrassed she thought he was waiting for money.

"Don't worry about that; whenever you are passing will do. Do you need anyone to stay, show you around the house?"

"I will be fine, thank you."

She sounded formal and he did not argue, saying he would see her the next day. He was a quarter down the back avenue when she called after him.

"Mr Conway, on the way out, could you pull over the gate at the back entrance? I will do the front myself. I just don't want anyone wandering through."

He looked oddly at her, but waved to show he had heard, before starting up his car.

She waited until she was completely alone, almost afraid to take the first steps into the house. Crows squabbled high up in the trees near the barn, the breeze lightly catching one of the stable doors, making it bang rhythmically, as she slipped across the yard to the back door.

The key fitted snugly, turning with only a little effort on

her part. Stepping into the kitchen, she had to push a net of cobwebs out of her way. It was a small kitchen with an Aga and a long rectangular table in the middle covered in a flowery oilcloth. The presses were open and empty, and the fridge was unplugged, its door wedged open with a piece of wood. Stepping through the kitchen to the hall, she stopped at the ornate mahogany table with a marble top. A bunch of lilies in a vase had putrefied, the vile smell piercing up her nose, the dust from the stamens staining the tabletop. Some blooms had fallen away, wilting dark brown, sticking to the marble. Others had congealed in a corner, a dark mess that made her stomach turn.

A mirror above the table had little notes stuck to it, reminders of court dates:

Tuesday, High Court No. 3, 10.30
Thursday, High Court No. 10, 11 a.m.

A shopping list had only four items:

Steak/Doyle's
Spuds
Carrots
Irish Times/Michael

It was written in a neat, tight hand. There was the sense of a life suspended, waiting.

The door to the drawing room was wide open. Despite it being a spacious light room in various shades of cream and gold, there was little about it she liked. Curious, she picked up the book left face-down on the small table beside the velvet fireside armchair. A notebook covered in silk, it remained splayed, as if it had gone that way permanently because it had been abandoned so long. The pages cracking as she turned them, she saw poems written out in longhand, notes, newspaper cuttings pasted in, recipes gummed in, others written in and dated. At the front, a short dedication:

From me to you.
With love
xx

The book creaked as she closed it. Looking over her shoulder, she was almost afraid its owner would return and ask what she was doing. The mug beside it was dark brown inside, holding a gelatinous sludge where once there had been tea.

Sitting back into the armchair, she took in the painting over the fireplace: a man and a woman, sitting stiffly on these very chairs in front of a warm fire. Strange in its composition, the woman was wearing a ball gown, the man in what looked like a dark tweed suit.

The dress was navy with a lustre of chiffon about it. A row of tiny gold buttons fringed with navy clustered down the centre of the bodice before it pulled into a tight waist, giving way to soft folds of fabric. Short puff sleeves caught into a plain band above the elbow emphasised the simple beauty of both the dress and its wearer.

The woman sat, her hands held together on her lap, her book closed on the table beside her. Around her neck was a necklace with a purple-red stone in a gold setting.

The man was crouched in his chair, a newspaper scrunched in his hands, as if he was unaware of the artist at work, or that the woman next to him looked so fine. Lingering on her face, Connie was drawn to the woman's eyes, gazing into the distance, as if she was deep in thought about something she could not share. There was, she thought, something about the woman's eyes, a sadness lingering in the gaze.

Connie moved across the worn old carpet to the front window, stuck with grimy dirt on the inside, cobwebs, dust and spiders huddled in the corners of the outside frame. A soft lace curtain was hanging loose from its elastic wire, dipping in the centre, giving the aura of a place uncared for. Gold brocade curtains were stiffly in place, tethered to hooks in the wall with gold fabric tiebacks.

She looked beyond to the gravelled front driveway, the bank of rhododendron marching across the sweep of grass to where it turned off towards the yew walk. Standing inside the window, she saw the woman with her two dogs, both frantically barking, one digging a hole.

Angry, Connie whipped out of the sitting room, through the kitchen, rounding the house to the front, where the woman was already making her way down the driveway.

Connie ran after her. "Pardon me, pardon me."

The woman swept around. The dogs cavorting across the field did not slow down.

"I am sorry, but you can't walk your dogs in here any more. This is private property."

The woman's smile turned to a frown, as she eyed Connie up and down.

"You are the new owner?"

"Yes, you cannot let your dogs loose here any more."

"Ludlow Hall has always been open to the public; there is a right of way."

"There is no right to let your dogs run amok, digging holes, barking and making a nuisance of themselves. I am asking you not to return. How did you get in here?"

"What, are you saying that I jumped the wall? I came in like any decent person, through the gate."

Clenching her fists close to her, Connie shook her shoulders in an effort to remain calm.

"Please close the gate on your way out and make alternative arrangements for walking your dogs."

Her voice was dead calm, but she was furious, becoming even more incensed when the woman shrugged, calling her dogs with a piercing whistle.

"You won't be welcome in these parts if you continue down

65

this road," she snapped at Connie, clicking a lead on both her dogs. With a whip of her shoulders, she turned away to stroll down the avenue.

Connie, her chest heaving, walked over to sit on the seat at the front of the house. Her breathing too fast, she pulled in a gulp of air to calm herself. A light breeze rustled through the fuchsia bush, making it sway; an old leaf curled on the stone step was lifted and dropped back down, landing precariously on the edge of the next step. Connie shut her eyes, letting the billows of air tumble over her.

Why had she come here?

His words worried and wormed into her brain, exhausting her. Inside her head was a din of words: his words.

There was the light flutter of wings as a wagtail, sensing her stillness, landed nearby and watched her intently, the rustle of the rhododendron leaves as they shifted with the breeze, two crows on the roof of the house squawking out, harsh, monotonous. Tears pushed through her lids, cold on her cheeks as the breeze mopped them away.

"Mama, Mama!"

She grimaced, jumping up too fast, so her head began to swim in a swirl of words.

"Mama, Mama!"

Pins and needles of fear coursed through her.

"Mama!"

The cry was more desperate, more anxious.

Connie ran down the path to the yew walk and the lake, cold sweat forming on her temples, pains shooting through her.

"Molly, Molly!" she called out.

Blinded by the words in her head, she tripped over a tree stump, landing on the spent cherry blossom and rhododendron flowers.

"Mama!"

A woman with a buggy laughed out loud and reached for her toddler daughter.

"Silly sausage, Mummy is not going to leave you."

The woman turned around to see Connie on the ground, her face contorted in pain, her forehead shiny with sweat.

"Are you all right?"

The woman and child moved closer. Connie jumped up, making a big thing of brushing the petals from her clothes, so she had time to regain her composure.

"Silly me, I was in too much of a hurry," she said, smiling at the young mother and daughter.

"If you are sure."

Connie nodded and the woman moved on. She watched them go, a pain in her heart so big she thought she would pass out. Turning away, she bolted for the back of the house, desperate to be alone, where nobody would ask any questions.

Once in the back yard, she leaned against the wall of the barn panting, her hands shaking, still clammy. She could not go inside. Walking over to the back door, she pulled it hard, locking it, before jumping in her car.

She drove too fast down the front avenue. A man walking with his three children rushed to pull his youngest daughter out of the way. Clenching his fist in the air, he shouted, but, blinded by the tears, Connie wasn't exactly sure what he said. The front gate was open, pulled back to the limit as if in defiance, but she did not care. She turned left, back up the hill to the town.

When Hetty saw her coming in, she noticed Connie had been crying, but she did not pass comment. After ten minutes, she followed her up to the bedroom with a mug of tea.

"I thought you might like a cuppa. I will do something for you to eat, if you are hungry."

Connie, her make-up streaked with rivulets of tears, thanked her host and took the mug.

"I don't usually have the beakers, but I know there are those like yourself who prefer them. Do you mind me asking, are you all right?"

"Just a bit homesick."

Connie made to step back into the room and close the door behind her, but Hetty kept talking.

"I know we don't know each other very well, but you are welcome to come down to the sitting room. We can have a chat, or not."

"I am fine. I might go for a walk after the tea," Connie said. Disappointment swept across Hetty's face.

"Might be just as well, the ladies will all be in soon. If you are up to it, I could introduce you to everyone."

"Maybe," Connie said, and Hetty thought she closed the bedroom door a little too hastily.

Connie immediately poured the tea down the sink in the ensuite bathroom, before lying on the bed. She must have fallen asleep, because the ping of the doorbell woke her up. The buzz of conversation seeped up to her, making her burrow into the pillow, afraid Hetty would invite her downstairs.

★

All the ladies arrived together expect Eve, who doubled back because she had forgotten a new bag of cloth.

"You know that Yank has only closed up Ludlow Hall. The town is locked out," Dana Marshall said the minute Hetty opened the door. Not convinced she had the right reaction from Hetty, who stood ushering Dana towards the sitting room, the woman spoke out, louder this time. "It is an absolute disgrace. Eve won't be happy."

The other women all nodded in agreement, the buzz between them heightening as they aired their grievances.

"Has she moved or is she still here with you?" Eithne Hall asked.

Hetty's neck and cheeks flushed red. "She is upstairs. I told her if she was at a loose end, she could join us. I had no idea what happened." Hetty was wringing her hands, afraid Connie would overhear.

Kathryn Rodgers threw her eyes to heaven. "The last thing

we need at this meeting is that one telling us our business," she said.

Dana Marshall, a stout woman with glasses, made for the door. "I won't stay in any room with her. She ordered me off the property, you know."

"Now, now she may not come downstairs at all. Why don't we all calm down," Hetty said, directing the women to the seats and gently pushing Dana towards the couch.

As they fussed like hens, arguing over who got the armchair and who had to sit on the sofas, Hetty retreated to answer the doorbell.

"For God's sake, Eve, will you talk to these stupid women? They are nearly ready to lynch the American and she is in the room directly above us."

Hetty, flustered, was talking too fast. Eve burst out laughing.

"They are all just talk, you know that." Eve patted Hetty on the shoulder and slowly pushed her towards the sitting room. "Let's put the same energy and vigour into our work," she said.

The women, responding to her firm tone, took out their squares of fabric, some threading their needles, others stitching straight away. She let them sew a few stitches, to get into the rhythm, before she spoke again.

"What does everybody think about the exhibition? If we pull together, we might end up chatting to Michelle Obama."

"We should be discussing what is happening at Ludlow Hall," Dana piped up and the others murmured in agreement.

Hetty put her hands up, calling for hush. "For God's sake, will you let Eve speak."

Eve sat on the edge of the armchair beside the fireplace.

"I think this is a great opportunity for us. I, for one, would consider it an honour if Michelle Obama cast her eye over my work. It is a challenge, but a very good and exciting one," Eve said.

"We need to up our game if we are going to be picked to meet Mrs Obama," Kathryn Rodgers said.

"We can't take on anything too big," Dana said and, nodding to Hetty, continued. "No offence, but this place is tiny."

Hetty felt a bristle of annoyance run through her, but she said nothing.

Eve clapped her hands lightly to garner the attention of all the women again. "The Rosdaniel Festival suggested something with a connection to life in the town."

"That is a lot of work," Rebecca Fleming said, but the others hushed her.

"I was thinking of something a bit different," Eve said.

"What do you mean?" Hetty asked.

Dana Marshall snorted.

"Remember the year we did cushion covers with Rosdaniel houses on them. That was bloody difficult," Eithne said.

The women murmured in agreement.

"I liked the year we just did our own thing, big or small," Bernie Martin said primly.

Eve stood up and everybody quietened down to listen.

"How about memory quilts? Quilts made of the bits and pieces of fabric of somebody's life? They tell their own story. It could be a nice way to remember our loved ones." Eve turned to Hetty. "You still have a lot of Barry's shirts, don't you?"

Hetty nodded, but did not say anything.

"If you did not mind cutting a few things up, you could sew a memory quilt, patches of his clothes to bring back all the memories."

The other women began to mumble in agreement.

"Sure, we all know Barry was a snappy dresser," Eithne laughed and others giggled.

Hetty, not sure how to respond, made to sit down. Two women shoved over on the couch for her.

"I realise it is a bit of a shock," Eve said. "I could do one about Ludlow, cutting up old dresses worn at special occasions. It is not as if I have anywhere to wear them these days."

All the women began to chat excitedly, but Hetty remained silent. Eve turned to her.

"I did not mean to upset you, Hetty. If you can't do it, don't worry. It is just the whole town loved Barry, such a lovely fellow."

Hetty heaved in a deep breath. "I have not touched his clothes in so long."

Eve put a hand out, touching her knee lightly. "You don't have to give a decision right now. Have a think about it."

Bernie Martin, by the window, stood up. "Where are we going to make all these quilts? None of us has a room big enough."

"We must apply our minds to that, but not tonight," Eve said.

Eithne Hall, who lived outside of town, giggled. "It is all right for you, Eve, and you, Hetty: your husbands were something big around here. My Robbie was only ever a small farmer. We buried him in his Sunday suit, so that only leaves the cotton PJs and a pile of dungarees. Nobody wants to have sight of them."

Other women began to murmur in agreement and Eve held up her hands.

"Ladies, ladies, don't be silly. We can do a Rosdaniel quilt to represent all facets of life in the town. And Eithne, bring in a strip of dungarees, we will find a place for it."

They all laughed, talking excitedly as Hetty slipped away to make the tea and plate up the scones she had taken out of the oven before they arrived. She leaned up against the counter, forcing herself to take deep breaths in an effort to calm down. How could she make a quilt remembering Barry? How could she cut up his clothes? If she did not agree, the others would find it odd. She would have to do too much explaining.

Date: March 26, 2013
Subject: THE LUDLOW LADIES' SOCIETY

Ludlow ladies!

Memory quilts it is, and with any luck America's First Lady will be throwing her eye over them very soon. Thanks to Eve for coming up with such a brilliant idea. Jack Davoren can put that in his pipe and smoke it!

On a less competitive note, what better way to draw in the whole of Rosdaniel than to remember our finest in the most unique way? Hetty has agreed to sew a memory quilt for her late husband, Barry, who we all know was a man who gave his time to every organisation in this town, helping at the church, bingo nights and the Rosdaniel Town Committee. Hetty will be taking samples from Barry's shirts and suits and bringing this fine man to life again in patchwork form. We very much look forward to seeing that. There is no better way to remember Barry: we all knew him as a dapper dresser and a gentleman.

Eve, formerly of Ludlow Hall, is to bring Ludlow Hall to life in patchwork using fabric from all those lovely outfits she wore over the years.

I will personally oversee the Rosdaniel memory quilt. I am hoping Dana, Eithne, Bernie and Rebecca will give their time. Anyone else who feels they can pitch in, please come forward. We need everybody to give 110 per cent. The timeframe is short, only eight weeks or so, but the rewards will be high.

Let's get to work, ladies, we can do this!

Kathryn Rodgers,
Chairwoman

P.S. Ludlow Hall has a new resident *in situ*. It is not clear if the lands will remain open to Rosdaniel residents for public access, but we at the Ludlow Ladies' Society will appeal to the new owner to consider how dear Ludlow Hall is to all of us and how important it is in our community. Neither are we happy Dana and her dogs were ordered off the lands this week. We will continue to monitor the situation.

9

Hetty was up and had coffee made when Connie came downstairs the next morning.

"How are you feeling? Are you up to having a bit of breakfast?"

"I am sorry, I hope you have not gone to any trouble, but I will just have some coffee."

Hetty beamed. "That is what I thought. I said to myself, if you come down feeling a great hunger, I can throw it all in the pan. Come into the kitchen and we can have the coffee together."

Connie followed her, sitting at the small counter while Hetty fussed, taking down her best china mugs for her visitor.

"I hope the ladies did not disturb you last night."

Connie smiled, allowing Hetty to pour milk in her coffee. "I didn't hear a thing," she said, and Hetty fretted she was just being polite.

"We are a noisy lot. We have a lot to talk about." Hetty was drumming the counter with her fingers, because she was nervous.

"I am moving into Ludlow Hall today."

"It won't bother you, staying in that big old place on your own?"

"It is my home now, so the sooner I get used to it the better."

"Eve loved it there. She was devastated when she had to leave."

Connie swirled the coffee in her mug. "Why was that?"

Hetty rummaged for some biscuits. "It is not really my place to tell, but that husband of hers took out a huge bank loan and could not repay it. They came knocking on the door early in the morning. Poor Eve had to walk away from her own home."

"That is terrible."

"It has nothing to do with you. I suppose there is no harm in you knowing about it."

"Is that why folks are so agitated about me being here?"

Hetty guffawed out loud. "It is easy to get the good people of Rosdaniel hot and bothered; it will all die down in time. You are the owner of Ludlow Hall now and that is that."

"My husband was the person who wanted to come here, but he died. I was left with the estate."

Hetty reached over and took her hand. "Don't be worrying about what people around here say. You have a friend in me, and the others will just have to get used to it." She fiddled with a spoon on the counter. "Do you mind me asking what are your plans for the place?"

Connie looked startled. "I don't know exactly."

"What did you do back home?"

Connie did not reply immediately.

"I don't meant to pry," Hetty said quickly.

"I was a dance teacher, but I have not danced in a long time, that's all."

Hetty clapped her hands in excitement. "Ooh, that sounds mighty. You have to give us dance classes. I always wanted to be able to dance properly."

Hetty began to move her hips, taking mincing steps across the floor, clicking her fingers to an unheard beat.

Connie laughed. "I honestly don't know. I guess I will have a better idea when I move into Ludlow Hall."

"Dance classes would be so fantastic, but promise me if you do go ahead with any of those plans, you won't confine it to the kids. We in the Ludlow Ladies' Society would love to tango." Hetty laughed.

"I have to settle in first." Connie, flustered, got up to go.

Hetty reached out and hugged her. "Don't forget us ladies when you are making the dance plans." She pulled back to look Connie in the face. "Just remember, if it all gets too much for you today, you can come back here. I mean it, any time, day or night, there is a bed for you here." She waved off Connie from the door, a tune in her head, memories flooding back, her hips swaying.

Barry was a lovely dancer, in the early days waltzing her around the kitchen, his hand lightly resting on her waist, softly singing in her ear. Early days, happy memories, she thought, climbing the stairs to the little room beside the attic guest suite.

It was where she kept all of her dead husband's paraphernalia. Not able to look at his clothes, not able to throw them away since he had died five years ago, she had had the carpenter division off this type of dressing storeroom. On rails were the suits he loved, tweed mainly and some twill, and for the summer light grey and brown blazers, all covered in plastic. He had had special plastic covers made for each suit, saying a man who did not look after his suits was a man you could not trust. His leather shoes, still with the patina of polish, balls of newspaper stuffed in to help them keep their shape, were stacked underneath in a row. To one side hung his good overcoat, long and dark. On the other end of the rail were his Sunday best shirts.

Barry was so particular about his shirts, insisting they had to be starched and rinsed in cold water, and pressed with a handkerchief between the heat of the iron and the linen of the shirt. He spent his money on heavy linen shirts, once ordering from a fancy place in London, but more often than not saving up and purchasing them in Arnotts, Dublin. She should have buried him in the London shirt, but she didn't. Instead she went to Tesco in Wicklow and bought a light blue shirt. When they lowered the coffin, all she could think of was Barry in his supermarket cotton. But she later worried she would pay dearly for her actions, staying awake into the night, afraid he would come back and haunt her. Most of his other clothes, she kept in neatly stacked boxes, except for his ties, which were wound up and arranged in rows like doughnuts in a drawer.

Quickly, she closed the wardrobe doors, the memories hitting her hard. He was gone five years next week, but it felt as if it was only yesterday. Under the skylight was his dressing table. She sat down, her breathing becoming faster, reaching out, fiddling with his brushes. In her distraction, trying to stay calm, she tipped against the aftershave bottle, making it fall over with a thud. As she put the bottle back in its place, a drop seeped under the seal on to her fingers. Even after all these years, his smell was strong, the aroma snaking around the room, clinging to her, making her nostrils twitch.

Nervously, she straightened on the seat, expecting to hear his step on the stairs, his clearing of the throat. She checked every-thing was in its place before bolting to the guest suite, where she washed her hands, soaping away the aftershave in a lather of soap and hot water. After he had died, that aroma of his aftershave often stopped her in her tracks, curling around her, drifting past when something of his was disturbed. Sometimes she found a certain comfort in sitting into the fireside chair he used. Every night after dinner, his aroma was so strong she could sometimes imagine him. Other times, the smell of him sneaked up on her, making her recoil and collapse in tears. It had happened when his bolts of fabric, the tools of his trade were collected to be handed out to the pupils of the local school so they had enough fabric for their needlework classes.

She smiled to think she once thought his smell was such an exotic one. She was proud that this man, who had a hint of sophistication, should be so interested in her. She had worked in Driscoll's drapery in Arklow behind the fabric counter, calcu-lating how many yards were needed and cutting out reams of fabric for the farmers' wives when they came into town on a Saturday.

Barry was one of the reps who called twice a month, his sample fabrics neatly folded in a battered old leather suitcase.

Hair slicked back, his fingernails cleaned and clipped, his shoes polished, Barry Gorman was very much the professional man. Every day he wore a navy pinstripe suit, even though he was only a salesman. His only concession to winter was a grey wool jumper under his suit jacket, his tie tucked underneath.

He was a handsome man, and she fell in love with his style and his warmth and, later, his attention to every little detail about her. Barry smiled and winked at her and, being a silly girl, she let her heart be captured. On his third visit to the shop, he asked her out to a dance. Six months later, they were married and Barry the rep had become Barry the shopkeeper, snapping up the fabric shop when old man Driscoll decided to sell up.

Pulling a finger along the top of the dressing table, Hetty found it neat, everything in its place as if he had only stepped away for a while. He was dead five years now, but she still did not know what to do with his things.

A crow flew on to the roof and peered in the skylight. She laughed, making it flit away, leaving only rumbles of clouds and sky. Closing her eyes, she remembered those first days, when they had so little, Barry working so hard in the shop, she spent the whole time waiting for him to come home. Picking up his watch, she looked at it. A fancy silver watch with a bracelet fastening, it had stopped a long time ago. Every night when he came home from work, he took off his watch and placed it on the sitting room mantelpiece, transferring it to the dressing table when he came to bed. He always picked the same spot each night, gently pushing the watch into place as if a special place had been marked out for it. Beside it was a box with his good gold cufflinks. He had bought them with his first and, as it turned out, his only bonus as a salesman.

Hetty made to put out her hand to touch the watch, but, like every other time, she felt his eyes on her and withdrew. Suddenly, she got up from the dressing table and left the room, making sure to lock it behind her. She fumbled about the house, straightening cushions that were already straight and wiping down the kitchen worktops for the tenth time that morning, still not sure if she was brave enough to make a memory quilt.

★

At Ludlow, Connie got out of the car to close the gates after she drove through. As the gates rumbled shut, she felt out of sorts, not wanting to be here, but compelled. The back avenue was a grass track through some fields, so she drove slower, bumping her way to the house.

At the back door, a mouse, surprised, scooted across the yard to the barn. Disgusted, she let herself in, dropping her handbag on the kitchen table. Wedging the back door open, to air out the room, she next pushed up the window by the sink, shoving it up as far as it would go.

Moving to the hall, determined to get a through breeze, she took the big key down off the hook on the wall. Pushing it into the keyhole, she made to turn it, but there was no give. She tried pushing and pulling the door, jiggling the key all the time, but it would not budge.

Disappointed, she went into the big room used as a library and study. A light, airy room, even with every available space covered in books, its long, wide window overlooked the fields and part of the lake in the distance. Pacing across the floor, she jigged up and down, hoping what was underneath the dark carpet was a wooden floor. It was a wide, long room with a high ceiling. If it had a good floor, it would be a start. Could she even dance any more? She had not taken a step since that day, afraid to let go, immersion in the pain of loss draining all life from her.

She sat at the big heavy desk in front of the window, angled so that the sitter could view the fields beyond. The leather office chair was comfortable and well worn. Idly, she opened the drawers, each one stuffed with bunches of receipts, as if whoever had placed them there had scooped them from a full pocket with the intention of sorting them later. The last drawer was empty except for a key in the far corner: tiny, the blade short, the tip chunky, the bow an ornate design. There was no doubt it was for something specific, but there was nothing to indicate what. Connie looked around, but there was no obvious place to put it, so she replaced it in the drawer, before standing to look out the window.

The woman with the two dogs was back, the animals barking and happy, speeding across the grass. Moving to one side, so she would not be seen, Connie watched, envious of the bond between dogs and owner. Frustrated, she turned away, making her way upstairs, trying to ignore the happy yelping. The first room she peeped into was dark, the shutters closed, so she moved gingerly to pull them back.

A man's room: the furniture mahogany, embossed wallpaper on the walls, the accoutrements of shaving in a cup. Bottles of aftershave were lined up on a table in front of the window. A small dressing room off still had rows of men's shoes, but was empty otherwise.

Feeling she was intruding, Connie moved to the next room. Here the shutters were already back, the room full of light. Stepping in, she knew this was the room she would use. The dressing table was empty, its drawers pulled out. Only a few pieces were left on the hangers in the dressing room. She pulled up the sash windows to air out the room and dragged an old patchwork quilt from the bed to reveal a bare mattress. She folded the quilt onto a chair, the bed and mattress ready for collection when the Arklow furniture shop delivered her new sleigh bed.

Sitting at the walnut dressing table by the window, she looked at herself in the mirror. She looked tired, bags under her eyes. Once so particular about colour and cut, her hair was now almost completely grey, long, scraggly and shapeless. If she was to go back into teaching, she would have to clean herself up.

Unable to bear the scrutiny any longer, she jumped up, in her haste knocking over the stool she had been sitting on. As she righted it, she spied the woman from the other day standing on the stone seat at the front of the house, her dogs around her as she teased them with a bag of treats.

Connie bolted down the stairs, cursing when she could not open the front door. She hurried out the back and around the house, until she could see the woman dancing like a madwoman and firing treats into the field. Connie faltered, watching the antics. Realising she had not been spotted, she slipped back, scuttling around the house, as she saw the woman walk to the rhododendron, before whistling for each dog and clipping on their leads.

She must ask Michael Conway to find the opening in the fencing this woman saw as her own private entrance and block it up.

10

Eve picked a generous bunch of lilac from the bush in her front garden and wrapped up the stems in tinfoil and newspaper, before getting a nice square of tissue paper to place around the bouquet. She set off early for Ludlow Hall, not wanting anybody to see her walking down the main street holding a huge spray of flowers.

Michael was the only person moving about Rosdaniel. He knew her mission, so he waved, giving her a thumbs-up. The night before, she had told him she intended to call on the new owner. He endorsed the idea and even offered to take her there.

"I think it is something I have to do on my own, Michael," she said quietly.

She always liked the walk down the hill to Ludlow and this morning was no different. Stopping for a few moments at the bridge, the water hurrying and gushing over the rocks, she remembered all the times Arnold had threatened to get rid of this treacherous narrow bridge, have the road widened. Puff talk, she called it, and it annoyed her. It saddened her, too, that he could not appreciate the little bridge and stream, which offered an oasis of calm.

Letting her hand plane along the top of the bridge until the end, she continued on the journey to the front gates of Ludlow Hall, dragged across and closed, with a sign hanging crooked: "Private Property. Keep Out."

Slipping through the stile, she trekked slowly up the avenue, her step heavy with trepidation. How many times had she done it in the past, irritating Arnold, making him give out?

"Darling, you don't need to walk anywhere," he said, and she knew he was annoyed, not wanting to give the impression that they could not afford to run their gas guzzler of a car.

The house looked quiet as she approached, the sun glinting on the top windows, the wisteria like a ghost crawling across the façade, dipping into the crevices. Shutters upstairs were still pulled across and she wondered if she was too early. In her day, nobody would have got this far without the geese chasing them across the field, the dog turning out from the back. She stood and listened, the breeze tousling the polished leaves of the rhododendron, the branches creaking heavily. In the distance, she could hear the Dublin bus rev up the hill to Rosdaniel. She did not want to be seen wandering around the place, as if she still owned Ludlow Hall. Not sure what to do, she perched on the stone seat at the front. She liked the view from here: the avenue, the paddocks when they were lush, the fences mended, the horses sometimes cantering over to push against her, searching for a treat. The geese had flocked over too, sometimes giving away her hiding place on the seat as they hissed and croaked too loud, traipsing across the flowerbeds so that the housekeeper ran out to shoo them away.

She realised that if the American looked out her window now, it would seem odd that she was sitting here, so Eve got up and climbed the stone steps to the front door, stopping to flick dried moss off the rusty balustrading.

Pressing the bell, she heard it *brrinng* through the house, twirling across the rooms.

She pressed a second time, and was about to leave when a woman came to the window of the drawing room and beckoned to her to go around the back. Eve smiled, dashing down the steps, a little self-conscious that she was carrying a big bunch of flowers.

The American, wearing a heavy dressing gown which was too

long and tied with one of Arnold's old belts, stood at the back door.

"I am sorry, did I get you up?"

"I'm not much of a sleeper."

"Eve Brannigan, from the village. I wanted to say welcome." Shyly, she handed across the bunch of lilac.

"This is very kind of you."

"They are nothing special, just from my patch of a front garden."

Eve did not quite comprehend, but she detected a certain reticence from the American about the gift. As if she was aware of the observation, Connie smiled brightly.

"Won't you come in, Mrs Brannigan?"

"No need to offer, I just wanted to make you feel welcome."

"I know you owned the place for a long time. Maybe you can help me: tell me how I get the front door open?"

"Do you have the key?"

"Yes, but I can't turn it."

Eve laughed. "There was always a special knack with that door. My mother-in-law said we would end up trapped in this house and burned alive, our bodies piled up inside the locked front door, just because we could not turn the key. I am sorry, it is a sordid story from a melancholic old hag."

Connie laughed. "Dramatic. Now I really have to get it open. Maybe I should get a new lock."

"It is an old door, best to learn how to open it." Eve was afraid she sounded too sharp, so she stepped back, lest the American change her mind.

Connie, beckoning Eve to follow, walked ahead to the hall. Tentatively, Eve stepped into the kitchen. It was cold, the cobwebs netting high up across the ceiling. The stove had not been lit, but a bowl had been placed in the middle of the kitchen table in some attempt to make the place appear lived in.

Stepping through to the hall, a pain drifted across her chest. The paintings were still on the walls, the hall table, mahogany, dark with the cold marble top, in the same place. She had hated it from the word go, tried to soften it with pots of geraniums, but Arnold said it made it too showy, only allowing a glass vase with roses.

"Otherwise, it makes us look like any house down the main street of Rosdaniel," he said. She acquiesced, not wanting a big show of words about a few flowerpots.

"There is a huge amount of post here. I stacked it all up; I presume you will want to take it with you."

Eve looked at the wire milk-bottle basket, piled high with brown and white envelopes and flyers advertising things from years before.

"Throw it all away, if you don't mind. There is nothing there I want to read. I am gone out of this place a few years. If there are any bills, I think they know at this stage they are not getting paid."

Connie thought better than to pursue it and handed the key to Eve. A big old-fashioned jailer's key, it was usually kept on a hook high up beside the door. Eve put it in the lock and pushed against the door, slightly lifting the key before turning it. The lock snapped back and Eve stepped aside.

"You should open it: it is your front door now."

Connie pulled at the door, but it did not move.

"It has been shut a few years. I don't know of anybody who came to the front, even in my last year here. Let me help."

Eve prised a grip on the letterbox and they both heaved. The door gave way slowly, the paint loudly unsticking. Connie gave a last pull, so that the door opened wide, spiders and earwigs running for cover.

"There is a beautiful vista from this hall door," Eve said quietly, stepping back, hardly able to take it in, only seeing it the way it used to be when sometimes she sat out on the step, her sewing on her lap. It was always when Arnold was away from Ludlow Hall, because otherwise he complained that sitting on the front step was a common pastime.

Michael had put the stone seat there for her. He came across her one day sitting out on a cushion on the top step; the next day, she woke up to see him busy at work out the front.

"I notice you like to sit out, so I thought I could make it a bit more comfortable for you," he said.

She brewed some tea and they sat together, when the stone slab was in place, watching the geese and the horses, the dog at their feet. It was days before Arnold noticed the stone seat.

"It is a gift to both of us from Michael, such a kind man," she said.

Arnold looked at her oddly. "I wish he had asked before he put it in place. It is so heavy. But there is no point moving it now." Arnold's irritation made his voice boom through the rooms.

"Do you miss it?"

Eve at first did not realise Connie had asked her a question.

"The memories are flooding back, being here, but I have a simpler life now, which suits me. I miss Ludlow, but not as much as I originally thought I would."

"Come and have tea," Connie said, closing the front door.

"Maybe double check you can open the door first."

Connie did, and made to leave the key back on the hook. "It is a stretch. Why so high?"

"That is another mother-in-law story I am afraid. When Arnold, my husband, was young he was quite the sleepwalker. One night Martha, his mother, was lying in bed listening to an almighty racket, worrying somebody was coming to kill them all. By the time she got her husband to wake from his deep sleep, she was terrified. He went down to find the front door wide open, the wind raging through the hallway, making the paintings knock off the walls. He closed the front door and was quite cross to be disturbed. Martha looked in on a then eight-year-old Arnold, but his bed was empty. That is when the panic started. They found him down by the lake, wading in up to his chest, trying to catch a fish. After that, the key was put at an unnaturally high level for a child. I think they also had a makeshift alarm set up, a piece of string attached to a bell, so if Arnold went sleepwalking again, they would be alerted."

"I guess you have a lot of stories like this."

"You should have stopped me: when I get caught up in the memories, I tend to prattle on."

"It is nice to have such lovely memories."

Eve thought there was a whiff of sadness about this young woman, so she put her hand on Connie's shoulder.

"I am sure you will make your own good memories here."

They walked together to the kitchen, where Eve remained standing until Connie indicated to her to pull a chair up to the kitchen table.

"Should we have tea in the sitting room?" Connie asked.

"No need on my account."

Nervously, Connie switched on the kettle, standing waiting for it to boil. Plopping two teabags into mugs, she poured the boiling water in.

"Will a slice of lemon do? I don't have milk, I have yet to do a grocery shop."

"You should get Michael Conway to do all that for you. He delivers and will never leave you with the bad stuff."

"I only have myself to look after, so it is not so bad."

Eve shifted uncomfortably on the chair. "You are a brave woman to come this far on your own."

"Brave? I hardly think so, but thank you." Connie picked up a teaspoon, feeding it between her fingers. "Stupid is a more accurate word."

Eve did not answer.

"Mrs Brannigan."

"Eve, please."

"Eve, how do I get to know people in the village? I smile, I greet, but I can never seem to get past introductions or comments on the weather. Everybody is polite – well, nearly everybody – but nobody really talks to me."

"I had a few problems when I moved here too. Rosdaniel is

a great spot; it just takes a while. After several decades I don't think I am a blow-in any more, but it takes time."

Connie let the spoon drop onto the table with a clatter.

"I'm thinking of giving up before I even start. I have never come across anything like this before."

"Ludlow has been part of this village for a very long time. People take it personally if they can't walk through the grounds for fear of prosecution."

Connie sighed loudly. "Pardon me if I want a little privacy."

"Not everybody is bad. Maybe when you get to know us ..."

"But how am I going to do that? Mrs Gorman and Mr Conway are the only people who converse with me, and now you." She stopped, knowing she sounded hysterical.

"Now, now, Rosdaniel never makes it easy at the start. You just have to know how to deal with everyone. You just have to find a way, like I did."

Eve let her chair swing back on two legs as she told the story of how, in her day, she turned around the ladies of Rosdaniel and averted a crisis.

It was not long after Arnold had taken over the running of the Ludlow estate. He was incensed when the locals strolled through the fields and down to the lake, nodding hello to him as if they had a right of way. Often he marched over and told them he would prefer if they walked elsewhere. He told them his mother might have accepted that intrusion but he and his wife would prefer to have some privacy. At first, Eve felt it was not her place to get involved, but when Arnold closed the gates of Ludlow Hall, putting up a "Keep Out. Private Property" sign, there was uproar. Locals who crossed over the fields regularly were the first to register their fury, but were quickly followed by the rest of Rosdaniel's citizens, who saw the Hall as their recreation park all year round. While there was no legal right of way, there was a long-held tradition on both sides that those from Rosdaniel could walk the lands around Ludlow Hall.

When all the apples from the orchard were stolen in one

night, Arnold was furious, his opinion of Rosdaniel as a hotbed of vandals now entrenched. A delegation of local men seeking to meet Arnold was ordered off the property. It was only when, for two days running, supplies were not delivered, no post arrived and the housekeeper did not turn up for work, that Eve fully realised the ramifications of her husband's actions.

Michael suggested she intervene, but in a quiet way.

Not telling Arnold, she walked into the village to the weekly coffee morning of the Rosdaniel Women's Club. Outside the village hall, she could hear the buzz of conversation as the ten or twelve women inside had coffee and cake. Knocking lightly on the door, she walked in. The postman's wife was the first to see her, quickly elbowing Margaret Kelly, the Ludlow Hall housekeeper, beside her.

"Good morning, ladies. I was hoping I could join," Eve said, a smile on her face.

Hetty Gorman walked towards her and put out her hand.

"You are welcome, Mrs Brannigan, but you must realise this is difficult."

Eve took Hetty's hand a bit too tight, to stay firm in her resolve.

"Ladies, my husband has been stupid. I am here to make amends. I was hoping we could work a way around all this, without the men realising anything."

One woman laughed loudly. "My man is in a right pickle because his boss told him to get off his high horse and deliver to the Hall or else."

"I want to go back to work, but my husband won't hear of it," Margaret Kelly said quietly.

"What will we do?" Eve asked.

Hetty Gorman clapped her hands loudly. "We will all sit down. Finally, the ladies' group has something exciting to do."

Eve was introduced to each woman. In turn, they stood up, Kathryn Rodgers vigorously shaking her hand, Bernie Martin grunting her greeting, Dana Marshall using the opportunity to say Ludlow Hall did not belong only to Arnold Brannigan but to the whole of Rosdaniel. Rebecca Fleming gave a formal handshake. Eithne Hall and Marcella Lyons were the only ones to stay sitting, nodding a quick greeting.

Eve, nervous, gabbed on to cover the awkwardness they all felt.

"My Arnold is a city man. He is not like his father, but he loves Ludlow Hall and is deeply upset by what has happened."

"So upset that he was off in his big car early this morning," Marcella Lyons sniped.

"He has business in the city for the next two days, which is why I think we could work this out while he is away. I will open the gates and take down the signs when I go home. You will come back to work," she said, turning to Margaret. Nodding to Helen O'Dea, the postman's wife, she said, "Your husband will deliver as normal." She spun around to a shy woman, Nell Beecham, who was on the outside of the circle. "Aren't you the woman who tends that beautiful garden just back from the main street?"

"Mrs Beecham. My husband is the Church of Ireland reverend here, though it is a very small community."

Hetty Gorman, a sweat forming on her brow, pushed in with her words. "We don't exclude anyone, Mrs Brannigan, not in this group anyway."

Eve turned to Mrs Beecham. "My husband returns at lunch-time on Monday. Could you pick some of the best flowers from that lovely garden and make up a bouquet and have your husband deliver them to Ludlow? Address the card to me, inviting me for tea. And Hetty, could you send a letter inviting me to the women's club?"

"I can, but what good will this do?"

"No man will go against his wife wanting to be accepted into the local community."

Mrs Beecham pulled her chair closer. "But won't the men be upset if it is all taken out of their hands?"

"I think we can get around that," Hetty said, her voice almost a whisper.

The rest of the women leaned in to listen.

"Nell Beecham, you ask your husband's advice about the sending of the bouquet. He is sure to recommend this kind gesture. Forgiveness and all that."

"I will try."

"Why don't we all remark on the fact that we heard the gates have been reopened, start a conversation about Ludlow Hall being open to all again."

Eithne Hall, who had not spoken yet, piped up. "That just leaves the whole thing about the apples from the orchard."

They all stared at Eve.

"Arnold said it was a bumper crop," she said.

Bernie Martin got up and walked across the room, where there were crates stacked on top of each other. Hetty could feel the sweat pumping from her.

"I am afraid we all went mad and supplied the crates. The lads handed them over the wall once full, and we drove them here. Don't worry, we have the apples wrapped in newspaper, they will hold."

There was silence as each woman eyed up Eve, trying to guess her reaction. Eve looked from face to face, straightening in her seat, her two hands clenched tight on her lap. Eithne Hall sighed, Rebecca Fleming fidgeted and Hetty seeped sweat. When Eve laughed out loud, their shoulders slumped in relief. Hetty took a tea towel and wiped it across her brow.

"I am sorry, ladies, but the tension is mighty," she said and giggled. They all joined in and Eve felt the happiest she had been since she moved to Ludlow.

"That is a lot of apple tarts," she said.

"Enough to feed the whole village," Hetty said, and they laughed again, until the tears streamed down their faces, streaking their make-up.

Mrs Beecham was the first to bring them back, saying they

had better quieten down or the people passing might think they were up to all sorts.

"We had better get down to business. We are supposed to be discussing new premises," Hetty said, turning to Eve. "Your husband owns this small hall too and he has given it over to the school, a very worthy thing on his part, so the children can put on plays and maybe do some gym work. Until we can find a permanent home, we will just have to use our sitting rooms. Otherwise the group will fall through. We will all go back to just nodding to each other on the street."

"I am not sure Arnold will allow the Ludlow Hall sitting room to be used."

"We will bombard him with apples and flowers," one woman said, and they all began to laugh again.

Eve waited until Arnold had returned from a short trip to the States to ask his permission for the club to use Ludlow Hall.

"It is an honour: they want to call the group after Ludlow Hall."

"What name exactly?"

She decided to say something pompous to grab his attention.

"The Ludlow Ladies' Society."

"A suitable name. If you want it, the Society can have meetings here, but only in the kitchen."

When she told the women they would have to call the club the Ludlow Ladies' Society, they all agreed it was a small price to pay for a regular meeting place.

"There is nothing wrong with a fancy name. It gives our little group gravitas," said Kathryn Rodgers.

"You wouldn't be saying that if he wanted us to be the Rosdaniel Rabble," Eithne Hall said, and they all laughed.

Connie got up from her chair and stretched.

"You think I should do the same?"

"I might have a way to help you."

"I just want peace and quiet, Eve. I have a lot going on; I don't really want a big deal."

91

"You are right. You have just moved here all the way from the States and have this enormous old house to sort out and here I am going on about village politics. My apologies. When you are ready, we can look after the rest."

She scratched at a flower on the table oilcloth. "Do you mind if I speak plainly?"

"Please do."

"Open the gates and let the town in. Ludlow was always a place where people liked to walk with their kids. Some even dipped in the lake when the weather was good. Lock them out, you play into their hands."

"But I am here on my own. It is weird meeting strangers in my back yard."

Eve stood up. "It is up to you. I won't overstay my welcome."

Connie stood up and asked Eve to wait: she had something upstairs that might be hers. When she came back down with the charm bracelet, she thought Eve might faint.

Eve reached out, her hand enclosing the charm bracelet, letting the different charms fall through her fingers.

"Where did you find it?"

"Underneath one of the beds."

"The bed with the patchwork quilt: my room." Eve desperately tried to compose herself. "My husband gave me the charm bracelet on our wedding day. The first charm was the diamond heart. I am afraid the bracelet got rather crowded after that, especially when Arnold insisted on bringing me so many charms back from his numerous business trips to New York. I tried to put it on the morning when the bailiff came, but I was so upset I couldn't close the clasp. So addled was I, the next thing I knew, I was out of Ludlow Hall and had no idea where the bracelet was."

"Would they not let you back in to search for it?"

Eve snorted loudly. "The bank would have bloody well stopped me walking by on the road, if it could."

Connie could see Eve was trying to conceal that her hands

were shaking, so she placed the charm bracelet on the table, to allow her to pick it up when she was ready.

"I am so glad to have been able to reunite you with the bracelet. If there is anything else in the house you want to take, please do."

Slow tears rolled down Eve's cheeks. Embarrassed, she quickly wiped them away.

"You must think I am a right one. They are happy tears, I have not felt like this in a long time."

Connie smiled and Eve thought there was a huge sadness about her.

"Where are my manners? I never sympathised with you on the loss of your husband. I am so sorry." She took Connie's hand and squeezed it hard. "Why don't you join us at the Ludlow Ladies' Society?"

"I don't know much about sewing or anything like that."

"We are also good for a cup of tea and a chat, if you change your mind. We are all in my place tomorrow night, No. 5 on the terrace as you go into town."

"I am not sure."

"We meet at seven. If you call before that, you won't have to walk alone into a crowded room."

Connie did not answer and Eve turned out into the hallway to the front door. For a moment, she swung around, taking in the wide, high hallway.

"I hope you find the peace you want here."

Connie did not answer, but waited until Eve passed the rhododendron and out of sight before closing the front door.

11

Hetty was the first to arrive at Eve's the next night.

"I am a bit behind," Eve said. "Aoife Meehan insisted on waiting while I turned up a pair of trousers she wants to wear at an interview tomorrow. She pays well, but Mrs High-and-Mighty Meehan thinks we are all on this earth to serve her."

"At least you are not that poor husband of hers. Have you heard the latest?" Hetty bent forward, as if there was a danger the empty room might soak up her words. "She has engaged the services of a landscape designer for their patch of a lawn or, as she insists on calling it, 'the grounds'. That one thinks she has a palace rather than a former council house on the Ballyheigue Road."

"A good garden is always worth paying for," Eve said, making Hetty pull a face.

"She is putting in a big water feature. Where does she think she is living, Ludlow Hall?"

Eve laughed out loud. "She certainly would bring the old place into the twenty-first century. In comparison, the American does not seem so bad any more."

"Is she coming tonight?"

"I don't know, but if she does, we will make her welcome," Eve said, placing a plate of sliced lemon cake on the coffee table in front of the fire. "What about the memory quilt, Hetty?"

Hetty concentrated on ripping open the box of chocolate fingers, letting them slide out on to the plate. "It seems like an awful lot of work. I am not sure I could do Barry justice."

She could not help it: her voice trembled, so that Eve put her arm around Hetty's shoulders.

"You are a lucky woman, Hetty Gorman, in so many ways."

Hetty, tears bulging at the corners of her eyes, nodded, setting off around the room, plumping up cushions. Eve concentrated on getting cups and saucers out on a side table as they heard the first of the women arrive.

Hetty, picking a stool at the far side of the room, let the others take the main seats as Eve opened the meeting.

"We have to get started as soon as possible. The Festival organiser said maybe three quilts max."

Eithne Hall, the farmer's wife, guffawed out loud. "Who the hell wants to be cutting up old clothes?"

"Not all of us have old clothes, Eithne. I am sure you can contribute some of the lovely flowery fabric you wear to Mass every Sunday," Kathryn Rodgers said, immediately continuing on so Eithne did not have a chance to respond. "Yes, it is work, but it is our chance to shine, ladies. Surely everybody can see that?"

Eve straightened in her seat in the middle of the room. "So, who have we got to help out the memory quilt teams?"

A few women shuffled their feet; others concentrated on twisting the rings on their fingers. Everybody was quiet, the silence loud between them. Eithne threw her hands in the air and shook her head.

Eve looked anxiously from face to face. "What is eating everybody?"

"Maybe dipping into the past is not such a good idea," Dana mumbled, and the others nodded in agreement.

Eve sighed loudly. "I have given my word. The Rosdaniel Festival has reserved a space for us. I am going to take on the Ludlow memory quilt."

She looked at Hetty. Hetty's face flushed pink.

"It is only a bit of sewing," Hetty said.

She elbowed Rebecca Fleming, to her left, making the other woman shift and sit stiffly on her seat.

95

"I will contribute to a Rosdaniel quilt, but only if everybody does their bit," Rebecca said, her voice low but firm. When nobody answered, she threw her eyes to the ceiling, her cheeks quivering pink, as the other women sniggered.

"I will oversee the Rosdaniel quilt, and Eithne, Dana and Rebecca, we can't do without your steady hands," Kathryn said, and the other women nodded. Bernie Martin put her hand up to indicate she was in.

Glad that business was over, they took out their patchwork.

"Is the American going to make an appearance?" Kathryn asked, and the other women laughed.

Eve, who was cutting out squares of purple and black lace, turned around sharply. "Don't you think that young woman has enough on her plate, without us turning against her when we don't even know her."

"She is not in a rush to meet us all, is she?" piped up Marcella Lyons, who was squashed between the sofa and the wall.

"I am not sure I would be brave enough to walk into a room full of women I did not know," Hetty answered, her head down, as she busied herself examining the edges of two pieces of fabric. "She probably has more to be doing with her time anyway than sewing patches," she said.

The others, sensing an unhappiness in Hetty, returned to their sewing, the room going quiet as each concentrated on the work at hand.

Eve made two pots of tea and was about to serve when Hetty said she had to get going.

"You will do the Barry quilt?" Eva asked gently.

Hetty hesitated.

"It is a quilt everybody would love to see made," Eve said.

"I might be able to do a small one," Hetty replied, anxious not to draw the attention of the other ladies.

Grabbing her things, she let herself out. Not even stopping to pull on her coat, she set off up the hill home. The town was dead. She was itching for a cigarette, but she was too nervous to light up. She waited until she got home and into the kitchen before pulling the cigarette box from her handbag.

Anger pulsed through her that, five years after his death, the women of the Ludlow Ladies' Society revered her husband so much. How did they know what it was like to be Barry Gorman's wife? So charming, they said. How many times had she paid for the charming persona he put on outside of the house, the frustration of his daily existence building inside him, like a powder keg ready to ignite with a smile from her or maybe a word or often just a look his way.

The first time it happened, she excused it: it had been a bad week, with two repeat orders cancelled. He ignored her when she put the dinner on the table, stabbing at the roast potatoes, saying they were too crispy, the beef tough. Suddenly he shouted, setting the plate spinning across the table until it crashed to the floor.

Bending down to pick at the porcelain, she pulled at the beef, wondering if she should have let the roast sit for longer once out of the oven. Letting the dog wolf what was left on the floor, she dropped the remains of the plate in the bin.

Tears jugged through her, her hands shaking, her voice feeble when she spoke.

"Barry, I am sorry."

"You had the whole day to produce this swill."

"I can do something else, I am sorry."

"What can you possibly do in the next half-hour?" he said, his lips bulging with sarcasm.

"A nice creamy scrambled egg and some toast?"

She expected him to spit out a reply, but instead he reached for the newspaper. Taking his silence as a signal, she began to work cautiously around him. Carefully, she cracked the eggs on the edge of the bowl, fearful the noise would disturb him.

When he lit up a cigarette, she did not complain. Head bowed, she worked over the gas cooker until the eggs pulled into a soft mess. Spooning it out on to the plate, she kept the scrambled eggs warm over the saucepan, until the toast was ready to butter. Just before serving, she asked him quietly if he would like some salt. She stood, holding the plate, waiting for his answer.

"A sprinkle," he said, lowering the newspaper.

She got down the tub of salt, letting a small amount fall into the palm of her hand, kicking off a pinch across the eggs, before sliding the plate in front of her husband.

He said nothing, but folded the newspaper carefully, making sure to keep the crease. He raised a triangle of toast and spooned some egg on to it, before placing it neatly in his mouth.

She was filling the sink with boiling water from the kettle when she heard him shout.

"Who said you could throw the whole of the salt cellar on top of my dinner?"

"Just a sprinkle, Barry, nothing else."

Not bothering to look around at her husband, she started to pile the dishes into the hot, soapy water.

When the blow came, she had no idea what had happened. Pain punched across her head as she reeled across the floor, hitting against the dresser, so her display plates and the china tea set her aunt had given her for a wedding present clattered. The sugar bowl fell off, smashing to the floor. Barry shouted at her to get up, his face so close she felt the hot spray of his spit. He put a hand out and she made to grab it, thinking he was helping her up, but he pushed her, so that she was bent over. Catching her by the hair, he dragged her up. When she cried out, he clenched her hard, snarling in her ear.

"Who the hell said you could throw the whole of the salt cellar on my dinner, bitch?"

"I didn't, Barry. Stop, please stop."

He released his grip and she staggered away. Instinctively, she put her hands up to shield her head. When the blow came, it was the hardest yet, sending her careering across the room, hitting the wall before falling in a heap on the cold tiles.

She must have been knocked out, because when she woke up

she was woozy. Pain swelled through her, and blood caked into her hair and head, staining the ruffled collar of her good blouse.

She did not know where her husband was, so she went back to the sink, scrubbing the dishes hard, the lukewarm water a strange comfort. When she was finished, she dried the dishes, before making sure to stack them neatly on the dresser. Next, she straightened her china cups and saucers, being particular the plates at the back were secure. On her hands and knees, she brushed the broken delph into a discarded cereal box.

That was the night she started smoking. She saw the pack of Major thrown in the bowl on the dresser, and ripped it open. Reaching for the box of matches, she struck one, making sure to hold the cigarette well away from her face when she lit it. Sucking in a long draw, letting it down into her lungs, it made her wheeze and cough until her stomach heaved. She had to bolt for the back door, throwing up in the flower bed. Standing, looking out into the pitch dark, she worried where her husband was. Leaning against the back door, she pulled on the cigarette again, a short puff this time, observing the smoke as she exhaled curl off into the black, away from the pool of kitchen light.

As more puffs followed, she began to feel better. Leaning against the back door of the kitchen, inhaling, exhaling, the nicotine made her feel strangely lightheaded, the pain throbbing through her, pulsing at its own beat.

The click of the front door indicated Barry was back in the house. Quickly, she grabbed the cigarette pack from the kitchen table and put it back in the bowl. Catching the handle of the back door, she fanned the door swiftly back and forth to clear the air in the room.

Barry, his coat hanging open, walked in, pulled out a kitchen chair and slumped down. He looked at his wife.

"You look a mess. After you have made me a cup of tea, go clean yourself up," he rasped.

She lit the gas under the kettle, waiting for it to whistle, busying herself taking down his mug, swiping it with a teacloth to make sure it was clean.

"Stop fussing, woman, get me the tea," he said, and she felt a chill crawl through her, that he might lash out again.

When she brewed the tea, she poured it into a mug and nervously placed it in front of him. He took a sip before pushing the mug away.

"I will have a full Irish breakfast in the morning, on the table at 7.30 a.m."

He stood up, the chair tilting back, before marching out of the room. She heard him tramp up the stairs. His footsteps sounded over her head, as he walked across the bedroom to place his watch on the dressing table. Moving to the bathroom, she heard the thud of his shoes as he threw them into the hall for her to take away and polish. Finally, she heard the creak of the bed, but she decided she would wait until she was sure he was asleep before venturing up the stairs.

Grabbing the pack of cigarettes she had bought for him earlier that day, too afraid to steal from the box in the bowl again, she sat down at the kitchen table to light up. Pulling long and deep, she threw her head to the ceiling and exhaled slowly. Her hands shaking, tiny flecks of ash flicked across the table, but she did not care.

Halfway down the cigarette, she got up from the table, her bones aching, flashes of pain vibrating across her skin. Taking her coat from the hook on the back door, she made to go outside. She wanted the cold air to soothe her throbbing head. Before she went out the door, she switched off the kitchen lights, in case anybody noticed and commented on the funny hours the Gorman household was keeping. Quietly, for fear he might hear her, she lifted the latch and pulled back the door enough so she could slip outside.

The cigarette tip her only light, the darkness crawled around her like a comfort blanket. Here, she let the tears flow; her nose full of snot, she swiped it with her coat sleeve as she stumbled around the side, to the seat Barry had installed on the lawn last week. The seat was hard, the cold seeping up through her, but she liked it because it reminded her she was alive.

Tears flowed down her neck, soaking the velvet collar of her coat. Why he had beaten her like a thug on the street, she did not know. Neither did she want to know. How was she going to get his egg right for breakfast? Tears clogged her throat. She wanted to shout at the stars to go away, to tell the moon to stop shining, in case he woke up and saw her sitting on the garden seat, installed just for show.

She had been so excited when the seat arrived. Last Saturday he arranged for a man in a van to collect it and help him put it in place. After they decided on the angle, she went to sit on the seat, but Barry pulled her back.

"You don't want to be sitting out here, where all the neighbours can see you. They will say Barry Gorman's wife is gone bone lazy sitting, taking the sun."

She giggled but bypassed the seat, returning to weed the bed of dahlias.

Hetty sat down, pulling her feet up under her coat. Shivers of fear shuddered through her, combining with the cold, so that she ached all over. It must have been two in the morning, but she didn't care: while he was sleeping, she was safe.

Could it be that he would wake up later full of remorse? She did not think so. They were married, and that was the way it was going to stay.

Her mother was the only one not taken in by the charming Barry Gorman.

"I don't care how good he is to you now, girl. He was once a salesman, too skilled at putting an image across; you remember that. Ask yourself: do you know the real man?"

"Of course I do."

"He is asking you to give up your job. You are going to be very dependent on him."

"Mum, Barry has picked me, can't you be proud of that?"

Her mother placed her two hands on her daughter's shoulders. Quietly, she took a bundle of notes out of her pocket, slipping them into Hetty's hands.

"For you and you only. Use it when you need to. It will get you a guesthouse, if you ever need one in a hurry. If you want to dash for home, we are always here."

Hetty pulled away from her mother's embrace. "For God's sake, Mum, will you stop telling me I am a failure at marriage before I even start."

"Keep it for a year. If I am wrong, you can fritter it after that."

Hetty snatched the notes tight, before throwing back her hand and firing them across the room. "Don't think I will be talking to you any time soon, the way you insult us."

Hetty sobbed to think she had not even invited her parents to the wedding, choosing to get married in Rosdaniel with just Barry's family and a few of his friends as guests. Her mother died suddenly a few years later. Barry refused to take a day off for the funeral, so she went on her own, her sisters barely civil to her, her father too caught up in his own grief to realise her anguish.

Spotting a car coming up the hill, she rushed from the seat back into the house. Shaking out her coat in the night air, in case he got a whiff of smoke from it, she also left the kitchen door open while she arranged a bed for herself on the sitting room couch. She couldn't face cleaning his shoes just yet.

She lay on the couch, his snoring shuddering through the house, counting down the minutes and the hours until she had to get up.

Date: March 27, 2013
Subject: THE LUDLOW LADIES' SOCIETY

*****SPECIAL NOTICE*****

Ludlow ladies,

This is an urgent request for help. We need premises, any type of permanent structure. Please keep your ears close to the ground and your eyes peeled.

Creating as many as three patchwork quilts in one go is a big enough job, we so badly need space, somewhere to store the fabric and where we can hold meetings and join together stitching these quilts. It must have electricity for light, the machines and the irons. Anyway, who can sew for any length of time without a cuppa?

We need premises urgently if we are to keep our commitment to provide three works to the Rosdaniel Festival.

We hold on to the belief that when the Ludlow Ladies' Society puts its mind to something, there is no stopping us.

Kathryn Rodgers,
Chairwoman

12

Connie woke up early, the white mist curling in across the fields, the birds competing in song, the sun peeping through, touching off the windows at the front of the house. The mist lightly skimmed the grass, huddling into the fuchsia bushes, skirting around the trees. Ludlow Hall was quiet, but all around it, the day was beginning.

Connie took in the scene from the bedroom window, the calm that was Ludlow soothing her tired eyes, stroking her heart.

Every morning for the last two years, she had got up and done her stretching exercises, maintaining the routine of before in an effort to make sense of the now.

In her head, she told herself she must keep supple, toned, so she did not lose the ability to dance.

Every day as she limbered up, she longed to lose herself in the movement of dance and every day she froze, unable to step out, unable to let her grief give in to the music, unable to allow herself to be transported to another world.

How could she dance, indulge herself in the beauty of the communion of music and movement, when her heart was shrivelled with grief?

For two years, she half existed, staying in Amy's house, unable to communicate the pain that consumed her, unable to speak of what happened, unable to find any reason to continue a normal life, unable to dance.

But she knew too, as she knew maintaining the warm-up

routine was vital to her being able to take any dance step, so too to lose herself in dance would be the only way of journeying from this state of existence to living life again.

This morning she woke up with a firm resolve in her head, which she tried to keep strong until she had finished her stretching exercises.

Walking down the stairs, she felt the skip of movement ripple through her, so when she got to the study she felt ready. Slipping the switch on the CD player, she stood listening as the music permeated the room, surrounding her, teasing her to move, so that she felt a frisson of excitement that this time she would let the music lift her away to a place where nothing bad happened, to a place where she felt satisfied and content.

Tentatively she stretched, stepping out, letting the music lift her, letting her talent be her partner. She danced like an audience of one thousand watched her. She danced this audition to be included among the living. Her body tingling, her muscles straining to the limit, she moved across every corner of the room, the pain of dancing replacing momentarily the pain of her loss, the beat of the music and her steps bequeathing a freedom on her that felt good. Every effort in her being she put into the dance, the sweat jumping off her as she twirled across the floor, the music taking over her body, her spirits soaring as she flew almost like a bird, the music holding her aloft. Sweat ran down her face, but she worked harder and harder, almost out of breath when the music stopped. Slumping on the floor, the joy of flying evaporated, she was afraid now the dance was over reality would again consume her.

Exhausted but buzzing, she moved to the kitchen. She had been up since gone past five. Energised by the dancing, she set to work. Boiling kettles of hot water and using a thick disinfectant, she tackled the kitchen presses and fridge first, scrubbing away years of neglect, before throwing a cloth over the brush bristles to trap the cobwebs in the high corners of the ceiling. She scrubbed the sink until the stainless steel shone and wiped down the window glass with hot water and vinegar until it gleamed. Not sure what to do with the Aga, she cleaned the outside and rubbed a cloth on the inside of the ovens.

Draping a new oilcloth from the Rosdaniel hardware shop in tones of yellow and red across the table, she felt at last she was making this room her own. She was so busy she did not hear Michael drive up and park near the barn. When she opened the door, she saw the wide box he was carrying first.

"Eve said you might need a bit of help, so I brought you a few things, a few staples for the cupboard: tea, bread, milk, that sort of thing. Some things from the delicatessen."

She did not know what to say, but Michael Conway did not wait.

"I will put this on the table," he said, pushing gently past her.

"I did not order anything."

"I know, but Eve, Mrs Brannigan, thought you might need a nudge in the right direction. You can't just live on tea and biscuits."

He placed the box down, pushing it in from the edge of the table, rubbing his hands together, nervous of her reaction.

Peering into the box, she saw a paper bag with slices of freshly cut ham, vine tomatoes, salami and fresh bread rolls. There was a box with two cream cakes and two packets of chocolate butter biscuits.

"She told me to pick savoury and sweet. If you don't like anything I can bring it back, bar the ham of course, but who doesn't like a slice of ham."

He was prattling on, feeling uneasy. She giggled, reaching into the box to take out the paper bag, salty wet with ham.

"There is enough here for a party, Mr Conway."

"I may have overestimated with twenty slices," he said, jiggling his car keys in his trousers pocket.

"What do I owe you for this?"

"Nothing at all, see it as a welcome gift. About time, too, that somebody around these parts made you welcome."

"Mrs Brannigan brought flowers."

"Lilacs, her favourite."

"Sit, stay a while."

She moved to switch on the kettle, as he pulled out a chair to sit down. When he saw the small book on the table he reached over and picked it up.

"Eve wondered where she had left this."

His hand trembled as he held the book.

"It was on a side table in the drawing room."

He shook his head. "I offered to break in and search for it, but she said, knowing the bank and the type they employ to protect repossessed properties, they would have me charged and thrown in jail. I came up early one morning to pull off the hoarding and get into the house, but I was not early enough. I only managed to dislodge some of the wood nailed into the frame on the side window when I saw the security men come up the avenue."

"What did you do?"

Michael Conway traced a pattern on the oilcloth with his finger. "God forgive me, I pretended to be surveying the damage, said I found the place like that."

"Weren't they suspicious to see you so early?"

"If they were, they kept it to themselves."

He picked up the book, flicking through it, as Connie threw two tea bags in a teapot and got down the mugs.

"Eve should have asked me for the book. I am more than happy to return what is hers."

"Ludlow Hall is hers. She loves it with all her heart." He stopped, frowning, knowing he had said too much.

Connie, reaching into the box, selected the cream cakes, setting them on a plate beside the mugs.

"I inherited this place, Mr Conway. I am down the chain from the bank."

He slopped milk into his tea, splashing spatters over the sides in his confusion.

"I did not mean it like that. I was just trying to explain how much the old place means to Eve. She adores Ludlow."

"It must have been terrible for her, having to leave."

He did not say anything. They sat quietly, the antique upright hall clock wound up the day before ticking loudly, biting into the silence.

Michael reached over to cut an end off one of the cream cakes.

"You know about the eviction?"

"Mrs Gorman might have mentioned something."

"I am sure she did."

Connie straightened on her chair.

"Mr Conway, I am not responsible for Mrs Brannigan's eviction; neither was my husband. It was before our time."

He sighed loudly.

"We all know that, it is just it is so hard for Eve, to see somebody else live here. You know the bastards who evicted her came three hours early? The night before, she stayed up most of the night, reading her little book in the drawing room and walking from room to room, saying goodbye. I offered to stay with her, but she was not having it. At five she fell asleep. Next thing, at seven, there was a loud banging on the door. She just about got her clothes on. When Eve went to the front door, they wanted her out straight away, would only let her take her coat from the stand in the hall. She took a tin box of buttons on the hall table and they even looked in it, to make sure she was not taking anything of value. She was treated like dirt, start to finish."

Connie picked up the book.

"The book, is it important to Mrs Brannigan?"

He fumbled with the handle of his mug.

"As far as I know it is," he said, pushing back his chair, and standing up. "I had better get along. I was thinking I would tidy a few things around the lake. The path is very overgrown in places."

"Thanks for keeping the gardens under control. I presume you had some arrangement with my husband."

"He sent me $500 every Christmas for myself and another $300 towards upkeep of the equipment, like petrol for the mower and all that."

"But you have not been paid in a while."

"I kept working on the upkeep: it's very hard to pull a garden like this around if it goes too far."

"Thank you. Do you mind continuing on the same terms, if I catch up with the arrears owed?"

"I enjoy it, so I will," he said.

"Would you like to give the book to Mrs Brannigan?"

"Best it comes from yourself, I don't want Eve thinking I was sitting gossiping about her business."

Connie put her hand on his arm. "I am very touched by the grocery delivery, Michael. I will personally deliver the book to Mrs Brannigan."

"She asked those bastards could she go into the drawing room to look for it; they refused point-blank. When she asked why, they had the cheek to tell her everything in the house was the property of the bank. For all they knew, it was a valuable first edition that she was trying to hide from them. She told them the book was precious only to her, but still they wouldn't have any of it."

"I will give it back to her today."

"Don't let on you know any of this." He made his way to the back door, turning around as he put his hand on the handle. "If you don't mind me saying, you are a right fit for Ludlow. Give it time and it will all work out."

He was out the door and crossing the yard to get his shovels and rake from the car before she had time to answer.

Waving, he walked past the window on the way to the lake, as she emptied the box, finally plugging in the fridge so she could store the butter, milk and ham.

Picking up the little book, where, over the years, poems and recipes had been handwritten, she decided to call on Eve straight away. Rushing off to get dressed, before she changed her mind, she stopped when she heard the ping of the shovel in the distance. The sharp scraping sound tearing across her heart, she only heard the whoosh of the loose earth, the thud as the earth landed where it should. She clung to the bannister, suspended between the past and the present.

His words hammering in her head.

Pain shot through her, like a knife through the butter Michael Conway had put in the box. Moments like these were as devastating as the first time, crueller maybe, because of their frequency. She stood and listened to Michael Conway working, the sound of his shovel travelling in the light breeze buffeting around the house.

Pushing herself to continue the climb up the stairs, she looked out the side window, to a swathe of yellow daffodils, the paddocks green-brown with moss. Forcing herself forward, she climbed to the landing.

When she got to the room, she pulled on her jeans and blouse and ran a comb through her hair before tying it in a ponytail. Grabbing her bag and car keys, she rushed downstairs, snapping up the book from the kitchen table on the way to the car.

Michael Conway, looking up from his work, saw her drive too fast down the avenue. He wondered had he said anything to upset the new owner of Ludlow Hall.

Eve was sewing inside the window, when she saw Connie's car pull up. She waited to see if she was coming to her house or just availing herself of a parking spot near the town. When Connie opened the front gate, Eve jumped up, gathering stray threads into a ball, closing the door to her sewing room, plumping up cushions on the couch.

Connie's knock was short and sharp.

"You are a day late for the Ludlow Ladies' Society, but come in," Eve said as she opened the door for her guest.

Connie, slightly embarrassed, edged into the front room.

"I found a book in the drawing room. I thought maybe you would like to have it, that it means something to you."

Eve showed her visitor to the couch, as Connie handed her the book.

"I thought it was well gone, where was it?"

"Where you left it, I would imagine, in the drawing room. I put it back in the library, but after I talked to you the other day, I thought maybe you should have it."

"It is very dear to me. I call it my Ludlow Bible. A dear friend gave it to me in my first few weeks at the Hall. All sorts of things I like are in it: poems, recipes, quotations. Did you have a look?"

"I flicked through. I saw the inscription."

Eve lifted the cover, reading the personal note as if she was seeing it for the first time.

"So important to me. Thank you."

"Michael Conway called this morning with a box of food."

"You did not think it was too forward of us?"

"I think it very kind. I suppose I have been hiding away."

Eve sat down on the couch beside Connie. "It is easy to hide out, but ..."

"I want to hide out."

"As long as you know you have friends."

Connie took out her car keys. "I had better get along."

Eve put her hand out, as if to stop her. "I wanted to ask you something. You can refuse and there's no harm done."

She paused, until she saw Connie relax back down on the seat.

"We are making these memory quilts for the Rosdaniel Festival. None of us has enough space at home for fabric storage or even to spread out the quilts. We are hoping we will win a prize and a chance to show our quilts at a special exhibition for the visit of the Obamas to Ireland." She felt she was going on a bit, her throat tightening because she was nervous. "We wondered, as the Society used to meet at Ludlow, could you find any room for us? We are ten at most, but there are only a few of us taking on the quilts. We meet once a week, but near the deadline we might need access more often, if you don't mind, of course."

Connie was silent.

"Have I overstepped the mark?" Eve asked gently.

Connie shook her head. "Is this your way of keeping an eye on me?"

Eve twisted the ring with the ruby stone on her right hand. "Yes and no. We all know how difficult it is trying to move on, after losing a husband."

Connie jumped up. "Mrs Brannigan, I know you mean well, but I am not prepared to discuss my grief."

Eve put a hand out to Connie, but she brushed it away.

"You and the women can have a room at the Hall, just please don't expect me to open up about anything else."

Eve got to the front door, as Connie opened it.

"I am sorry, I forgot how raw grief is, even after time has passed. I have been a fool, I am sorry."

"It is not your fault, Eve. I have too much grieving left to do. And I mean it about the room. Call up on Friday morning, you guys can have a look around."

Eve nodded sheepishly, almost sorry she had suggested the idea. She watched Connie leave, the car shuddering as she wrestled with the gears.

Feeling shaky, Eve picked up the book. Turning it over in her hands, she noticed it did not close as it should, stuck after being left face-down on the drawing room side table for too long. All she had wanted that early morning was to pick it up, to bring it with her into the unknown. It would have given her so much comfort. She smiled to think of how angry Michael Conway had become when she told him, pacing up and down this sitting room, his eyes staring in anger.

Even if they had tried to sell the book, it was worth nothing to anybody: only the owner and giver. The memory of the day he handed it to her flooded back. In his shy, reticent manner, he put it unwrapped into her hands.

She liked that it was not wrapped: it made it more important, more a necessity of life than a gift easily accepted and discarded.

"You won't have to scribble on scraps of paper any more."

"How did you know that?"

"The time I asked you for the lemon drizzle recipe, you had it on the back of a Shaws bag."

"Did I really?"

He shook his head, his smile broad and indulgent.

"I thought it would be handy to write down your favourite things, like that poem you were talking about the other day."

It was only when he was gone that she saw the inscription.

From me to you.
With love
xx

From that moment, she knew Michael would always be a big part of her life, and she liked that.

Date: April 6, 2013
Subject: THE LUDLOW LADIES' SOCIETY

*****NEWSFLASH*****

Ludlow ladies,

We have the most exciting news!

Thanks to the extraordinary generosity of Ms Connie Carter, the new owner of Ludlow Hall, the Ludlow Ladies' Society is to be allowed to return home.

Connie, who hails from the United States, has allowed the Ludlow Ladies' Society access to Ludlow Hall. Wherever she decides to put us, it means we will have plenty of space to carry out the arduous work of completing our memory quilts. This means a great deal to the Ludlow Ladies' Society, and we are most grateful to Ms Carter and to Eve Brannigan for organising it all.

The first meeting of the Ludlow Ladies' Society in our new surroundings will be next Tuesday. We must have a good turnout, so we can thank Ms Carter in person.

It is fantastic Ms Carter has not only decided to keep the grounds of Ludlow Hall open for the community, but has reinstated the Ludlow Ladies' Society in a place where we had so many happy years.

We are all very excited about the move. There is no excuse now not to put all our heads together and do a fine job of finishing our memory quilts.

This is a huge step forward for the Ludlow Ladies' Society and will not be forgotten. While we have not put it to the vote, we have asked Connie to be an honorary member of the Society and we are very happy she has accepted our kind invitation.

I think, if I may permit myself a level of coarseness, it is also two fingers to Jack Davoren.

Kathryn Rodgers,
Chairwoman

13

Eve's front door was open and several boxes were stacked on the step.

"I thought I was bad with my two suitcases. This makes me feel much better," Hetty said as Eve came out, locking her front door behind her. Together, they placed the boxes on top of the cases in the back seat.

"What do you think Connie will make of all this? I hope she knows what she is letting herself in for; it can get quite messy, threads and all. We don't want to be watching ourselves too much."

"I think, for her, it will be a nice diversion," Eve said, as they turned up the avenue to Ludlow Hall.

Connie was in the kitchen in her dressing gown when they arrived.

"I thought the drawing room would be a nice spot, as it catches the sun nicely throughout the day. You can have the sun on your backs while you work."

Eve, a little surprised to be offered such a grand room, did not comment. It was Hetty who said what they were both thinking.

"Are you sure? Eve here only ever used that room for special occasions; she said it was the best room in the house. I will be afraid to get a thread on the carpet there."

Connie looked confused. Eve tugged at Hetty, telling her to stop her silliness.

"This is Connie's house now, I am sure she has her reasons. We are just glad of the room."

Connie tightened her dressing gown around her. "That room has the nicest view of the outside. I know it is special to Eve, and it is also beside the front door. I could give you a key and you could come and go as you please."

Eve stepped forward.

"All very sensibly and sensitively worked out, and we are delighted to bring the Ludlow Ladies' Society back to the Hall."

"Of course we are, thank you so much," Hetty said, reaching over, catching Connie into a tight hug.

Pulling gently away, Connie turned to the two women. "I have plans of my own. The big room opposite the drawing room, I have workmen coming to clear it and decorate it. Maybe it can be my dance studio."

"Dance?" Eve asked, and Hetty clapped.

"Well done you."

"I am thinking I might give dance lessons," Connie said shyly, turning to face Eve.

Hetty, swinging her hips and throwing her hands in the air, called out to Eve. "Are you ready to salsa?"

Eve put her hand up to hush Hetty. "Connie, I admire your get-up-and-go, but I hope you are not expecting me to step out."

"Dancing is so good for us, Eve. I am sure we can persuade you."

Hetty, her hips swaying, began to move heel to toe across the kitchen, elbowing Connie to follow her. Eve giggled, her body rocking to the imaginary beat.

"Well, you are the right pair. But this won't get the memory quilts done in time for the Obamas, and we have to set up before the others arrive," she snorted, a smile creeping across her face.

Connie and Hetty finished with a flourish, holding hands, bowing low. Eve clapped and they laughed, the sound of their laughter echoing through the downstairs of the house.

Connie, her eyes bright, felt a quiet joy running through her, which she tried to hold on to for as long as possible.

"I have to go out this morning, so I will leave you to it. I will lock the back door on the way out, so please use the front door and make yourselves at home. There are cookies in the jar. Help yourselves to tea or coffee."

Eve, savouring the lightness of the mood about Ludlow Hall, beamed at Connie.

"That dancing of yours sure makes us all a bit happier and I have not even taken a step yet."

"I told you so," boomed Hetty, who was filling the kettle at the sink.

Eve, clicking her teeth, pointed to the car. "I am going to dance out and bring the boxes of fabric in, if nobody minds."

As Eve left the kitchen, Hetty loitered by the sink.

"You are very good to give us the room, for Eve. This is so lovely, to be back at Ludlow. It means a lot," she said, placing a hand on Connie's shoulder, before scooting after Eve, giving out that she was taking the lazy man's load.

Connie slipped upstairs to get her coat, the chat downstairs wafting up as she sat at the dressing table applying her make-up. She did not have anywhere to go, but neither did she want to get caught up in the plans of the Ludlow Ladies' Society. Instead, she decided to pay a visit to the auctioneer to find out exactly what her husband had had planned for this place. Pushing the perfume bottles out of her way as she placed her handbag on the dressing table, she thought she must ask Eve if there was anything else she wanted to take from the Hall.

Eve was nowhere to be seen when she got downstairs, but Hetty was brewing up a pot of tea in the kitchen.

"Eve went for a stroll down to the lake. I think it was her favourite spot, when she lived here."

"It must be hard for her, coming back like this."

Hetty poured the boiling water into the teapot. "I hope you don't mind, I had a rummage, tea tastes very different when it comes from a teapot. I found it in a jiffy: everything is the same as the day she had to leave it."

Connie noticed a kitchen chair had been moved. She put it back near the window.

"Eve automatically put the chair where she was used to it. She did not mean anything by it."

"It's okay, I understand."

Hetty pretended to be busy fiddling with the cookie jar, but raised her head as Connie went out the door. "You have done a good thing, letting Eve back into the place. None of us will forget that."

"I have to go," Connie said, smiling shyly.

As she drove down the avenue, Connie saw Eve stroll around the front of the house from the yew walk, slowly treading across the grass, all the time her eyes on the house. So caught up was she, she never even noticed Connie drive by.

Eve wandered, the softness of the spent cherry blossom petals and rhododendron blooms a plush carpet under her feet. It had not changed one iota; neither did she want it to change. A robin flew low across her path. Pulling up, she watched as it landed on the branch of the holly bush. When Arnold was in the States, Michael came every day, helping out with this and that, chatting and often staying for lunch. How often had she and Michael wandered here, away from the gaze of the house, just talking, sometimes not even that. Sometimes, too, their hands had brushed against each other, making each stumble back. Often, they went as far as the lake, to sit watching the ducks and the two swans, side by side, gliding together.

She crossed the grass to the front of the house. The windows were clean and the door washed down, but it looked its age. She wondered what the American would do to the place. Out of the corner of her eye, she saw Connie leave. Waiting until the car had cleared the house and turned the bend, Eve sat on the stone seat, breathing in Ludlow Hall, the call of a heron at the lake faint in the wind.

Hetty rapping on the window made her look around. Giggling, she stood up as Hetty, gesturing wildly, thumped on the glass once again. Slowly, she made her way to the front door, where Hetty was fighting with the lock. She heard her scurry off; next, the sash window in the drawing room was pulled up.

"I can't open the front door, Eve, what will I do? She locked the kitchen door from the outside when she left."

"Throw the keys to me, I will unlock it from this side."

Hetty fired the bunch of keys. They landed two feet away from Eve.

"You will never be in the Olympics, Hetty," Eve laughed, as she scooped them up.

Rarely had she used the front door to go in the house, preferring instead to walk around the back and in through the kitchen. But once Arnold's body was found, she changed her routine, slipping into the house through the front door, to avoid the memories and the sadness that there was nobody, not even the sheepdog, to welcome her home.

After she freed the lock on the front door, she stopped to take in the fields. It was easy to think it was all hers again, too easy to pretend, even though the fields were mossed up and the fences were leaning. No animals had been there in years. There was a time when if she even opened the door for a few seconds, the geese strutted up cackling, fussing like a group of gossips.

"Do you think we should have a look around, while we have a chance?" Hetty was standing in the middle of the hallway, waiting for the word to go upstairs.

Eve swung around, her face angry.

"May God forgive you, Hetty Gorman. Connie has been nice enough to give us a room for our silly society meet-ups and you want to invade her privacy."

Hetty marched off to the drawing room, her head down, her face upset. When Eve arrived after her, it took Hetty a few minutes to regain her composure and speak up.

"I was only thinking of you, Eve. You might want to look

around the old place, see what she is doing with Arnold's study."

"Don't I know every nook and cranny already? What good would it do me?" Eve's voice softened, because she saw Hetty was upset.

"I don't mean to pry. I was trying to help," Hetty said, her voice shaky.

Eve bit the side of her lip and put her arm around Hetty.

"Let's get some of the fabric out before the rest of the Ludlow Ladies' Society comes in on top of us. We will need a few more mugs; no doubt they will all want tea," she said, and Hetty, glad of the subject change, immediately volunteered to set up refreshments on the kitchen table.

Eve stood, surrounded by the boxes in the drawing room. Closing her eyes, she felt the old place talking to her, the house come in around her: the tap in the kitchen gushing too hard when Hetty turned it on, the fridge revving like an old car, the chirping and tapping of young birds in a nest in the chimney, because a fire had not been lit there in so long, the pile of the carpet deeper in the middle of the room than at the fireplace, where the indentations fitted her shoe size. Tears brimmed up, but she shook herself awake, pulling at the nearest box, dipping in and taking out carefully cut pieces of fabric. Taffeta in one pile, and the grey silk she had not dared cut all these years despite her grand ideas to make a shawl with a fringe.

Hetty knocked gently on the drawing room door.

"I have made you a mug of tea. I found your favourite china mug out there, I am sure Connie won't mind."

Eve took the pink flowery mug and smiled. "It is an awful long time since I had a drink from this. It was one of the few things I bought myself. Arnold hated it, never allowed it into this room."

"Wasn't he the fusspot?"

Eve looked at Hetty. "He was a good man, but a snob." She held up the mug to the light. "This 'beaker', as he called it, offended him greatly."

"Hadn't he little to be worrying about," Hetty said, bending down to lift a mountain of fabric from another box.

"As it turned out, you are right," Eve answered, sitting into her armchair at the fireplace. She sipped the tea as Hetty worked quietly around her, emptying boxes, creating neat piles on the carpet based on fabric types. Cupping the mug, she examined the pink flowers, a cacophony of colour that could have been one of her flower borders at Ludlow Hall in its heyday. It was a simple china mug, stained brown inside, because she liked to drink her tea without milk.

The gold rim had faded over the years, rubbed white where she sipped. She had bought it at the Tinahely Agricultural Show. Arnold was on one of his trips to America, and Michael Conway persuaded her to accompany him to buy some sheep for the back fields.

The business done, they walked together looking at the stalls. Twice she went back to look at the mugs, but it was Michael who suggested she buy some.

"Arnold would never drink from a mug," she laughed.

"I know that, but what about you?"

She moved off, but just as they were about to tramp across the fields to where they had left the car, she had a change of heart, running back to buy the mug for herself.

"Now, what will Arnold have to say about that?" Michael laughed.

"He can say what he likes, he won't have to drink from it," she said, wishing she was as brave as she sounded.

Two cars came up the driveway. Eithne Hall pulled into the front, rather than slipping around the back, as agreed with Connie.

"That Eithne is a cheeky one," Hetty said, making for the front door to open it. She shouted back to Eve from the hallway, to help.

"You are going to have to learn, Hetty, I won't be here all the time." Pushing gently on the door, she turned the key and pulled back the door. Five women were waiting on the steps.

"Eve, it must be so strange to be back and not in charge," Bernie said.

"It is just nice to be back. Now, let's get to work, plenty of time to chat later."

"Is the American joining us?" Eithne asked.

"Connie has the good sense to leave us be."

Marcella leaned into Eve. "Have you had a gander about the place?"

Eve sighed loudly. "Why would I do that? I am the one person who knows the place inside out. It is all somebody else's problem now."

The women fell silent, concentrating instead on laying out the patches, helping to figure out the designs for Eve's quilt.

Eve joined in, sifting through neatly folded good outfits, not yet cut up in squares. When her hand touched the turquoise silk, she rubbed the rich softness of it between two of her fingers. These days she had nowhere to wear a fine Chinese silk ensemble.

Arnold had travelled to China for a trade fair, bringing her back a bolt of the softest silk she had ever come across. It was the one present, bar the first piece of jewellery he ever gave her, that pleasantly surprised her. She was touched, too, that he had put so much effort into getting it right.

"I know you like to get outfits specially made, so I got the lot. Thought I could not go wrong with a whole bolt. It cost a fortune, so maybe go to one of the big fashion houses in Dublin, let them design something fitting for such expensive fabric."

Unfurling the bolt, the silk shimmered in the light. Sometimes it appeared green, sometimes a deep blue flashed across the folds, and sometimes it appeared sombre until disturbed once again.

There was enough for a long dress or a long skirt and top. Deciding the fabric was too delicate for the type of jacket she liked, afraid that it would pucker if she strengthened it with iron-on stiffener, she opted for a dress gathered at the waist, long sleeves pulled into cuffs, a discreet neckline with a peplum collar, the simple design letting the fabric speak for itself. Tiny covered buttons close together ran down the bodice, fastened with tiny loops of silk: a nod, she thought, to the dress's Chinese origins.

She bunched up the silk, letting the smooth softness caress her cheeks, and she knew she was not ready to let this dress go just yet.

Eve looked around. The other women were unusually subdued, whispering like they were waiting in church for the priest to come out. Never had the women dared to go into the Ludlow drawing room with their patchwork. "I suppose we could sit around the kitchen table and have a cuppa, discuss what we want to do," Eve said quietly. There was a collective sigh of relief as the women jumped up, eagerly leading the way like excited children told they could have something nice.

"Do you think Connie will mind if we decamp to the kitchen?" Hetty asked.

"With any luck, we won't have to tell her for a while," Eve said, pulling out the chair at the head of the table: the same seat she always took when the Ludlow Ladies' Society met. Each woman sat in her usual place, Hetty bustling about like normal, handing over plates of biscuits and cake for the middle of the table. Eithne Hall got down the mugs for the tea and coffee.

"She has spruced up this room nice," she said, her voice begrudging.

"I still think she was high and mighty at the start," Dana said, pulling out a chair and sitting at the table.

Kathryn Rodgers remained standing. "We have to put out an appeal for fabric and stories for the Rosdaniel quilt, otherwise it will just be the bits and pieces three or four of us can find."

"What fancy piece are you bringing to the table?" Eithne asked.

Ignoring Eithne's sarcastic tone, Kathryn beamed with

pleasure and whipped a bag of cloth from her large handbag. "There are several pieces, of course, but my favourite is the dress I wore when I was elected town councillor. It was a very onerous job and only lasted a few years, but it was an exhilarating time for me personally and for the town." She pulled the red silk fabric with blue flowers from the pile. "I loved the dress and it still fits me, but it is important to give our best to the memory quilt," she said, and the others, not wanting to encourage her more, just nodded in agreement.

"It is like we have never been away," Marcella piped up. Dana elbowed her, grimacing and pointing towards Eve.

"You don't have to be on pins because of me," Eve said, as Hetty slipped back to the drawing room for the flowery mug, rinsing it under the tap before placing it at Eve's elbow. "I am glad Connie is here. I have a feeling she will have us all on our toes very soon," Eve said, making Hetty stifle a laugh with her fist.

Eve, listening to the rise and fall of the conversation, thought maybe life was coming back to Ludlow Hall after all.

14

Connie was sitting in a coffee shop in Rosdaniel when her phone rang.

"Connie, it's Bill."

Pain coursed through her; blood drained from her face, making her go pale; her stomach turned sick; shock streaked across her brain as she heard him speak.

"How are you, Connie?"

Turning towards the wall, so that the woman sitting having tea across the way would not see her distress, she spoke in a low voice.

"Bill, why are you calling me?"

"Amy said you were in Ireland. I am in London; it is only a short flight away. Can I come visit?"

"She should not have told you anything."

"Connie, we need to talk."

"And then I will get my family back, I suppose."

Her teeth ground together; tears flowed down her cheeks. She wanted to howl in agony. She cut him off.

She only realised she had been shouting into the phone when she turned and saw the café owner looking down at her. The woman having tea opposite nodded to Connie before gathering up her shopping and making for the till. Leaning her head against the coldness of the rough stone wall, she closed her eyes, thinking that if she banged hard enough she might pierce her brain, so she was no longer able to feel. She might even die.

His voice was the same: strong and reassuring.

She loved him. She had then, she did now.

When she had asked him to stay away, he respected her wishes, though she knew he wanted to rush to comfort her. Was she ready yet to allow him back in her life? Honestly, she did not know if she ever would be.

Under the pretence of clearing a table, the café owner came close.

"Mrs Carter, are you all right? You don't look very well," she said gently.

Connie, dragging her hands across her face to wipe away the tears, pulled out a five-euro note, slipping it onto the table.

The owner pushed the note back. "Don't worry about it, we can run to a cup of coffee. You sit and get yourself sorted before going out on the street. You don't want to be feeding the gossips."

Gently, she pushed Connie back into her seat, before disappearing behind the counter and noisily changing the coffee filter.

Connie sat, not thinking, not feeling, examining the wall. Bill rang again.

Quickly, she turned down the volume of the phone, watching it as it pulsated and shivered across the table. She was not being fair on him, she knew that, but then none of this was fair. Gathering up her things, she again tried to leave the five-euro note on the counter, but the woman stopped her.

"You will be in another day. Look after yourself," she said, lightly tapping Connie's hand.

Not wanting to return to Ludlow Hall yet, Connie got in her car and headed for Arklow, to call on the estate agent.

Roger Greene greeted her with a strong handshake.

"I am not sure what I can do for you, Mrs Carter, but I will be of whatever assistance I can. You told me to take Ludlow Hall off the market; we have done so," Roger Greene said, ushering her to sit on a chair in front of his desk.

"Please, tell me why my husband bought Ludlow."

Roger Greene looked taken aback. "I was very sorry to hear of Mr Carter's death. What a shock."

Connie did not answer.

"Mr Carter, I believe, had big plans for the development of the land around the house."

"How was he going to do that?"

"Mr Carter was a man in a rush but he was stymied before he even had a chance to fail. We did advise him that the planning process here can be quite drawn out."

"Why build on those fields? It would ruin the estate."

"A lot of people in these parts thought so too, lodged objection after objection. The effect of it all was to delay everything; the longer it went on, the more stressed Mr Carter became." Roger Greene shifted uncomfortably in his chair. "He had no patience, said he was running out of money before he even started."

"Do you think he intended to move his family here?"

Roger Greene carefully flattened beads of sweat on his temple with his fingers. "Mrs Carter, this may come as a shock to you, but Mr Carter never mentioned a family."

The estate agent fiddled with a pen, rolling it through his fingers until it leaked ink, staining his thumbs. Throwing the pen to the side, he rubbed his hands together, before looking directly at Connie. He settled himself back into his chair and cleared his throat.

"Mr Carter phoned up out of the blue asking about Ludlow. We wanted to arrange a viewing, but he said he did not need to. He offered the asking price there and then. He was determined to own Ludlow Hall."

"But why?"

"I don't know. He never even came over to visit the place. For somebody who was so determined to own Ludlow, he made no attempt to get to know it or Rosdaniel. I said to him, would you not come over, get to know people, maybe do up the Hall, even as a holiday home. He gave me an odd answer: 'I hate the place, I only ever bought it to tear it down. Why would I ever want to stay in the place?'

127

"To him, it was about the money. He said it had sapped everything from him. He said it was bleeding every last cent from him. He fought it all, if I may say so, took it all a bit personally; it sapped money and energy from him. 'There's not even the consolation of making a quick buck,' he said. Finally, defeated and running out of money, he told me to put it back on the market and make sure I got a good price for it."

"Why would he want to tear down Ludlow Hall?"

"He said it was personal."

"Personal?"

"I did not enquire further. Every week after that he rang me for a progress report, until the calls stopped coming." Roger Greene, worried he might have said too much, shifted uncomfortably in his chair.

Connie buckled, her shoulders hunched, tears taking over. Pain pulsed through her. She held herself, her arms wrapped tight around her body, almost as if there was a danger that if she did not, the pain would split her open like an axe on a lump of wood.

Roger Greene opened a file on his desk and pretended to study it.

"None of it makes sense," she whispered.

Roger Greene scratched his bald head fiercely.

"That is pretty much it. The country was gone down the tubes and nobody was buying or selling property, but Mr Carter thought somebody out there was going to fork out millions for a dilapidated mansion beside a small town." He straightened in his seat. "There is still the question of the outstanding bill, Mrs Carter. We could come to some arrangement."

"I don't have any money, Mr Greene. Whatever bit I have, I intend to put into Ludlow Hall."

"Maybe you will think of this office if you ever decide to divest yourself of Ludlow Hall."

Connie stood up. "I have taken up too much of your time, Mr Greene."

She moved to the door as the estate agent rushed around from

128

his side of the desk and grabbed her hand in a strong handshake. Her phone vibrated in her pocket. She ignored it.

Once out on the street, she walked across the bridge, down the quays, picking a seat so she could look across the harbour to the sea.

A text message beeped.

We need to talk, clear the air. I am coming to see you.

She did not need to enquire as to how he knew where in Ireland she was. He would turn up at Ludlow Hall; Amy was going to make sure of that. Her phone vibrated. Connie accepted the call, already shouting.

"Why did you tell Bill where I was?"

Amy, taken aback at the strength of her sister's aggression, waited a few seconds before answering.

"I didn't exactly. I said it was Ludlow Hall, Ireland. He did the rest himself. None of this is his fault, Connie. You can't keep avoiding him. He deserves a chance, you both do."

"I am not dealing with this right now."

"Or ever, Connie? It is time to start building a new life. He loves you, Connie, he understands."

"Understands the loneliness, the raw pain that I would trade him in a minute to have things different? I don't think so."

Amy sighed loudly, the tears choking the words in her throat. "Connie, let some light in, please," she said, her voice wobbly with emotion.

Connie cut off the call, letting her phone drop, bounce and spin across the ground. An elderly man walking his dog bent down and picked it up.

"Another foot and it was gone into the sea."

When she did not take the phone, he placed it on the seat beside her.

"Things can't be that bad for a beautiful young woman like yourself."

She did not answer. Suspecting he was intruding, he called his dog and headed off to where the trawlers were tied up at the far end of the harbour.

Connie sat, her hands punched into her pockets, looking out to sea, the only sound the water as it gently chafed the harbour wall, making the smaller boats further down lean to one side. The elderly man, passing back again, his dog running ahead of him, stopped beside her.

"Tell me to mind my own business if you like, but are you all right?"

"Not really."

"Is there anything I can do to help?"

Connie jumped up, staring at the man.

"Bring my child back from the dead?"

Picking up the phone, she bolted for her car. She did not turn around to see the shock on his face, the concern as he quickened his pace behind her. What could he or anybody else do? She'd had over one thousand, eight hundred and eighty-nine days with Molly. All she wanted was one more day, even half a day, to hold her, talk to her, play with her, be with her. She desperately wanted to change the ending, tormenting herself with what might or could have been.

The man tried to flag her down as she reversed the car, but she ignored him, driving up the quays towards the bridge, where she turned right for Rosdaniel.

★

The first meeting back of the Ludlow Ladies' Society at Ludlow Hall lasted over two hours. Hetty had to go to a doctor's appointment after tea, so one of the other women did the wash and tidy-up, while the rest sat around the kitchen table talking and sewing until gone three o'clock.

"I had forgotten what a lovely house this is," Rebecca Fleming whispered, flinching when she was elbowed in the side.

Eve laughed. "This was my home for so long, but no longer.

They are calling it the new reality, whatever that means. I am no better or no worse off than a lot of people. We are in different times."

Rebecca peered over her glasses. "Very true, Eve, but not everybody was the innocent bystander, like yourself."

"When it comes to the end, that matters little to the bank: they are there to get their money back at all costs."

"At least you are not like Hannah Humphries."

"Hannah Humphries?"

"She lived the other side of Rosdaniel; I think she came to the Society once or twice."

Eve remembered well the small, stout woman, blonde hair clipped into a tight bun at the back of her head.

Everybody turned to Rebecca Fleming. Not usually one to impart gossip, they knew the story was bound to be good if Rebecca felt she had to share it. She blushed, her voice squeaky, as she felt the pressure of the others listening.

"Poor woman, they had paid off their home mortgage years ago, but their son remortgaged the place to finance his business. Her name was on the remortgage along with that son of hers. It all went belly-up. He went off to Australia and has not been heard from since. The bastard left his mother trying to deal with the banks. Eventually, she gave up. Her health failed. She was in and out of hospital, had chemotherapy, the whole lot."

When a few of the women around the table sighed, Rebecca Fleming, now relishing being the centre of attention, pitched her voice higher, so she could more easily be heard.

"Hannah told me herself she stopped opening her post, let it pile up rather than be frightened when she read yet another nasty threat from the bank. She was at her wits' end over it all. It was when she was recovering at her sister's house in Arklow, after another bout of chemotherapy, that they came and repossessed her home. All her personal belongings were thrown in a skip."

Marcella Lyons put her hand up, like she was at a meeting.

"They hardly threw out her furniture. How could they do that?"

"The banks can do anything they like, we all know that," Eve said, and the others murmured in agreement.

Rebecca Fleming, afraid she would not be allowed to finish the story if the conversation shifted, cleared her throat loudly.

"Cute enough, they threw any piece of furniture that might be worth selling in the back of a van. All the personal stuff, that was only precious to Hannah, was chucked in the skip: books, clothes, photographs. The neighbours phoned Hannah's sister, but by the time they made it up from Arklow, her whole life was piled high in the skip."

"I suppose I should count myself lucky the same did not happen here," Eve said.

Not noticing or deliberately ignoring the sarcasm behind Eve's comment, Rebecca Fleming continued.

"The worst thing was when Hannah in her dressing gown and slippers got out of the car roaring and shouting, calling for her husband, John. Everybody thought the fright had badly affected her: John had been dead four years. It turned out the silver and gold urn containing John's ashes had been dumped with everything else. Even the plaque she had specially made, saying 'John Humphries. Gone, But Never Forgotten' was ripped from the wooden mantelpiece."

"Jesus, don't tell me this is true," Eve said.

Rebecca Fleming looked around the table, taking in the shocked faces.

"The urn and plaque were gone. They must have been tipped into the skip along with everything else."

"What did Hannah do?"

"What could she do? Her only hope was that the urn might have broken and John's ashes were scattered along the garden and road they loved. She clings on to that thought. She is in the last stages of cancer now, and she has made it clear she wants to be cremated and her ashes scattered on the same lane and the garden of the old family home."

"The new owners might have something to say about that."

"She says even if it is done in secret or under cover of darkness, she does not care: her only wish is to reunite with her husband."

Those around the table fell silent for a while.

"Maybe she should be scattered over the dump, to be sure," Dana Marshall said quietly.

Others began to snigger, the sniggers turning into snorts of laughter, followed by loud guffaws. Laughter rippled from one woman to another, until they were all heaving, thinking of the Humphries on the dump.

"They could name the dump after them," Eithne Hall guffawed.

Chortling, the ladies' shoulders shuddered at the misfortune of Hannah Humphries.

"After that, maybe we had better go, in case Connie thinks we are laughing at her expense," Eve said, and the women bustled about, tidying up the kitchen, putting everything back as the American would like it.

"Before you pack up, remember we need to be super organised by next week. We may even have to schedule two meetings, so we can plot the quilts and decide on patterns," Kathryn Rodgers said, raising her voice over the noise of the women chatting and tidying up.

"Did anybody have a cookie?" Eve asked. The others shook their heads and Eve picked a few out of the jar. "Just so she doesn't think we are too high and mighty to be eating her biscuits." She pushed them in her pocket.

"Who is going to offer Eve a lift?" Kathryn Rodgers piped up and Eve, already making to open the front door, put up her two hands, as if to hush an audience.

"I am going to walk back. I might wait a bit for Connie, to thank her."

Nobody said anything, but they all knew Eve was finding it hard to leave Ludlow Hall.

They were right: she was. After the last woman said her good-byes, Eve leaned against the door, tears rolling down her cheeks. How often before had she been keen to have them gone so she could have the house to herself? She did now, but these walls were hers no more, the pain inside her unbearable. She might have stopped Hetty leading a prying expedition, but she really wanted to peep in the study. Hesitating at the door, she knew she could not bear to think anything could change there. It was Arnold's room, and she had not been there in so long. Even after she found him in the barn and later had to go through his things, she could not bear to throw any of it out. Even then she had not sat at Arnold's desk, and now a stranger was going to clear the room out.

Turning swiftly away, she moved to the drawing room to sit by the fireplace. Sinking into the velvet armchair, her feet exactly fitted the slight indentation in the carpet. Examining the painting over the fireplace, she was cold in her assessment. She didn't want it. The day it was painted had not been a happy day. Arnold insisted she wear that dress. She felt uncomfortable, wanting instead to wear her own choice.

"What is it with you, Eve? This is a beautiful dress from Bloomingdale's, New York. You won't get finer this side of the Atlantic. It cost me a bomb."

"For this occasion, I want to wear something more representative of me. Not something picked by a fancy shop assistant who does not know one thing about me."

"And what about me? Has your husband no say in this?"

When he presented her with the beautifully wrapped box, she found it hard to rustle up any excitement. Somehow, she could not see Arnold going in Bloomingdale's on his own to buy her a dress. When she questioned him on it, he became cross.

"Why the inquisition? I buy something different and get the third degree."

Arnold, in all his trips to the US, had only ever brought her back jewellery, pieces that were more his taste than hers, though she would never say that to him. Jewellery for him was a safe, small option. Initially, she wore the pieces, regardless of whether she liked them or not, but later she did not bother, thinking her husband did not notice.

"I am damned if I do, damned if I don't, Eve. You hardly ever wear the jewellery I select for you, now you turn your nose up at a beautiful dress. Pardon me if I am fed up of my wife not dressing as she should. It reflects badly on me and on Ludlow Hall."

"You know you are being unfair, Arnold. I run this estate more and more. I can't be expected to do that and look like a model every day."

"My mother seemed to be able to do it well enough."

She whipped out of the drawing room and up to the bedroom, afraid that her answer, if she gave it, would ignite a bigger row.

The artist from the city was due within twenty minutes. It would intensify the rift already present between herself and Arnold if she did not wear the dress. Reluctantly, she lifted the navy gown from its shop box. Slipping it on, she saw it suited her beautifully, accentuating her waist, swishing around her ankles, a perfect fit. Why it made her feel uncomfortable, she did not quite know, but to even wear it for the several sessions required for the portrait would be a trial.

When she came downstairs, her husband tersely introduced her to the artist, but said not another word to her. Neither did he comment on the family necklace she clipped on at the last minute, in an effort to appease him.

Looking at the painting now, she knew Arnold was feeling sore: his shoulders hunched, crouched over his newspaper, tightly gripping the sides, almost as if he wanted to maintain a barrier between them.

When Eve heard a car, she thought it was Connie coming back, so she grabbed some fabric and pretended to be concentrating on her sewing. A knock on the drawing room window made Eve jump, the sewing needle dropping onto the carpet.

Michael Conway, outside, pointed to the front door and Eve went to open it.

"I met one of the Society ladies, she said you were going to walk. I thought you might appreciate the lift."

"You mean you are checking to see if I am all right leaving Ludlow Hall."

He smiled. "Something like that."

"I was going to wait for Connie to come back, but she might not like the intrusion."

"I think she will be good for Ludlow, Eve."

"I hope you are right," she said, as she got her coat and checked that everything was unplugged in the kitchen, as she always had in the past, before making for the front door.

Michael turned the car and was sitting, the engine running, waiting for her, when she came out on the top steps. She did not hurry; he was not an impatient man.

"What did it feel like, having the place to yourself?" he asked when she got in beside him in the car.

"Just fine. The ladies liked it too. I am back again tomorrow, to get a good head start on my quilt. Hetty might come. You know, our quilts might be shown to the Obamas. What do you think of that? I might learn to dance too."

He laughed. There was an excitement in Eve's voice, something Michael had not sensed in her in a long time.

15

Connie was glad there was nobody at Ludlow Hall when she returned.

Letting herself in the back door, the lingering mingled scents of the ladies' perfumes clouded around her. Peeping into the drawing room, she took in the neat piles of fabric set along the carpet. The chair by the fireplace had been moved slightly, as if the sitter was angling for a better view of the painting. The house appeared different, the buzz of conversation from the Ludlow Ladies' Society blowing away the stagnant air. Stepping into Arnold's room, she itched to get started. Yet she worried. Could dance steps be forgotten? Would she stumble? When it came down to it, would she be able to dance day in day out, be able to teach again? She stepped along the carpet, tentatively pacing out the dance in her head.

That is what she had been doing when she met Bill the first time. At first she did not see him standing in the doorway of her small dance studio, a cup in his hand, waiting to borrow a teabag. When he made to steal away, she heard him, because he fell over a student's discarded rucksack, crashing to the floor, his mug sliding away, making her step smartly to the side to avoid it. Studying for his masters, he gave French classes in the room next door twice a week.

She smiled to think how they got to know each other, as she began to teach him to dance, step by step together, intense, their love deepening, the music sweeping them along. That was ten years ago, but it might have been a lifetime ago, it was so different. Abruptly, she stopped dancing, leaving the room quickly.

All day, Bill sent too many text messages, each saying the same thing. She tapped out her reply.

> Bill, I am finding it very hard to cope. There is no doubt I will always love you, but it is not going to help anything if you turn up on the doorstep. I need time alone to figure out where this place fits in the whole jigsaw of events. Please understand. C x

Straight away there was a return message:

> I love you, Connie. I want to help, no more, no less.

She wanted to scream. How could he help, how could he soothe the agitation inside her, calm the grief, understand the pain and the guilt which consumed her? She loved him, but she had nothing left for him.

She put the phone away, her head weary, her heart aching. Was it so bad that she could never regret meeting him, loving him, missing him? Leaving the phone in the kitchen, she went upstairs.

Wanting to go back to happier times, she opened the laptop to read the blog she had started when baby Molly was born. It was now her escape and her torment. The Mommy Blog. Was life ever so sweet? Scrolling through, she sat in bed, the night looking in on her because she had not bothered to close the curtains. If anybody was close enough to Ludlow Hall, they would think she was hard at work. She was, rolling back the past, a place she preferred to dwell, because the future held almost nothing at all.

Lingering in the baby years, she traced her finger across the screen, following the shape of Molly's face, her eyes, the scruff of black hair. Pushing her hand against the perfect little fingers, remembering her tight grip, the gurgle of contentment, like a pain now through her heart.

WELCOME BABY MOLLY
MAY 2006
She has ten fingers and toes and the most beautiful smile and, would you believe it, her daddy's black hair.

She is our princess, born at 3 a.m. on Friday morning, screaming her little heart out and telling us she was ready for this life.

We feel blessed and lucky, and thank you all for your lovely gifts and messages. We as a family are going to spend precious family time together, and when Baby Molly is ready to meet you all, we will throw a lovely welcome party, so you can meet our special girl.

It is so overwhelming to think this little person has come into our world and already we love her so so much.

She might be an astronaut, a hairdresser, a college professor, a mathematician (not of course if she has my head for figures) or even an entrepreneur like Ed. Whatever she wants, she can be, and now it is our responsibility to give her the love and the values to reach her potential.

Above all, we want for our lovely Molly to be happy.

Connie xx

JANUARY 2007
Poor little mite, she has such a snuffly cold. I stayed beside her cot all night, worried she would be uncomfortable or maybe afraid. I think this is what it means to be a mother, to love and care so much for this little person. She woke up at one stage. I rested my hand on hers and it seemed to calm and comfort her. I was going to sing, but she settled. I stayed sleeping on the divan beside the cot. I didn't wake up until Ed came in the next morning, saying he had two sleepyheads in the family. Sometimes it is such hard work being a mom.

Connie xx

Connie felt a stab of anger reading the post. She remembered it well: the little snuffles from Molly, Ed complaining bitterly every time she crept out of bed to check on their daughter, so that she stayed in Molly's room, curling up on the divan, nodding off, only waking up when she heard her husband turn on the shower as he got ready for work. He had not even put his head in the door, citing afterwards the important meeting of district managers he had to prepare for as an excuse for his lack of concern.

MARCH 2007
Molly's first steps. Why are we always in such a hurry to reach the milestones? How I longed for her first steps, and now I know she is growing up. She danced across the carpet to her daddy. I was supposed to capture it all on camera, but I was so entranced I did not even think of holding up the camera. To see her move like a ballerina into Ed's arms is something I will never forget: her joy at reaching him, his pride in his daughter. Memories don't have to be recorded to be special forever. I am an especially proud mom today.
    Connie xx

Connie shut the laptop. The real story: Amy was holding Molly, Connie was cajoling, pleading, smiling, her arms outstretched almost a foot away as they sat on the sitting room carpet. Two jumpy steps she took, her achievement beaming across her face, falling into Connie's arms as the two women whooped in joy. She told Ed when he came home from work later, but he became sullen and cross when Molly would not give a repeat performance.

SEPTEMBER 2008
There are mornings like this. Ed was busy with what Ed does best, wheeling and dealing in business. I was rushing about and little Molly turned around, her two hands open wide, and said "Hug."

We laughed, we hugged and the world was put to rights. Just sometimes the smallest person in the house is the wise one. Remember, there is always time for a hug.

Connie xx

Connie got out of bed and began to pace the room. So much time for a hug now and nobody to hug.

Understand. Forgive.

The words pounded inside her brain, pain coursed through her, the room twirling about her. Her head was dizzy, but she could not stop pacing.

For two days, she was not allowed to even see her, touch her; only when she was stiff cold in the coffin could she place a hand on her. She would not leave the coffin either; she insisted it be this way, that she sit and keep vigil at Molly's side. She wanted to scoop her into her arms, to warm her up, to make the life start coursing through her. Instead, she rubbed her hair ever so gently, sang her favourite song. Her voice soaked with tears, she managed to get to the end. In a little white coffin, Molly looked frail and gentle, as if she had forgotten to wake up.

When he had placed the pillow over her face, had she felt the pressure straight off or was it only when she was deprived of air? Was she terribly afraid? Was she hurting so? Did she know her father was the one hurting her, sucking the life from her?

Had he ever hesitated, reconsidered, regretted? Was it too late when he came to his senses, which is why, like a coward, he continued with his plan, or did he feel the life seep away from her, numb to all feeling but a compulsion to persist? How could he have calmly locked the doors of the house as he left Molly dead in her bed that morning? Did he wave as normal to Mr Singh?

Questions, too many questions, but no answers.

She had calmly asked the detectives first, the pain numbing her reactions. Later, screaming, she scratched at the big detective, clawing at him as if he could provide some answers. Amy held her back as she lashed out, before crumpling like a rag doll in a heap on the floor. They looked at her with kind faces and eyes full of pity, because they knew she was taking on more than any mother should have to bear.

They had pity, but no answers. Not even the post-mortem results could tell them why Ed Carter had killed his daughter and then himself.

They wanted to seal her coffin, but she needed to say goodbye. To say sorry. Leaning in, she touched her daughter lightly on the head.

"I am sorry I was not there, my little one. I am sorry."

She pulled and caressed each strand of hair she could reach, ran her fingers gently over her eyelashes, down the contour of her cheeks: life gone, nothing left but memories, regrets and a little girl who would never grow old.

Cupping Molly's hands, she told her she was sorry again, she whispered the words in her ear, sat with her daughter and thought how could she have stopped this, how could it have been different, this day in the funeral home marked in the calendar a long time ago as a promised girls' day out.

Instead, she sat and listed all the things that would never happen: Molly's first crush, sweet sixteen, the tears of a broken heart, college, silly things mothers and daughters do. Molly was to be forever moulded in her heart. One thousand, eight hundred and eighty-nine days of her, no more.

She wanted Molly to herself, the fading light lingering around the coffin, clinging, waiting to spirit her away.

Connie hummed softly. She tucked in Cuddly Cat, with his broken eye, beside her, expecting Molly to acknowledge his presence. There was nothing, only shouting silence where once there had been life. For the last time, she felt the starchiness of Molly's skin, the make-up delicately applied to the bruising left after Ed pushed Cuddly Cat's eye so hard into her cheek that it broke, leaving a jagged imprint. Connie licked her finger, rubbing at the make-up until it caked off. Anger swelled inside her. Had her baby felt the pinch of the plastic as it smashed under the pressure? Reaching into her pocket, she pulled out the faded blue-grey cloth that looked more like a dishcloth. Gently, she pushed it beside Molly's neck, using her finger to ease it underneath. Molly never went anywhere without her favourite blankie.

Later, they came to place the lid on the coffin, screw it down. She insisted on staying in the room, silently witnessing this end, worrying she would forget what she looked like or that the act of her father would stain her memory.

Connie did not remember much of the funeral service, only the kind, clammy hands which took hers, the words whispered to her, the journey to the crematorium, where she and Amy watched as the coffin slipped away.

The next day, Ed was brought to the crematorium early in the morning. She waited until the curtains were pulled across fully and his coffin was out of view. She stood with Amy, clutching Molly's back-up blankie, dragging it between her fingers. It hurt, but that was good, she wanted to feel this pain. How could she ever understand or forgive?

That night she had sat on the porch huddled in a corner where nobody could see her from the sidewalk. When the screen door creaked open and Amy stepped out, she knew by the determination of her step she would not take no for an answer.

"We are going for a drive," she said, handing Connie her sweater.

Amy drove through the streets at a slow pace, only pulling over when she got to the park.

"You need to scream."

When she did not move, Amy gently pushed her.

"Get in the gap at the side of the hedge. Nobody will see you. You have the whole park to yourself. Nobody will hear. Get out and scream."

Connie reluctantly got out of the passenger's seat, gingerly feeling her way through the hedge. When she was far enough away, she opened her mouth, but nothing came. Feeling stupid, she made to turn back, but Amy, coming up behind her, blocked her way.

"It is not fucking fair! Shout it out," Amy screamed, reaching over, squeezing her sister's arm.

Connie shouted out the words.

"Again," Amy shouted, joining in with her, until they were both screaming so loud the stars overhead could hear.

She screamed until her throat hurt, letting the words bullet into the sky, so that the other world knew her pain. She screamed, because it was the first time since it happened that she could.

Afterwards, Amy helped her to the car, sobbing into her scarf, until they got home, where she climbed into bed and Amy tucked her in.

Here in Ludlow Hall, Connie fell on the bed, exhausted. Not bothering to pull the duvet over herself, she curled into a ball, closing her eyes. The deep sleep of exhaustion took over, a sleep that brought no rest.

16

Eve rooted through her wardrobe, until she put her hand on the navy chiffon Bloomingdale's dress. She had almost forgotten it until she saw the painting at Ludlow Hall again. It was beautiful, well cut, stylish, elegant, and she hated it. It signalled the point in time when her attitude to her husband changed: a subtle change at the outset, but she could trace it back to that dress. Arnold had never frequented a women's clothing department in his life, as far as she knew. Why he suddenly should have done so to buy her a dress remained an absolute mystery.

The trip when he bought the dress came up unexpectedly and at a peculiar time, just days after they buried James.

"I will refuse to go, stay here with you, Eve. I will tell them the situation," he said.

She could see the agitation in his face, his brows furrowed into his eyelids, the nerve in his right cheek twitching the same as the night she had come home from the hospital, leaving baby James in the morgue.

"Arnold, I understand. It's work."

"I don't have to go."

"You do. It must be important or they wouldn't have asked you."

He sent word to the travel agent to book him a seat and began straight away packing his case. When she offered to help, he refused, telling her to rest.

He left early the next morning. Turning down breakfast, he

was anxious to get on his way. At the front door, when she reached out to him to kiss goodbye, his shoulders shook, tears streaking his eyes. Squeezing his arm as reassurance, she whispered in his ear.

"Go. We will be fine. I will be fine."

He nodded, and she thought she saw sadness glint across his eyes.

Standing on the front steps of Ludlow Hall, she watched the car go down the driveway, rounding the rhododendron and slipping out of sight. It was a crisp, cold morning, but she did not move back inside, dropping down to sit on the step, the cold damp seeping through her.

The sheep, normally huddled in one corner, began to drift across the field to the fence nearest the house. The geese pecked around on the gravel at the front as she sat, tears coursing down her face. The sheepdog, panting after following the car down the avenue, came and settled beside her, sniffing at the tears, gently nudging her face.

When Michael Conway drove up the front avenue an hour later, Eve was still sitting on the steps, the front door wide open behind her. Thinking something terrible had happened, he rushed from the car.

"What is wrong, Eve, what has happened?"

"Arnold has rushed off to America."

"Why?"

"Something at work, I don't know."

"Let's get you inside, you are frozen with the cold." Gently, he helped her to her feet, fussing about, guiding her to the upstairs bedroom. "Get into bed, I will look after things today."

"What do you think is so important, he has to fly all the way to New York?"

"I don't know, Eve. Best to concentrate on getting better."

Michael left her and went to heat a can of soup. When he brought a tray upstairs ten minutes later, she was sitting up in bed.

146

"How long is Arnold going to be away?" he asked.

"I don't know, maybe a few weeks."

"Do you have any family or anyone who can come and stay with you?"

"There is nobody to ask."

She paused, pretending to look towards the windows, but he could see she was upset.

"Do you think Arnold is going to come back, Michael?"

Michael Conway spluttered out his answer. "That is silly talk. You have been through a lot; it is putting silly ideas into your head."

"Things have been so quiet between us, since the baby died."

He rubbed his hands along the sides of his trousers, embarrassed that the talk was turning intimate.

"Maybe a break of sorts will give you both time to grieve."

"Or drive us further apart."

Clearing his throat, because he was nervous, he spoke in a gentle voice. "I can help you out, get somebody in at the shop while I tip around the farm for you."

"Michael, you are so kind, but what will Arnold think, or others in Rosdaniel? They will have something to say."

"I am not moving in, Eve, just helping out. Arnold will understand, and the gossips, they will blather about it for a day or so. Will you be okay on your own at night?"

"I have stayed a lot of nights on my own here already, Michael."

He shifted uncomfortably from one foot to another. "I have to go back to the shop just now, but I will call around later to see what needs doing."

When Arnold came back two weeks later, he looked worn out. When she enquired, he would not be drawn on the details of the trip. Neither did he explain why he was gone so long. He handed her the Bloomingdale's box before going upstairs to lie down, not even waiting to see her face when she opened it.

Standing at the bottom of the stairs, she watched as he trudged away. Taking the box into the drawing room, she did not open it immediately. Instead, she stood by the window, listening to her husband move around upstairs. She wondered if he would ever tell her what happened in New York.

Outside, the sheep bunched together. A young horse in the next field cantered into the middle of the plot, throwing its head about. The geese flocked down towards the lake, and crows in the far copse of trees kicked up a racket, showering spent twigs onto the avenue.

She turned to the box. Never had he given such an extravagant gift. Slowly, she nicked the tape on the outside with her fingernail, gently pulling up the top. Layers and layers of white tissue paper she pulled out, until she came to the dress, neatly folded, as if it had that minute been placed there. When she lifted it out, the full skirt fell to the ground in a swish of chiffon. She knew only a woman's eyes could have picked this dress. A man could never pick a dress that on first glance looked so simple.

An uneasy feeling came over her, making her reluctant to even hold the dress up to her. She knew it would fit perfectly, and that knowledge made her feel strange. Letting it drop back in the box, she hastily put back the cover, pushing the box with her foot under the long couch.

Eve caught the dress now, yanking it from the hanger and balling it into a bag. It was meant for a stylish city life, not an old house in a backwoods town. Maybe she would have a use for it in the quilt. God knows, for long enough she had wanted an excuse to put scissors to it.

Eve checked her appearance in the mirror, patted a tint of powder on her face and applied a slick of lipstick, before putting on her coat and heading for Ludlow Hall. She wanted to get a head start on Hetty today, afraid the deadline was making her rush, cutting lazy large pieces of fabric to cover a big span of quilt.

Hetty, with her tiny squares of suit and shirt fabric, had been

148

aghast when she saw the rectangles and squares howling with colour, drowning out the smaller neighbours.

"You can't get away with that, Eve, people will comment," she had said, and though Eve knew she was right, she would never admit it out loud. "Don't give in to fast progress and sacrifice the mystery and depth," Hetty said, a smug tone to her voice.

Walking to Michael's shop first, Eve stuck her head in the doorway.

"I am off to Ludlow for the best part of the day. Drop into the little house on the way home this evening, we can eat together."

"I can't do it tonight, Eve, I have the Scrabble Club."

She pretended to be in a huff, making a face, and he laughed.

"I am in the semi-final. This is my chance to knock Sean Mackey off his perch."

"I have a word for you: quagga. Remember that."

He picked up a pencil and attempted to jot down the word on a newspaper on the counter. "Spell it out, Eve."

She did, slowly, adding, "That better not be my *Irish Times*."

"What does it mean anyway?"

"Look it up. I can't stay gabbing, I have to get to Ludlow."

He waved goodbye as a few customers slipped by Eve for the morning newspaper.

Eve rushed along, anxious to get to Ludlow, a renewed vigour in her to make a go of this memory quilt. Beetling along the driveway, she suddenly stopped as she came to the rhododendron. There was Ludlow Hall, the sunlight streaking morning gold across the top windows, the pots of primulas at the front door, left there by Connie, the car parked where Arnold used to leave it, a sense of life there now. She expected the sheepdog to amble around from the back, the horses to raise their heads in the paddocks, the geese to start fussing, to hear the echo of a voice from inside the house. It was as if nothing had changed and everything had changed.

Sensing the house was silent, she let herself in as quietly as she could, holding the door until it clicked shut, for fear it would bang and make a noise. Tossing her bag of fabric in the drawing room, she headed for the kitchen to put on the kettle.

Eve was surprised when she saw Connie sitting at the kitchen table.

"You are very quiet. I hope you don't mind me turning up so early."

"That is why I gave you the key."

Eve felt awkward, loitering, not knowing if she should help herself or wait to be asked.

Connie, as if she sensed the other woman's discomfort, stood up.

"Why don't I get out of your way?"

Eve looked at her closely. "It may not be my place to say it, but you look like shit."

Connie smiled. "I was dancing, working up a sweat. I thought it might be a good way to clear my head."

"And did it?"

"What do you think?" Connie mopped her forehead with a towel she had around her neck. "I am sorry, I don't mean to be rude. It has been a bad night."

"I should not have walked in on top of you so early. Why don't I go and come back at a more decent hour?"

Connie shook her head.

"All the hours in the world can't sort some things out."

"We don't know each other very well, but I know a thing or two about grief."

"You don't want to hear my story, Mrs Brannigan."

Eve reached over, touching Connie on the arm.

"Ludlow is a huge responsibility. Is there anyone who can keep you company for a while?"

"A friend said he can come over."

"That is something to look forward to."

Connie slumped down on a chair.

"Not exactly. He was my lover ..." She paused, waiting for a reaction from Eve, but all Eve did was pull out a chair and sit into the table. "I was planning to leave Ed. I'd met Bill years earlier. He went off to California, but when he came back, we rekindled our relationship. This time I was ready to leave my husband. I am shocking you, I guess."

"There is not much in the world that shocks me these days."

"Bill is in London, working. He wants to come over."

"What is wrong with that?"

"I thought you would not approve."

"Firstly, you don't need anyone's approval. Secondly, take it from me, you should snatch happiness whenever it comes knocking, otherwise you will regret it."

"You sound like somebody with regrets."

"I have never met anyone on this planet who does not have regrets. It is the size of the regrets that matters: I would rather a big sack of small ones than one big one that colours your life."

Connie smiled. "It might be too late for that advice."

Eve got up and filled the kettle at the tap.

"Connie, I am no expert, but if I knew a man was interested enough to travel to meet me, I would dress up and bloody enjoy it."

"Even if you felt guilty?"

Eve put two mugs down heavily on the table.

"Tell me, what can either of us do about the past? We can't change it."

They sat together, waiting for the kettle to boil, the peace of the house cloaking around them. When the water spat and bubbled, Eve waited until the kettle switched off before getting up to make a pot of tea.

17

Eve was in the drawing room, her head down, busy at work, when Hetty arrived.

"Why do I get the impression the day started much earlier? I am late to the game," she said, picking up the new squares Eve had cut out. "A change of heart from a two-patch quilt?"

Eve put down her sewing. "I had a rethink."

"You have created a lot of work for yourself, Eve."

Eve smiled that Hetty was taking so much umbrage.

"Kathryn rang. She said they have a lot of fabric to sort through for the Rosdaniel quilt and they should be here around eleven."

Eve noticed Hetty was barely listening. She reached out and touched her shoulder.

"We have different memories, different stories to tell, but there is no competition between us." Eve noticed a shadow move across her friend's face.

"Mine is too sombre. I don't know if it is a good idea including fabric from the suits," Hetty whispered.

"If anything was to sum up Barry Gorman, it is the beautifully cut suits, the trousers sharply creased," said Eve.

Hetty did not answer, but spread her quilt over the rug in the middle of the drawing room floor. Pulling the blue suit from a box at the side of the room, she heard Eve sigh.

"See what I mean, Hetty, after all these years, I can see the trousers crease, like it is just pressed in."

Hetty let the trousers drop along one side of the quilt, a cacophony of delicate linen that once made up his expensive shirts.

"Why don't I add a narrow strip?"

Eve picked some black trousers from the box.

"Not those," Hetty said, handing her some grey trousers instead. "Use the brown and a pinstripe for the other sides. The black one is his wedding suit," she said, as if she had to explain why she did not want to cut it up.

"Lovely quality. Why would you want to destroy it?" Eve said, sensing a big upset in Hetty.

They stood back and considered the quilt.

"It looks bigger. Have you been working on squares at home?" Eve asked.

"I was afraid I would not get it done in time."

Eve did not quite believe Hetty, but she said nothing.

"The ladies will be along later for a full meeting and review, so we had better get cracking."

Hetty, moving towards the kitchen, mumbled she could not start without a coffee.

Eve watched her go, noting for the first time that Hetty's step was unusually heavy, her shoulders slightly hunched. Best to leave her be a while. No doubt if there was something big eating her, she would spit it out when she was ready.

Hetty shook the kettle to check there was water in it, before clicking it on. A streak of tiredness darted through her, so she sat down, jiggling her shoulders, in an effort to throw off the foggy feeling in her head. Most of the night she had sat looking at Barry's suits, wanting to slice them to shreds, almost afraid to touch the fabric that summed up all his parts.

His shirts she had easily slipped from their hangers. Picking his favourites, she carved through, cutting small patches, so when she sewed them together it looked like a wave of lilac and blue turning to grey and white. The linen was the right fit for patchwork and easy to work with, so she sat up at night sewing

153

the squares together, deftly stitching, all the time creating a new story for herself. Every time she turned up at Ludlow, she had even more to add to the memory quilt of a marriage, so that it was already much bigger than Eve's.

Eve might think Hetty was being competitive, making a big show to impress the town, but the truth was that once she started ripping his favourite shirts, she enjoyed it, revelling as the fabric shrieked in protest when she pulled with the grain, giving pleasure as she sliced with the shears up the back of the shirt in the first long cut.

Her husband's words, in her head, she slashed at random.

"The back of a shirt must be crease free, pristine."

"Show me a man who can't take off his jacket. If the shirt back is not ironed, show me a man who can't control his wife."

The first shirt she cut tentatively, nicking it at the side seam, picking away a few stitches, wrenching the seam hard with her hands so that it gave way. She cut out a neat square, almost the size of his back. The shape of him made her angry, making her slash erratically through the panel, his words fading as she stabbed with the scissors. So much she cut, and in all directions, that she was compelled to choose small pieces to achieve the number of squares she required. Handling the small patches, it no longer felt like Barry's shirt – like she had finally escaped him.

Eve came through to the kitchen.

"I don't know what is up with everyone this morning. Is there something wrong, Hetty?"

Hetty made a show of smiling brightly. "Nothing a cuppa won't sort out."

Eve knew better than to ask further.

"I brought out the black serge trousers, the wedding pair. You don't have to cut them up, if they mean so much to you."

Hetty busied herself, throwing a tea bag into her mug, fishing for a cookie from the jar beside the sink.

"You are not yourself this morning, Hetty. What is it?" Eve asked gently.

Hetty stopped what she was doing, swinging around so that her elbow hit against the cookie jar, nearly knocking it off the worktop.

"My head is a bit addled, Eve. What are you doing with those trousers?"

Eve handed them to Hetty.

"You should put them aside, so they do not get cut up by mistake."

"Mistake? It doesn't matter. Nothing will bring back the happy feeling I felt that day, nothing will obliterate the unhappy years I spent after that."

Eve stared at Hetty. "Sewing this quilt is not good for you, Hetty. I am sorry."

Hetty flopped on to a chair. "You are wrong, Eve. It has freed me from the clutches of that bastard. No longer will he have a grip on me from the grave."

"You are not talking about Barry?"

Hetty snorted loudly. "Barry Gorman and his wife, Hetty, the woman envied by the whole of Rosdaniel. What did they envy, Eve? The way he put his hand around my throat and squeezed? The nasty things he said, the time he pinched my tits so hard I howled like a dog in pain?"

Eve did not answer, but Hetty did not notice.

"A fine gentleman who beat up his wife if the crease in his trousers was not pencil sharp and straight, who insisted I steep his underpants in bleach so they were perfect white, even though he knew the fumes made me throw up. His socks and underwear had to be ironed and folded a certain way."

She stopped to pull in a deep breath, all the time registering the shock streaking across Eve's face. When she spoke again, it was in a lower voice.

"If I fell down on any of the things he expected, he docked my weekly allowance. Mind you, he still expected the same amount of food on the table."

She stopped talking when she saw Connie standing in the

155

doorway. Connie, pretending she had not heard anything, waved and retreated.

"Hetty, I had no idea," Eve said, reaching out and rubbing her friend's hand.

"Don't worry, Eve. Nobody knew. We were very good at keeping it a secret."

"Was it drink? What made him act that way?"

"I wish I could blame the booze, but it was just him: he was a cruel man. Don't get me wrong, there were some good years, but once he showed his cruel side he could not get away from the great sense of power it gave him. When the shop began to lose out to the fancy shopping centres, things got a lot worse. When he lost the shop altogether, it nearly destroyed him and me." Tears flowed down her cheeks and she squeezed Eve's hand tight. "Barry Gorman was no gentleman in his own home."

They sat, Hetty gulping her tears, her shoulders heaving.

"I am sorry about the quilt," Eve said quietly.

Hetty squeezed her hand more. "Don't be. I let go of the bastard's clothes, finally. I got to cut them up."

"And stick needles in them," Eve said, noticing a curl of a smile on Hetty's lips.

When Connie arrived back in the doorway with a bottle of whiskey and three of Arnold's crystal glasses, Hetty beckoned her in.

"Come in, we can't be taking over your kitchen."

"I thought you could do with a drink," she said, pouring a measure into each glass. "To the men in our lives, long departed." Connie's voice was strong, almost comical.

Hetty and Eve clinked Connie's glass, the three gulping large sips of the whiskey.

"I think doing the quilt you have had your revenge," Eve said, walking towards the drawing room, the others following to where all the sections to make up the Barry Gorman quilt were laid out on the floor.

"It is beautiful, even if it documents a horrible hero," Connie

156

said, bending down to examine the multitude of small patches.

Pushing the quilt with the toe of her shoe, Hetty spoke, her voice strong.

"Every one of these pieces represents the bastard my husband was."

Pointing to the centrepiece, where the points of delicate shirt colours wheeled out in a movement of gentle colour, she explained more.

"Violet and pink: they were his Sunday best, starched stiff, difficult to iron. If Barry's shirt was not immaculate, warm from the heat of the iron when he reached for it, as he carefully dressed for Mass on a Sunday morning, he punched me in the stomach. Never enough that I couldn't walk, but just enough that, as we made our way down the public footpath, my insides flared with pain.

"White for the work shirts, bleached and starched to the point that they wore out too fast."

Pointing to the mint green slit in the wheel of colour, Hetty's hand shook.

"Eve, he bought that shirt to come here, the time you decided to change the drawing room curtains. Remember he drove over to show you the bolts of cloth."

Eve did remember. Barry had been nervous, perspiring, mopping his forehead with a white handkerchief as he gabbed on too much, and she felt sorry for him. She was happy enough with a plain gold for the bay window and the three front single windows. She brought him tea and excused herself, so she could show a sample to Arnold in the library.

"You did not go for his samples, Eve," Hetty said quietly.

"I loved a plain gold basket weave, but Arnold would not hear of it."

Eve remembered he was so rude, flinging the bolt so that the fabric gushed across the library floor when he heard that his wife was going to buy from a shop in Arklow.

"Are we to have the same soft furnishings as everybody in

Ballyheigue? Over my dead body, I can tell you. At Ludlow Hall we pick the finest fabric, furnishings that endure, furnishings that fit in with the Hall and who we are."

She knew better than to argue, pulling out of the library, rolling up the sample as she went.

When she told Barry Gorman she was sorry, but her husband did not like the colour, he went from pale to grey. Stuttering his words in his anxiety, he offered every other colour under the sun, almost begging for another appointment. He persisted, not realising she was trying to let him down gently.

"What did he do when he got home?"

Hetty shook her head. "You are entitled to pick any colour you like for your curtains, he knew that well, but..."

Hetty's voice trailed off, as she walked over to the bay window and fingered the curtain.

"Somehow I never imagined you would go for a brocade, Eve."

"I didn't. I hated the heaviness of them all these years, way too formal and fussy for windows that look over fields with sheep and horses. I preferred the plain gold Barry had to offer. He knew what suited a window."

"Why didn't you order it?"

Eve picked up a panel of her patchwork and flattened it out with her hands.

"You are not the only one who had a husband who thought he knew everything. Arnold made all the big decisions: that day it was the drawing room curtains. The next morning, he rang Clerys in Dublin and a man was sent down to measure the windows. Arnold was taken in by the man's guff that brocade gave the room a hint of sophistication. Within weeks, the curtains were up."

"I never realised Arnold was like that," Hetty said quietly.

"Like the rest of us never copped on to Barry."

Connie moved to the window. Climbing up on the chaise longue, she unhooked the top of the curtain pleats, first letting one side drop to the ground, then the other.

"I think we are all in agreement it is time for these drapes to go."

She swung around to Hetty and Eve, standing staring at her, a look of admiration across their faces.

"You are leaving a lot of windows open to the world."

"All they will see is dancing."

"Hetty, you suffered because of Arnold's decision," Eve said.

"He must have felt really bad, because he forgot himself that night and punched me in the face. Barry did not usually leave evidence for the public eye." Hetty, with her finger, circled her right eye. "I had to stay out of sight for a while, or at least until the make-up could do a better cover job, once the bruising turned a yellowish colour."

Connie jumped down, put an arm around Hetty and hugged her tight."

"Help me take the rest down," she said.

Eve ran out to the kitchen and grabbed a chair. Climbing up, she reached for the top of the drawing room bay window. In all the years she had owned Ludlow Hall, she was never brave enough to suggest a change of curtains. Tugging so hard the curtain pole shook, yanking the hooks out of position, she felt a thrill of excitement shoot through her.

Hetty pulled over the couch and stood on the arm to tackle the second front window. They worked hard, unhooking, letting the heavy brocade curtains fall to the floor.

"The room is much nicer now," Connie said, surveying the bare windows, the mountains of spent curtains in piles across the floor.

"God knows what the Ludlow Ladies' Society will say," Eve said, making the other two chuckle.

Hetty turned to Connie. "We will blame you."

"I suppose the truth is out of the question."

"Out of the question," both Hetty and Eve chanted at the same time, and the three women laughed as they bundled up the gold curtains, helping Connie throw them in a heap at the far end of the hall.

Hetty took out her powder compact. She stood at the bare window, gently tapping the red blotches around her eyes. Snapping the compact shut, she turned to Eve.

"How do I look?"

"Like it never happened, any of it."

"Good, back to normal so," Hetty replied, picking up sections of the memory quilt and folding them neatly away.

Kathryn Rodgers, holding a neat little handbag, was the first at the door.

"We have to get more fabric in. We need to send out an SOS to the village," she said, standing in the hallway, directing operations as the other women carried in box after box.

Dana Marshall hesitated when she saw Connie loitering in the hall. Never one to let a moment pass, she called out to Connie, her voice high-pitched. "Don't worry, I am not hiding a dog in here."

Connie did not answer, but waved, disappearing out of view.

Kathryn rapped Dana on the knuckles.

"Don't be such a naughty girl. We have so much work to do."

"A bit of humour gets us a long way," Dana said, digging into a box and pulling out a pile of old clothes. "I am not too sure how we will get anything presentable out of this lot," she said, holding an old tweed skirt up to her. "If you ask me, a lot of people are saying they are donating fabric, but really they are getting rid of all their own shite."

Kathryn Rodgers clapped her hands loudly.

"Let's be clear that we'll only take fabric that tells a story. What you have in your hand, Rebecca, does it have a story?"

Rebecca, flushing pink to be singled out, held up an Ireland football jersey.

"A few people have asked us to include a green jersey. Nobody wanted to give up their Ireland shirts, but they were all talking about the time in the '90s when Ireland got as far as the quarter-final in the World Cup. Somebody put green dye into the river that flows through the Ludlow lands and the town and …" Rebecca turned to Eve. "Remember your Arnold went mad and called the Gardaí and insisted they find the culprit and look for the dye. He even had the priest announce at Mass that he was going to find who did it and charge them for any damage caused. If you don't mind me saying, he was way over the top."

Kathryn guffawed out loud. "Wasn't there quite a lot of talk when a crate of dye was found in the barn at Ludlow Hall? That silenced Arnold Brannigan."

Eve remembered it well, and the fury Arnold cradled for so long. When, a week later, she saw Michael and Richie slip the empty crate into the boot of their car, she said nothing.

Hetty began to giggle. "My Barry bought a fish in the river, caught only that day, and I poached it for his dinner. I thought the water was a funny colour, but I said nothing. The fish just smelled of fish. He threw up like a volcano that night. When, the following Friday, I put fish in front of him for his dinner, the poor man turned as green as the river."

"Maybe include the green as a meandering river through the quilt," Eve said, and the others, surprised, laughed heartily.

Date: April 10, 2013
Subject: THE LUDLOW LADIES' SOCIETY

Ludlow ladies,

We are living in such exciting times! Who would have thought a few weeks ago that life could be so good?

Ladies, now is the time for us to band together and produce the best quilts ever. As you know, the Americans know their patchwork, so we want to make sure that it is our best work. Ladies, we want to get this right!

We are asking all those members who may have lapsed in their attendance to support us now, as we arrange and sew our memory quilts. With any luck, we will receive the great honour of having our work examined by the First Lady.

Even if you can't give your time, please donate quality fabric that has some resonance with Rosdaniel. Spread the word, ladies, and please drop all fabric donations in to Bernie Martin on Parnell Street. Top-quality fabric only, no more football shirts please, and most definitely only clothes with a story!

May I say, ladies, that if our very good friend Jack Davoren deigns to donate, refuse. I hear he has a new Sunday suit and is only dying to get rid of his old one. The Ludlow Ladies' Society will not entertain Jack Davoren's cast-offs.

Let's work hard and dream of the honour of having the most beautiful Michelle Obama throwing an eye over our patches! This is an amazing opportunity for Rosdaniel to showcase its best and an incredible opportunity for the Ludlow Ladies' Society.

Kathryn Rodgers,
Chairwoman

18

Eve woke before it was light, images of Hetty bruised and in pain flashing through her mind. She wanted to talk to Michael, to feel reassurance in his voice, but she did not want to ring him so early.

Instead, she went downstairs and pulled out the button box, her hand stacking the buttons into a high mountain before letting them run to one side. Closing her eyes, she felt the heaviness of the button mound, hundreds of stories held in such tiny offerings. Piercing through with her fingers, she let the buttons of all shapes, colours and sizes rain down either side of her hand.

Opening her eyes when she felt the softness of the small Lady Washington pearl button, memories flooded back of the light blue dress with the angel sleeves she had made especially for the Ludlow Fete. After only four months in Ludlow, she came up with the idea of the fete and was cute enough to time it for when Arnold was on an extended trip to the States. The dress, made of cotton with tiny flowers on a light blue background, was long since gone, but she remembered it had taken her a week to run it up, stealing time on her machine when the estate was very busy, workmen tidying up the gardens and mending the fences for the fete. Using a Butterick pattern, she pinned the tissue to the fabric, which she had bought the summer before on a day out in Dublin, confident she could finish it in time for the fete. It was not a fancy dress, a simple pattern of the time, maxi length with a deep frill at the bottom and angel sleeves from a bodice tight into the waist. She placed three mother-of-pearl buttons on the bodice, trimming the angel sleeves with a delicate lace, which she replicated at the waist.

Eve smiled to think of the dress now. A dress for a sunny day, and they got just that for the fete in late July. Arnold was in America, and just as well, because he would never have approved of opening up Ludlow Hall to the public.

The first of the crowds came directly after Sunday Mass, laden down with picnic baskets and blankets to spread out near the lake. Children crowded around the old jetty, taking turns to jump in the water as their mothers stood watching and gossiping.

The Ludlow Ladies' Society set up a stall laden down with patchwork cushions, doilies and cushion covers. Eve had a separate stall selling rhubarb and ginger jam, along with apple chutney made in the farm kitchen. Michael stood with her, manning the stand, until the last pot had been whipped up. Afterwards, they walked together down the yew walk to the lake.

"It is still very busy at the lake. Will we give it a miss, walk over to see the horses in the far field?" he asked.

They strolled side by side, sometimes stopping to chat to those sitting out on blankets on the field nearest the house. Many did not take much notice of the two of them, but those who did remarked that Arnold Brannigan should not spend so much time away from home: Michael Conway was strutting about as if he owned the place.

Climbing over the locked gate that was marked "off limits", they made their way across the second paddock, where some of the sheep stopped to watch them as they crossed over to the field beyond.

"The gossips will have a field day," Michael muttered, making her giggle with nervousness.

"Arnold does not talk to anyone in the village. Anyway, we are not doing anything wrong," she said, sounding a lot braver than she felt.

It was a few moments later that Michael told her she looked beautiful.

Embarrassed, she ran her hands across her dress, saying it was new but only a dress she had run up herself.

"Stop putting yourself down, Eve. Light blue is your colour. The way the light sparkles off those buttons, they are a mirror to your eyes."

She had no answer to that, but it made her feel warm all over as they walked on together, not needing to say much more.

After a few moments, she turned to him.

"Do you always notice so keenly what a woman is wearing? I thought men did not take particular notice. Arnold notices nothing."

"Arnold is a fool. No offence, but it is true: he should not be leaving you alone here at Ludlow."

She laughed nervously. "I am hardly completely alone. I am always busy, especially with the Ladies' Society."

She skipped on ahead, and he watched her, the blue dress fluttering in the sunshine.

"He brings me back the most wonderful gifts from New York."

"Wealth can get you out of any situation," Michael said, and she put her hand on his shoulder to calm him.

"I am not sure you even like him any more."

He was about to answer when Eve heard her name being called. It was Hetty Gorman, half running, half walking, swaying and gesturing wildly at the two of them. When she got as far as them, she was puffing, using her hands to fan her hot, round face.

"You two are hard to keep up with. Eve, it has been decided you should make a speech. We need to do it before everybody starts wandering home."

"I am not very good at speeches, Hetty."

"You might as well start getting good at it: everybody wants to hear from Mrs Ludlow."

165

She pressed her hand to her mouth, making Michael guffaw loudly.

"I think Eve knows already everybody calls her Mrs Ludlow, Hetty."

"It is just a friendly nickname," she said, her face flushing red.

"And one I like," Eve said, linking Hetty's arm through hers for the trek back to the house. Hetty was pumping sweat and out of breath, Michael following behind.

Within minutes of her arriving back at Ludlow Hall, a crowd gathered at the front steps, with Eve standing on an old apple box on the top step. She spoke softly, thanking them all for coming.

"Maybe we can make it an annual event. It is so lovely to get together in a spirit of community. I am glad Ludlow Hall can play its part, and I hope it will continue to do so for many years to come. Thank you also to the Ludlow Ladies' Society for making it all possible."

The Ludlow ladies, she thought, clapped the loudest, and she wondered what would Arnold say if he ever found out she had stood on the top step of Ludlow Hall and addressed a crowd.

Michael stayed on until the last person left, walking, picking up bits and pieces of litter, and tidying away tables and chairs that had been dragged across the grass to favourite picnic spots and the lake, where mothers sat watching out for their children. After an hour, when everything was more or less back where it should be, Michael stepped in the still-open front door of the Hall.

"I hope everything is well here."

"You mean are all the family jewels still in place? If I knew where they were, I could tell you. I looked in on Arnold's study, in case anybody wandered in there, but nothing has been touched. I think everyone respected the sign saying 'Private' at the bottom of the stairs. Hetty said only a handful of people came into the house; the sunshine was a much bigger draw. There is nothing much anyone would want to take, big old ugly antiques and that's it," Eve said, running her hand along the marble-top table in the hall.

Michael laughed. "You are the boss, Eve. You could change it all if you liked."

"Arnold would have something to say about that."

She walked ahead into the drawing room.

"You will have a sherry, Michael."

He grimaced, shaking his head.

She moved to pour a drink for herself, but stopped in front of the drinks cabinet.

"What is wrong?" Michael asked.

"There was half of a decanter of sherry there before, but now it is empty."

"Somebody has gone home to Rosdaniel happy," Michael said.

Eve swung around to face him. "Hetty and Barry were looking after the house, they would never let anybody drain the sherry decanter."

"Barry wouldn't let anybody, because he would drain it himself first."

Eve was surprised at the venom behind Michael's words.

He coughed, almost as if to contain his anger. "Barry is well known for liking a drink, I doubt he could resist it."

Eve put a bright smile on her face, pointing to the kitchen. "Nothing for it but to make a cup of tea," she said.

Michael knew she was deliberately not getting too excited about either the sherry or his opinion of Hetty's husband.

"I am not particularly bothered about the sherry. I probably should have told them to help themselves," she said.

When there was a light tap on her front door, she knew who it was.

"I saw the light on and knew you were up."

"Michael, I was thinking back to the days of the Ludlow Hall Fete."

"They were good days, mostly, or is that just the way we think of life events so many decades on?"

"That was a good day. Do you remember when we set off walking across the paddocks?"

"I told you you were beautiful."

She stared at him.

"I did not expect you to remember."

He laughed.

"Eve, you blushed, the pink rising up your neck, just as it is now."

She busied herself, closing the button box and putting it away.

"It was such a pity Arnold vetoed the holding of a fete at any other time. Jack Davoren and his big mouth."

"I called to tell you that great word won me the Scrabble tournament. Mackey pretended to know what it meant, but I know he didn't."

"Oh good! What is the prize?"

"A weekend in Belfast, all expenses paid."

He sat on the edge of his seat.

"Eve, I was hoping you would come with me. We could get away from here, get to know each other a bit better."

She sat down suddenly, a strange feeling flowing through her.

"We know each other so well. You know everything about me."

"We are friends, that is for sure, but maybe we need to get away from the shadow of Ludlow."

Her mouth was so dry she could not speak.

"I hope I have not overstepped the mark."

Placing her hand on his arm, she managed to talk. "I don't know what to say, Michael. Thank you, I would love to go."

"Do you mean it?"

"I mean it."

Her voice was stronger and she looked him straight in the eye. When he stood up, she did too, and when he reached to pull her towards him and kissed her, she did not object.

"Shall we say next month? I would say spring in Belfast, but it does not have a great ring to it."

She giggled and he let her go. They stood holding hands, looking at each other, until Michael shook his shoulders.

"I have to go, the shop won't open by itself. Richie was up early and away to the swimming pool. He prefers keeping fit to standing behind the shop counter. Can I call back this evening, we can plan the trip?"

She nodded, and he reached over, kissing her on the top of her head, before making for the door.

Waving him off, she felt giddy with excitement. Not able to concentrate on anything, she got herself ready, waiting inside the window for Hetty to arrive, so they could go to Ludlow Hall together.

When she saw the car pull in, she went to the door.

"You are keen today," Hetty said, giving Eve an odd look.

She had pulled out on to the road, when Eve broke the awkward silence.

"Hetty, I have been asked on a date."

Hetty crunched the gears.

"What did you say, Eve?"

"Michael has asked me on a date."

Hetty swung into the Ludlow Hall driveway and stopped the car.

"Oh, my God, and about time too! Tell all." She was screeching, her knees jigging up and down in excitement.

"He has won a prize and we are going to Belfast together."

Hetty stopped, staring at Eve.

"Not just a day trip, Hetty, a weekend away."

Hetty threw back her head and laughed long and hard. "That is the best news I have heard in a long time. What will you wear?"

"I have plenty of clothes."

"Silly woman, you will need all sorts."

"I didn't think of it like that," Eve said quietly, and Hetty laughed again.

"How I envy you, Eve Brannigan, invited for a weekend away with a man, and at our age."

169

Hetty parked beside the seat at the front of Ludlow Hall.

"It is not for a while yet, so I have plenty of time to prepare," Eve said, almost as if she was trying to reassure herself.

They let themselves in the front door and went straight to the drawing room, hoping to get in two hours' work before the other ladies arrived.

"I didn't see Connie's car. She must be avoiding us. I told her we would be here."

"Maybe she took the opportunity to do something away from Ludlow," Hetty said, a tinge of disappointment in her voice.

"If Michelle Obama is going to be giving our quilts the once-over, we had better get cracking," Eve said, and the two of them headed into the drawing room to set to work.

19

Connie was up early waiting for the delivery truck. When notification had come a few days earlier that the boxes shipped from the States so long ago had arrived in Ireland, she was nervous. Now she was waiting to touch the bits and pieces that had made up her daughter's short life. That she would soon be able to do it was both painful and exhilarating.

After Molly's death, she had Amy go to the house and tip all of Molly's stuff into cardboard boxes, sealing them up quickly, so they did not have to face their terrible loss. She never went back into the house. Her sister did it for her, carefully selecting every last thing connected to Molly. Connie at that stage could not bear to look at it, ordering the boxes that summed up a precious life to remain sealed, stacked in Amy's basement.

As the lorry trundled up the driveway, she walked out to meet it, directing the men around the back, to unload the boxes into the barn. Box after box was lifted out carefully. When the truck doors were shut and all the boxes were stacked in the barn, one of the delivery men turned to Connie.

"Are you sure you don't want us to bring some into the house? They are heavy."

She did not answer, but took the clipboard and signed it, waiting for the truck to reverse, beeping its way down the driveway, before she walked across to the barn.

About thirty boxes were piled two high to the right inside the door. Tearing the nearest one open, she saw her funeral suit, the deep purple trousers and jacket she wore that day, because she knew Molly hated black. Why on earth had Amy sent it over? She would not complain, though. Amy was brave enough to go into the house to pick up everything, big and small, that was Molly. All that was Ed Carter she left for the cleaning company coming in behind her.

Pushing her hand down through the box, Connie pulled out a vacuum-packed plastic bag filled with the clothes and paraphernalia of a life not fully lived. Pulling at the cardboard box, tears rising through her, she lifted out hard plastic square bags, six of them, one for every year of Molly's life. Grabbing them, holding the stack out in front of her, she stumbled across the yard, pushing through the kitchen door, landing them on the table.

Only weeks before it all happened Connie had filled up six vacuum-packed bags with neatly folded clothes, the first five years' mementos of milestones passed. For the bag from when Molly had turned five years old, Amy had done her best, but it was a jumble of everything, reflecting the turmoil of the last day of packing in what was the family home. The bags were labelled Molly. The baby year, the first year, the second year, the third year, the fourth year, the part-filled fifth. Happily, Connie had folded and arranged the clothes, finding pleasure in picking the little outfits that summed up a year.

The night before, scrolling down through the Mommy Blog she had stopped at this one:

MARCH 2009

I don't want to throw away any of Molly's clothes, but let's face it, small kids generate a lot of stuff and we can't keep it all. This, her second year, she has so many darling dresses, but my favourite is the simple red-and-white gingham. It cost a fortune on a weekend away for Mommy and Daddy in Boston. It brings back such beautiful memories. It must be the first item folded neatly and kept as a talking point

172

for years to come. I am sure one day Molly will go through these memory boxes of clothes and find them all so adorable and, hopefully, a reflection of her young life.

Connie xx

Connie ran her hand across the little dress. In fact they never got to Boston that weekend. She was ready, but Ed was too busy, agitated, and in no mood for a weekend away. He shouted at her that she should have consulted him before booking a hotel. He paced the floor of the kitchen, snarling into his phone, and she wondered what had happened to the once kind and considerate man she had married. When he had turned into a man prone to terrible flashes of anger, she did not know. She was sure it was the tension around her that made Molly decide to act up that morning, crying and screaming, so that Ed marched out of the house and drove off.

Reaching for the blue pyjamas with the trains on them, Connie felt an anger rise up inside her. Ed had protested loudly and angrily when he saw his daughter wearing the pyjamas, shouting they were meant for a boy. When she said Molly loved trains, he became sullen and quiet, shrugging his shoulders, ignoring Molly.

Connie let the pyjamas drop and reached instead for bag six, clothes squashed and wrinkled, the pyjamas she had worn in the days before her death still inside out from where she had pulled them off, two nights before. Burying her head in the pyjamas, Connie breathed in deeply: a cold, clean smell of a life gone, a soft, fleeting innocence. She felt the stab of pain when she realised they were one of Molly's favourite pairs of pyjamas. Molly had picked them out because they were just like the ones Mommy wore. She left the top inside out; she could not bear to rearrange from where Molly's little hands had pulled that night, could not bear to uncrumple the pyjama legs from where they had rumpled down, as she stepped out of them – such a small step, a step that would never grow bigger or longer.

173

Connie felt cold, but she could not move. Flashes of pain racked through her, his words swiped at her.

Understand. Forgive.

She should have dressed her in these, her favourite pyjamas, for the last goodbye, but she was selfish, could not let them go, desperately hanging on to as much of Molly as she could.

Understand. Forgive.

The words assaulted her brain, menaced her so that she could barely conjure up the good times. Desperately, she gripped the pyjamas, willing herself to remember the day Molly picked them out: expensive, soft, in light pink with little flowers at the front. Molly was firm in her resolve to have them.

"We are sisters," she said when she pulled them on, kicking out with her leg to show off the cuff.

An emptiness overwhelmed Connie, dull emptiness, his words echoing around her, piercing her brain and heart, tormenting her so.

Swiping the bags hard from the table, pulling the pyjamas to her, she walked to the room the builder, John O'Reilly, had earlier that day promised to make into a dance studio. The carpet had been rolled back to expose a wooden floor, the desk pushed back, the shelves cleared and dismantled. Reaching behind the curtains at the far window, where she had left the bottle of whiskey, she unscrewed it, slugging deeply, letting the alcohol burn her throat.

Shaking herself free, she went back to the kitchen. The Year One bag was still on the table. Unzipping it, the tiny babygro Molly wore the day they brought her home from hospital tumbled out. It had tiny butterflies all over. It still smelled of her, she thought, pressing her nose into the soft fabric. Gulping some more whiskey, she reached for the bib: 'Molly's First Christmas'. Somewhere in a box were the photographs of Ed and Molly taken that Christmas morning. What would she do when she came across them? How could she look at a photograph of them side by side? Leaning against the edge of the table, angry convulsions gushed through her body.

How could she ever understand or forgive?

She reached for the pink velvet and taffeta dress Molly had worn on her second birthday. It had gone in the wrong bag, because Molly had insisted on wearing it even when it became too short for her. On her birthday she had pirouetted across the sitting room, bowing, waiting for her audience to clap. Connie had smiled, looking at her daughter, her black curly hair bouncing on her shoulders, her back straight, her hands resting lightly on the taffeta skirt, dancing to a tune only she could hear.

Where was her little girl now? Lost to her, because of what he did.

Thumping the table hard, Connie shouted.

"I will never understand, never forgive."

Her words ricocheted off the walls, pumped through the house. Swigging some more from the bottle, she caught the dress, flinging it across the room. Scooping up more of the clothes, she threw them hard, watching as they hit the fridge, landing on a pile on the floor. Tears fogging up her eyes, she stumbled up the stairs, the whiskey bottle in her hand. Falling onto the bed she cradled the bottle like it was her baby.

She used to lie with Molly to help her get to sleep, her arm lightly over her, sometimes humming a little tune, until she felt the heaviness in the bed, the rhythm of her breathing, the trust inherent in a child when they sleep. She had trusted Ed to look after her baby. Molly just trusted. What was there to understand? There was too much to forgive.

Connie sat bolt upright in the bed and fired the bottle of whiskey across the room, where it crashed against the wall, smashing, the liquid streaming across the floorboards.

His words thumped in her brain, but she would never give in.

20

Eve arrived early at Ludlow Hall. She let herself quietly in, careful that the front door did not thud too loud as she shut it. She heard Connie moving around upstairs and called up to her.

She wanted to get a good two hours in, before Hetty and the others arrived, so she set to work immediately, cutting the last squares of fabric, placing them, moving them again, until she was happy with the combination of colours. Rich greens and blues she had picked for this section, reflecting the fields and lake at Ludlow, flashes of colour radiating from a section with flowers, to remember the formal gardens at the Hall.

Standing up from where she had been on the floor, plotting out the final look of the quilt, she stepped to the window. A curl of mist pirouetted like a ballerina across the paddocks, massaging the trees, before skirting along the top of the fences, dancing towards the house. She was lost in the contemplation of this scene when she heard a fast step on the stairs, a rush across the hall, the door banged shut.

Connie was at the top of the front steps, dithering, stopping to check the door was shut, before hurrying away.

Eve, annoyed the peaceful morning had been interrupted, went back to her quilt, considering it now: a collection of gold, blue, green, purple, red and other colours in between, in rich and sumptuous fabrics to show Ludlow Hall was once a place where occasions were frequent and dressing up commonplace. Running her hand along it, she stopped at the black and purple lace, beside it a grey silk from a suit made when Arnold brought her to the Galway Races. Strengthened with a stiff backing, the light blue fabric with the little flowers from the dress she specially made for the Ludlow Fete was a centre square along with the pink gingham she wore the day Michael took her to Tinahely. If anybody asked, she would tell them it represented the simple and beautiful side of life in the estate when the sky was clear and the flowers grew and life was good.

What the inhabitants of Rosdaniel would make of it was another thing, she thought, reaching for a gold brocade from the long skirt she wore to the Lord Mayor's Ball in Dublin. The event was a long, drawn-out affair, where her husband spent most of the evening in conversation with a city businessman. She spent the time waiting to go home. She never wore the skirt after that, though she kept the cutting from the *Irish Press* newspaper, which included a photograph of herself and Arnold in all their finery.

Casting the skirt aside, she glanced out the window, expecting to see Connie on the avenue. It was quiet. Maybe she had reached the bend quickly in her rush. Eve had not heard her skirt around to the back either. A worry rose up in Eve. She tried to concentrate on the quilt laid out on the floor, but a tension twitched at her, making her go to the window again. Distracted, she checked the kitchen. At the kitchen door, she stopped: there were clothes everywhere. Items of clothing small enough for a child on the floor, strewn across the table, dumped in front of the fridge, even hanging from the dresser. Stepping further into the room, she saw the plastic containers marked "Molly". A huge cardboard box was on the floor beside the sink. It was half open, as if somebody had had a change of mind after ripping up one side. A short note had been thrown on the draining board.

Eve glanced at it.

Darling Connie,
I am not sure why you want Molly's clothes; you are hardly staying in that place. I hope this does

not upset you too much. Remember, I can come over. Just give me the word. You should not be on your own.

The local newspaper said it is going to do a big spread for the anniversary. We told them we won't cooperate as it is too upsetting.

I hope you are talking to somebody over there about all this and learning to cope. You are in our thoughts and prayers.

Love,

Amy xx

Eve sat on one of the straight chairs beside the table, a strange feeling curdling in her stomach. She picked up a pink taffeta and velvet dress. It was almost brand new. Beside it lay a sleepsuit, clean but well worn. A sparkly skirt was on the floor. Eve bent down to pick it up.

It was as she was doing this that the dread and fear consumed Eve, making her rush from the kitchen to the front door, letting it bang behind her. Scanning the avenue and the paddocks, she did not see anyone. Wanting to scream for Connie, she did not. Instead, she walked briskly down the yew walk, panic pushing her forward. She was cross at herself; she had not noticed earlier something was wrong. Never had Connie walked past the drawing room door without sticking her head in or waving a fast goodbye. Neither had she ever gone into Ludlow Hall but Connie had said hello, either walking up the hall from the kitchen or calling from upstairs. Fear radiated through Eve as she quickened her pace, approaching the lake and jetty.

She wondered whether to call out, but decided against it. The path was clear as she rushed along to where it opened out into the small jetty. Arnold had it built so he could launch a boat to cast a better line for fish.

Connie was further along, deep in the reeds, moving through

the water, as if it was the most normal thing in the world. Eve watched her for a few seconds before calling out softly to her.

Connie had catapulted through the yew walk, tears streaming down her face, but by the time she got to the lake, a strange calm had taken over. The water curled around her ankles, seeping into her shoes. The stones on the lake bed scraped her, the cold water hitting against her legs, making her tights stick to her, pinching at her clothes. Her legs heavy, she waded out further, the water washing up her thighs, invading under her blouse, curling up around her chest.

She could end it all here. She could do it: sit down and let the water rise around her, consume her. If they knew why, they would say who could blame her.

She could lie down and feel the water coming over her face, seeping around her neck, crawling down her throat, soaking her long hair.

She could do it, the water a balm on her tired head, soothing, caressing the ache in her heart.

The sunlight streaked a path across the water. She turned to follow it.

Eve's voice was loud and clear.

"Connie, turn this way please. Turn to me. I am here."

Eve was standing up to her ankles, holding a life ring.

"I am going to throw it, Connie, you hold on to it. Will you do that?"

Connie looked away, stumbling into a hole on the lake bed, the water above her chest suddenly.

Eve threw the ring.

"Grab on to it, Connie. I will guide you in."

Connie grasped the ring. Eve heaved hard to pull her in to shore, her breath going, her arms aching, but she was afraid to stop and rest, even when Connie was in the shallows. When Connie came close to her, she grabbed her arms, pulling her through the reeds up onto the jetty, where they both lay coughing and spluttering.

"What were you thinking of, Connie? We need to get you back to the house and out of those wet clothes or you will get your death." Realising what she had said, Eve shut up.

"It would be too bad if you saved me from the lake for me to die of a common cold," Connie said, a hysterical ring to her voice.

They ran together hand in hand through the yew walk, Connie shivering in her tights, her shoes slipped off by the weight of water at the bottom of the lake.

"We will get you up to bed and get some nice soup into you. The doctor will come out to you. We will say nothing to the other women, only Hetty," Eve said as they reached the house.

Rushing Connie through the back door, Eve gently pushed her to the stairs.

"Let's get you into bed," she said firmly, holding Connie by the elbow as they negotiated the steps. When they got to the bedroom, she pulled the wet clothes off her, pushing a shivering Connie into the bed. Taking Connie's mobile, she rang Dr Granger, who promised to call out to Ludlow directly. Next, she dialled Hetty.

"I can't leave her, not until the doctor has examined her anyway. Tell the others she has a stomach bug and needs a bit of help."

"Will she be all right, Eve?"

"Who knows?"

"We can pray."

"I guess it is as good a strategy as any."

She rang off, turning back to the bed, where Connie was curled up like a child afraid of the dark. Eve pulled over a chair and sat by her.

About thirty minutes later the doctor arrived, letting himself in the back door and up the stairs. Eve left him to it, retiring to the drawing room to pick up her patchwork, her enthusiasm for the sewing somehow diminished.

Three cars came up the driveway, all parking at the front.

Kathryn Rodgers, Hetty, Eithne and Dana led a group of women to the front door.

Hetty was surprised to see Eve in the drawing room.

"I am not going to stay, I will duck upstairs in a few minutes," Eve whispered as she bundled up some more fabric to take with her.

Kathryn Rodgers pulled Eve aside.

"We have some great workers here, do you think we can stay on a bit longer? I want to forge ahead today with the Rosdaniel quilt."

"Connie is not feeling well and in bed sick. As long as there is not too much noise."

Eve did not wait for an answer, but scooted out the door and up the stairs.

Hetty, who was sitting ironing flat pieces from Barry's shirts, smiled watching the others cut out patches from a pile of clothes they had thrown in the centre of the rug.

Kathryn Rodgers held up a long woollen scarf.

"Who in the name of Jesus gave us this?"

"Not Jesus, but near enough: it was Fr Dempsey," Eithne said.

"What does he expect us to do with it?"

"He insists it is a real test of faith: it is the scarf he wears for the 7 a.m. Mass in Rosdaniel every morning."

"So?"

"So anyone who recognises it has the faith and the dedication and devotion to turn up for 7 a.m. Mass," Hetty giggled.

"What a load of balderdash. He would be better donating some of the fancy clothes he wears ballroom dancing," Eithne said.

Kathryn threw the scarf aside. "Whatever do you mean?"

"Sorry, I thought the whole town knew. Fr Dempsey every Saturday night is twinkle toes himself, not in Rosdaniel, but far away in Wexford town."

"Is he allowed to do that?" one of the new women asked.

"Since when did a man of the cloth ask if he was allowed to do anything?" Eithne said.

Kathryn, worried at the turn in conversation, clapped her hands again.

"We need to get working, ladies. Eithne, would you start cutting out the patches in this lot?" She shoved a big box of clothes across the floor to Eithne.

"Funny, when you are talking about a priest, there is always somebody wanting to cover up the truth," she sniped as she opened the box and took out a long orange sparkling dress. "Who the hell would wear this sort of thing?" she asked.

"A priest going dancing on a Saturday night," Rebecca Fleming said in a matter-of-fact voice, a ripple of laughter pulsing across the room.

★

Eve did not exactly move into Ludlow Hall after that day, but she spent a lot of time there. She sat in the bedroom, which had the best view of the land at the front, keeping vigil beside Connie. Eve stayed there most days and sometimes at night in the house she had once called home.

Much as Michael had been for her as she grieved and her husband tore off to America, she was a comforting presence for Connie as she rested and waited for the medication to help her rebalance. Eve smiled to herself, thinking she was doing the same as Michael, singing a high tune as she came up the stairs each morning with a breakfast tray.

There were days when she had barely talked to him. He said nothing, just opened back the curtains, saying it was a fine day out. What was it, but the weather seemed to fill in the gaps in every conversation. He used to wait patiently outside the door while she got into her dressing gown and then helped her to the chair by the window.

She was sitting in that chair now, looking out over the driveway and the paddocks, bleak, tufted with moss, banked up with sodden grass, so they were more brown than green. It would take a few summers before the fields were worth anything, she knew.

Those days, Michael checked on all the animals very early before coming into the house to fix her some breakfast. Afterwards, he always rushed off to open the shop, returning in the afternoon, bringing something from the delicatessen for lunch. She came downstairs, watching him prepare the food. Sometimes they hardly exchanged words.

Later, he would lay a fire and they would sit in the drawing room, chatting or looking at the television.

Michael knew her well. Even without Ludlow Hall, he had stayed by her side. He was not a person who needed to visit a big house to sustain a friendship. He gave her the use of the little house she was in now when she was thrown out of Ludlow Hall. He was insulted when she asked him how much was the rent, but told her she must find something that would fill the gap the loss of Ludlow had left in her.

"Do what you love, Eve. So soon after losing Arnold and Ludlow, having a bit of in-and-out around your house and a bit of chat will help you no end."

She humoured him, setting up in a small way. She had not banked on Michael constantly advertising her business to his shop customers, so the number of people calling and looking for alterations went from a trickle to a constant stream. In time, many also looked for complete outfits to be made.

One early morning, after Eve had stayed with her all night, Connie caught her hand.

"Eve, I really appreciate what you have done for me, but you don't have to watch over me any more."

"I would not call it watching over you. It is more that I am here if you need me."

"The doctor said the tablets would help after a few days. I am feeling more together, calm."

"There is nothing wrong with giving yourself time."

"I suppose you are going to say next that time is a great healer."

Eve snorted. "For some grief, there is no healing."

Connie sat back, her head on the pillows. They did not talk further. The morning light threw shapes on the room, flashing off the mirror on the wardrobe.

When Eve saw Hetty and Eithne scurrying up the path, she stood up.

"Eithne will have a lot to say if she thinks I stayed here last night."

Connie giggled.

"Seriously, she has been asking every day where you are. I said you have taken to going on long walks. Do you know what she said yesterday? 'Connie must be hiking to Timbuktu and back, that one.'"

"I will come down when I am ready," Connie said as Eve rushed for the stairs to get the kettle on in the kitchen before Hetty and Eithne arrived.

She was halfway down the stairs when Connie called out.

"Eve, the clothes that were in the kitchen…"

"I folded them a few days ago; they are in a nice, tidy bundle," Eve answered.

The kettle was steaming and Eve was examining her quilt in the drawing room when they came in the front door.

"I think I am nearing the end of my quilt." Eve held up a lemon dress. "Do you remember, Hetty, I wore it the day I braved it and called into the ladies' club to try and sort out the crisis after Arnold shut the gates of Ludlow Hall."

"You were like a frightened rabbit in the headlights, but you knew what you wanted."

Eve touched the lemon satin dress. "I wore it to give me courage. Michael said I looked very chic, but I was worried on the day that I looked too much like a city slicker."

"Didn't you notice we all had satin dresses made after that?"

"If I had known I was going to be the fashion icon of Rosdaniel, I might have gone for something fancier."

Eve, holding the dress up to herself, walked in an exaggerated fashion across the drawing room carpet.

Throwing her eyes upwards, Eithne moved to where she had stored her own patchwork for the Rosdaniel quilt while Hetty moved to the kitchen to get the table set.

She was back in the drawing room almost straight away, carrying a high bundle of clothes, gesturing wildly at Eve.

"These kiddie clothes, what should I do with them?"

"They are Connie's. I will take them."

"There is a big box of them in the kitchen. Maybe leave those on top of it," Hetty said.

Eve went to the kitchen, where in the corner was a box marked "Molly's clothes".

"I didn't know she had a child," Hetty said quietly.

"I didn't know until a few days ago. Best not mention it, unless she brings it up."

"Why, has something happened?"

After she placed the bundle carefully on the box, Eve turned to Hetty.

"Connie's daughter died some time ago."

Hetty threw her hands to her face. "Oh, the poor thing," she whispered quietly, as if somehow her words could travel upwards and be heard.

Date: April 17, 2013
Subject: THE LUDLOW LADIES' SOCIETY

Ludlow ladies,

Just to keep everybody in the loop, Hetty is forging ahead with her quilt and very fine it is looking too. Eve is also making excellent headway on the Ludlow quilt.

We are sorry to say, but it is most disappointing that more have not come forward to lend their considerable sewing skills at this stage. We are in a bit of a pickle, having promised three quilts, including one on Rosdaniel itself, but we may not be able to keep pace.

Unfortunately, too many saw the request for fabric donations from Rosdaniel as a quick and easy way to dump old clothing. Poor Bernie Martin was so inundated with donations, many of which were dropped off quietly at night, that we had to hire a skip to remove it all. We were lucky to get a good price from Danagher Skips on the Ballyheigue Road or we would have been smothered under a mountain of hand-me-downs.

While the call to arms has received a disappointing response, we are forging ahead. We are glad to report we will at least have two stunning quilts to present at the Rosdaniel Festival and hopefully to the First Lady herself. Ladies, we need to get our act together on the Rosdaniel quilt.

There are three places available for the Obama exhibition and we have to get them. If we are not winners, Jack Davoren will make it his life's ambition to exclude us forever more. Now is the time to pull together and squash the snake Davoren and put down a marker that the Ludlow Ladies' Society means business.

Kathryn Rodgers,
Chairwoman

21

It was a few more days before Connie had the courage to walk downstairs.

Dressed in jeans and a jumper, her hair tied up in a ponytail, Hetty noticed she had made an effort with her appearance, dabbing on lipstick.

"Connie, I can't let it pass. I am so sorry about your daughter." Hetty, her two arms outstretched, walked towards Connie, pulling her into a tight hug.

"Did Eve tell you everything?"

Hetty drew away. "She did not. I didn't ask her either. Only the box of clothes is here in the kitchen ..."

Connie sat down at the table. Straight away, Hetty placed a mug in front of her.

"Eve is just finishing off a few things with her quilt. Tell me about your little girl. What age was she?"

Eve, rambling into the kitchen, spoke severely. "Molly was five when she died tragically, Hetty. I don't know if Connie is up to saying more."

Connie shivered, his words beginning to pound in her ear. Every night she stood at the upstairs bedroom window, shouting at the sky, "I don't forgive, I don't understand," before collapsing in tears, pleading to the night sky for her daughter.

"Where are you, Molly? Come to Mommy."

Up until now, she had half coped by pretending Molly was elsewhere – napping, out with Amy, playing in another room

– but since she had moved to Ludlow Hall, she could not so easily imagine that any more. She could not expect her to come tripping up the stairs, calling out over something or other, or placing her little hand in hers.

But last night was different. After weeks of pleading, of screaming to her in her head and heart, Molly spoke to her.

She felt her breath in her ear; she smelled her smell. Her heart and head were calm for the first time since she had lost her.

"Here I am. Just love me, Mommy."

As quickly as it happened, she was gone, like a shooting star in the night sky.

When she woke up this morning, she was not sure if she had dreamed it or not. All she knew was that his thundering words were banished and, no longer submerged in the details of the crime, she was free to love the little girl she had lost.

Relief flowed through her as she heard Molly's voice:

"Here I am. Just love me, Mommy."

Connie's brain did not hurt so much any more. The loss remained titanic, but happy memories were beginning to flood in.

Eve and Hetty sat observing her across the table.

"Honestly, I can talk about her. It feels good to talk about her. Molly was so beautiful, with the cutest giggle. I wish you could have met her. She would have loved it here."

Eve reached out and took one of Connie's hands.

Taking a deep breath, Connie began Molly's story. Like when they brought her home from hospital, she only slept at night if Mommy was beside her.

"Ed, my husband, was very unhappy about it, said we should let her cry in her crib, but I never wanted to let her cry. She was very much stuck to me, and me to her. We were best friends. I learned to look at life afresh, through her eyes. It was such a privilege."

The pain of the loss rising inside her, she heard Molly's voice again.

"Here I am. Just love me, Mommy."

"We were happiest dancing together. She loved to come to the dance studio with me and practise her steps. I miss the sound of her little feet scraping across the floor, her wobbly jumps. I miss her hand in mine, but mostly I miss the laughs and the fun. We had a lot of fun together."

Connie stopped to swallow hard.

"You have lovely memories. They must be a strength for you," Hetty said, pouring tea from the pot into three mugs.

"Beautiful memories, but when I opened the boxes containing all her things, I could hardly look at them. Even now, I can't even look at her clothes. It is a step too far. Holding her little bits and pieces from when she was a baby … is torture."

Connie's voice wobbled. She gulped the tea Hetty had slipped in beside her.

The silence of the house flowed around them. Hetty, uncomfortable with the stillness, spooned sugar into her tea and stirred. When Eve cast her a long look, she stopped stirring, gently placing the spoon on the table.

"Maybe it will come in time," Eve said.

"I don't think it will, but I can't bear to throw them out. It wouldn't be right."

"You could store them, until you are ready."

Connie looked at Eve and Hetty.

"It was nearly two years ago, when Ed killed my Molly."

Hetty let out a cry she tried to muffle. "Sweet divine Jesus, what are you saying?"

Connie did not answer. Eve put a hand on Hetty's knee, telling her not to ask further.

"I have to find a place where I can cope. I have to find a way. Maybe my time at Ludlow Hall will do that."

"Would you not be better at home in America?" Hetty flushed red up her neck. "I didn't mean that to sound as unwelcoming as it did. It is just that home is the only place, when there is so much grief and loss."

"Except there isn't a home any more. Our house was only rented. And anyway, Ed killed Molly in her bed. How could I even walk down the corridor to the bedroom again? I went into meltdown after that, maybe lost my mind. I don't know. It was so hard."

Hetty began to blubber. Connie put a hand out to comfort her.

"Thank you, you have a soft heart," she whispered to Hetty.

Distracted, Eve got up to get the cookie jar and put it on the table.

"Connie, do you want to make a memory quilt for Molly?"

Hetty looked up, wiping away her tears. "We could make it together."

"You mean from her clothes, cut them up?"

"Yes. We will have to cut out the patches, so you need to be sure you are willing to let that happen."

"It brings up a lot of memories, but in your case, it will be the sweet ones with Molly," Hetty said, her voice shaking.

Connie was silent, the only sound in the kitchen her fingers streaking across the table.

"It will be a beautiful quilt, you can rely on us to do a good job," Hetty said gently.

Connie smiled. "Can I help? Will you show me how to do it?"

"Of course we will," Eve said, Hetty clapping her hands in excitement. Eve stood up and looked in the cardboard box. "There are a lot of clothes here. How would you like us to arrange the quilt?"

Connie sighed. "Molly's favourite top was her train pyjama top. Do you think we could make that the centrepiece? It describes my independent girl so well."

Eve began searching through the plastic vacuum bags of clothes, picking out the pyjama top with a train engine on it.

"That would be a lovely centrepiece," she said, Hetty nodding in agreement.

"Will we sort through the clothes, cut out the squares and

present them all to you, maybe year by year, or do you want to take part?"

Connie swallowed her tears.

"I don't think I want to be around when you are cutting the clothes up, but I do want a memory quilt for Molly. Can you include everything in those bags?"

"We will do our best," Hetty said.

"Why don't you have a look at your dance studio? John O'Reilly said he will be back on Monday, as he has gone as far as he can. The mirrors are due to be delivered today."

Connie stroked the pyjama top.

"Thank you," she said quietly, before disappearing into what used to be Arnold's study.

The walls had been plastered and painted white, the floor lacquered in a heavy clear varnish. Arnold's desk was pushed into a corner. She thought she might leave it there to hold her music system.

The room was light and airy, the floor with just the right amount of give. Spotlights had been put in at the ceiling. When the mirrors arrived, the studio would be near finished.

Kicking off her shoes, she began to step out, slow tentative steps until she heard music in her head, then she pirouetted across the floor. Flopping into Arnold's desk chair, she wanted to ring Bill, tell him to come to Ludlow Hall. When she was ill she had had Eve explain the situation to him, to put him off from visiting. It was time to talk to him directly.

Swinging around to look out over the paddocks, she picked up her phone and hit his number.

"Bill?"

"Connie! Did you get the flowers?"

For a moment, she hesitated, remembering Eve arriving up the stairs with the flowers, her face beaming. She did not expect Connie's reaction: shouting, telling her to take them away, throw them in a bin. How could she tell him they had kicked up so many memories, of the white coffin hidden under bunches

191

and bunches of flowers, the house full of bouquets afterwards.

"They were beautiful and lasted so long. So lovely," she said, detecting his relief. "Bill, I have been in a bad place. I am not sure how much Eve told you, but I am getting there. Being away from the US, in this place, is helping."

"I understand, Connie. You know I will do whatever you ask."

"I want to see you, Bill. I don't know what is going to happen after that, but I owe you that much."

"This might be the time to tell you, I have accepted a position at University College Dublin. I start in the next few weeks. Maybe one weekend I could call on you."

"I would like that."

"I love you, Connie. I will give you all the time you want."

"Bill, I love you too. Just be patient."

"I will ring when I arrive in Dublin, we can talk some more."

Amy was right: it wasn't his fault. He was not the one who made the decision to kill Molly. He was not the one who waited until her mother was out of the house, stole into her bedroom ... But her burden of grief had pushed him away.

Connie jumped up, pacing the room to clear her mind.

"Here I am. Just love me, Mommy."

She walked back to the kitchen.

"I was thinking I would like to help," she said.

Eve pulled out a chair. "You can do some tacking, while we cut out the rest."

Hetty ran off to get the sewing box in the drawing room.

"The first thing you have to decide is if you want others to know what the quilt is commemorating or would you prefer that to stay private. We can insert a piece saying 'In Memory of Molly'. Rebecca Fleming is very good at the embroidery."

"I am not sure I am ready for too many questions. Let's not tell anyone anything, just yet."

"You are lucky, there are quite a few of us for the Ludlow Ladies' Society this week. We can get a good start on the quilt.

We are thinking the usual size of a throw, and four big squares incorporating many little squares." Eve faltered. "The squares make up the complete years. I suppose the fifth-year fabrics can be used to link up around the train pyjama top."

She laid out the blue pyjama top on the table, taking other pieces of fabric – the floral dress Molly had worn the week before, the combat jeans she had on at the zoo the month before, and the sparkly skirt she wore at the birthday party at the end of the road – and laid them carefully around the pyjama piece.

"We will have to line the pyjama piece, but that is all right, we are never stuck for fabric. We will build up year five in small squares around it."

Eve felt she was gabbing on too much, so she stopped.

"Am I doing the right thing, do you think?" Connie asked.

Hetty, who had returned with the sewing box, pulled out a chair and sat down.

"Keeping the good memories has to be a good thing. It is a giant comforter, a part of Molly to keep close."

Connie looked straight at Hetty. "Your quilt has caused you so much upset, dredged up so much."

"Because the good memories in my marriage were so few, completely obliterated by his abuse. But you have so many good memories, Connie, so much to cherish," Hetty said, threading a needle and taking two patches of fabric, lining them up together and starting the stitch for her.

Handing the fabric to Connie, advising her to hold the patches together so they stayed even, Hetty helped her guide the needle in and out in four long stitches along one side.

"Now, flatten it out right side up and you will get an idea of it all. Eve will run them up with the sewing machine later."

Connie did as she was bid, using her fingers to smooth out the two pieces of fabric with her hand.

"That red corduroy was from her favourite trousers before she could walk. You hardly got the patch from the knees; they were mostly worn out. The black piece with the flowers, a little coat I bought in Macy's for Molly. There was a hat to match. She looked so sweet, with her black curls pushing out under the hat."

"You see, already the memories are flooding back," Hetty said, making Connie smile.

Eve got out the iron and pressed the two squares. "We need to get everything cut before you decide on the layout. You know I won't be back here until Monday."

"I can come tomorrow," Hetty piped up, "while Miss Fancy Pants is off for her dirty weekend in Belfast."

Eve, reddening, swiped at Hetty with a tea towel.

"That is terrible. Michael Conway has asked me to Belfast for the weekend. Can't we all be adults here?"

"Sounds very romantic. Michael is such a nice man," Connie said, and Eve, realising she was not getting anywhere giving out, concentrated on filling the steam iron with water from the kettle.

"She will come back with a ring on her finger, I am sure of it," Hetty said.

Eve clicked her tongue in annoyance, doing her best to ignore the two women beaming brightly.

22

Eve was ready the next morning early when Michael Conway called in a taxi to bring her to the train station.

She had packed and unpacked twice, worrying about what she should bring with her. Michael, in jeans and a jacket she had not seen before, looked very smart. They did not talk much in the taxi, a little nervous the driver, McDonald from out the road, would overhear.

At Arklow station, they stepped onto the Dublin train, sitting opposite two people from Rosdaniel on their way to work in the city. Eve snoozed until the train became so packed with early morning commuters that the carriage was stuffy and uncomfortable.

"We are first class to Belfast from Dublin," Michael whispered, reaching under the table and holding her hand.

On the Belfast train, they had four seats to themselves, but still sat side by side, her head leaning in to him as he stroked her hair. By the time they got to Belfast, neither of the two of them cared if the whole of Rosdaniel saw them checking into the Europa Hotel as Mr and Mrs Conway.

Like two children, they delighted in the room, checking the softness of the bed, oohing and ahhing over the free toiletries and standing at the window overlooking the city view.

When Michael put his arm around her, Eve let him kiss her, kissing him back. When they moved to the bed, she trusted him, crying when he made love to her. He kissed away her tears.

"Eve, I have loved you so long. I tried to convince myself I was just happy to be in your orbit, but I am not prepared to ignore it any more."

"Neither am I," she said, taking his hand to her and kissing it. "I did not see it for a long time, but after James died, I realised I not only relied on you, but I looked forward to your arrival at Ludlow every day. If you had not been there, I am not sure I would have stayed at Ludlow Hall. You were always my rock, my friend, and probably the only person who understood me."

They lay in each other's arms, watching the lights switch on over Belfast.

The next morning when Eve woke up, Michael was standing by the window, his back to her.

"Is there something wrong?"

"Eve, I want it to be like this every day. I want to do all the ordinary, everyday things with you. I want us to marry."

She sat up, trying to damp down her hair, which she knew was sticking out. Michael knelt beside the bed.

"What do you say, Eve? I want to shout out my love for you, not hide it."

"Yes."

She thought she had said it too low, so she shouted it, making him beam and laugh, jumping up to hug her. Briefly he pulled away, doing a funny dance as they both giggled with joy, feeling young again.

"A ring. I want you to go back to Rosdaniel wearing a ring."

"Hetty was right about one thing."

"What?"

"She said I would come back from Belfast with a ring on my finger."

"That Hetty is too good at observing other people."

"I think with Hetty there is no real badness, she will genuinely be happy for us."

"Eve, I don't care what anybody says, I am not letting you go back to living alone when we get back to Rosdaniel. My house is bigger and more comfortable; you can make any changes you like."

"I don't know, Michael. I like being near Ludlow Hall. I like the little house."

"I wish I could have bought Ludlow for you."

"Connie needs Ludlow now. She needs to open her dance studio and start a new phase of her life."

"She will surely sell it."

Eve reached over, running her hand down Michael's face.

"We will start a new life. I don't need or want to go back to Ludlow Hall. I want to create new memories with you, not be pulled down by the old ones. What about Richie?"

"Richie told me a long time ago I should ask you out. He will be behind us."

He kissed her, climbing into bed beside her.

"I have a feeling we may not see much of Belfast this weekend," he said as he pulled her to him.

"You promised me a ring and for that we will get out of bed, but later," she said in a mock firm voice.

"Yes, Mrs Conway, and I have to tell you, I will not let anybody call you Mrs Ludlow from now on."

She smiled, feeling safe and happy for the first time in a long time.

★

Hetty was working quietly at the kitchen table when Connie got up.

"I thought I would get a head start; we don't want Eve to think we were slacking while she was off gallivanting."

"I wonder how she is getting on."

"With Michael Conway by her side, I imagine very well indeed. It is about time those two got it together."

Connie sat down opposite Hetty. "And what about you, Hetty, will you let romance back into your life?"

Hetty put down the fabric she was sizing up. "When you are

battered and bruised, like I was, you don't give anyone a chance to come close. That is just the way it is."

"I know what you mean."

Hetty slapped the table hard. "What are you talking about, girl? You can't let this happen to you. You have to move on with your life."

"Maybe I don't want to move on. Maybe staying still is the best I can do."

She jumped up to the window overlooking the yard.

"I am sorry, Hetty, I did not mean to snap your head off. I have lost my beautiful child in such a violent way … There are times I can hardly get through the next minutes, never mind the hours and the days. Trust, for me, is only a five-letter word, nothing more."

Hetty came behind Connie and put her arms around her.

"I am not preaching. I know what it is like to live with pain in the heart. It is exhausting."

Connie turned around, letting Hetty embrace her, tapping her on the back, like you would an upset child.

"Come now, if you do the tacking, I will finish the cutting out of the squares, so we can start laying out Molly's memory quilt."

Connie liked that Hetty used Molly's name so easily and sat into the table, working awkwardly with the needle and thread. Hetty passed no comment on how long it was taking Connie to loosely sew two patches together.

"I would have loved a daughter. It must have been so special spending time with Molly."

Connie did not answer immediately. When she spoke, it was as if she had forgotten where she was, caught up in the reminiscence, reaching into the recall to find a type of comfort.

"I would throw everything away to get one more minute, even a few seconds with Molly. We were so close, I wondered could either of us ever live without the other. Look at me now. I am nothing. I have lost the one job I wanted forever."

Hetty sighed loudly. "All the special times, if we could return ..."

Connie, after a while, bit into the tacking thread to cut it and finish, flattening out the two pieces: one khaki green, the other pink and flowery.

"When she was three, she lived in those combat jeans. She loved them because they had side pockets and patch pockets down the legs. She insisted that the patch pockets were for candy, walking around with some in there like she was carrying gold. To think I worried about her teeth."

"Each worry has its time and place. I used to fret people would find out my husband was hitting me. How strange was that?"

"Did you never look for help?"

"Where would I go? Everybody thought he was a great fellow. Anyway, if he found out, he would have killed me."

Connie did not know what to say. She fingered the pink fabric with deep pink and purple flowers.

"Molly's dress when she was two. We went to a wedding. She looked so cute. She loved all the attention, but would not sit still for the photographs. She had such a lovely flower in her hair. That day, I could see the adult in the contours of the child's face."

"How do you manage?" Hetty asked.

"How did you manage with that husband of yours? You just do."

Hetty dropped the scissors, so that they banged on the table.

"Connie, I did not manage at all, I just pretended, so when others saw me on the street, they passed little remark. Giving off an aura of being able to cope is inherently reassuring for those around you."

"I went into the lake, did you know that?"

"What do you mean, the lake?"

"I walked into the water ..."

"Ludlow lake?"

"Nearly over my head. If it wasn't for Eve, who got me out and looked after me, I might not be here today."

"Oh my dear Lord, Connie, don't talk like this. I can't take it."

"Eve looked after me well."

"Of course she did. She and most of the Ludlow Ladies' Society are good eggs, not that I could ever open up about Barry."

"A pity."

"I am well rid of him anyway. Did Eve tell you?"

"An accident five years ago, she said."

"If you want to call it that."

"What do you mean?"

Hetty checked around her, as if she was afraid somebody might be listening.

"Did Eve tell you what sort of accident?"

"Only that you found him beside the bench on the front lawn the next morning."

"I did. I called the Gardaí and the doctor. He had a gash on his head. They think he fell on the way back from the pub, keeled over in his own front garden."

"I am sorry."

"Don't be, Connie. The bastard was finally dead. I thought I was free of him. There was quite a spectacle of grief at his funeral, women openly crying, but his widow unable to shed a tear. Everybody put it down to shock." Hetty's voice was shaking. "I thought I was well rid of him. I never thought his hold on me would reach beyond the grave. I could not let go of him, I was still too afraid of him, or maybe that somebody would find out what really happened that early morning, when he died."

"What do you mean?"

"I am not afraid any more. It is a funny thing to say, but slicing up the bastard's clothes, especially his shirts, cleared the fear which was festering in my heart."

Connie listened without saying a word.

"He beat me black and blue before he went out to the pub,

something about his shoes not polished the night before, forcing him to buff them up with a rag that morning. He said it made him late all day." Hetty looked at Connie. "It never had to make sense to get Barry angry."

She leaned closer to Connie.

"He went off to the pub, I crawled upstairs to the spare room and lay on the bed. He was gone about three hours or more. The front gate clicked in the late night as he opened it. I could hear him muttering under his breath. There was a fierce ground frost that night. He was swaggering across the lawn; I could just make him out in the beam of the outside light. I don't know why, but he diverted to the garden seat. Suddenly, his legs were gone from under him; he slipped, hitting his head on the bench.

"I was frozen to the spot, waiting for him to get up, but there was no movement. I opened the window, quietly listening. God forgive me, I heard him moaning. I heard him call out. His voice was low and weak."

Hetty pulled in a deep breath of air, her chest heaving bigger.

"I stood in darkness at that window. I was shaking all over, no part of me could move, even if I wanted. All I knew was: if he survived this, he would kill me. Does it make any sense?"

Hetty did not wait for an answer.

"I waited a long time, I don't remember much of it. I know the moaning continued and I closed the window, sitting in the dark. At six I went downstairs, that was the usual time for the light to go on in the kitchen. I began to get his breakfast ready. I am not sure I ever thought it through. I was in a state of shock, I can't say more than that.

"The strange thing was that I called him for his breakfast as normal. It was only when he did not arrive that I checked outside and found him. I ran to the neighbours and they dialled 999."

Hetty got up from the table and went to the sink, where she fiddled with a tea cloth.

"My distress was real. I was not sure what had happened the

night before. All I knew was that he was dead. It appeared to be a dreadful accident.

"It was months before I acknowledged I had a part to play in his death."

She swung around to Connie.

"I never regretted it. However, I will never forget the feeling of that night. It has haunted me. I have paid the price all these years, unable to move on with my life."

Connie went to Hetty, catching her up in a tight embrace.

"I understand, Hetty. I understand."

Hetty burrowed into her shoulder, tears raging through her, the relief of finally telling flowing through her.

After a few minutes, she pulled away. Beckoning Connie to follow, she made for the drawing room, where she laid out her quilt on the floor.

"Do you see that deep-pink square? That was the shirt he was wearing that night. He looked a right peacock in it." She began to blubber again. "I can't bear to show this at the town festival, but Eve will never understand. It is beautiful, but for me it is the past that needs to be banished, not celebrated."

"What do you want to do with it?" Connie asked gently.

"Take it out to the field and watch it burn."

Connie picked up one side of the quilt.

"Let's do it."

"Eve will be so cross."

"I don't think she will."

Hetty did not need persuading. Grabbing a box of firelighters and matches from the bucket beside the fireplace, Connie let Hetty carry the quilt.

They walked together down the stone steps at the front, climbed over the fence and marched out to the middle of the paddock.

"What will we do if anybody comes along?"

"You can blame the crazy American," Connie said, making them both giggle.

Connie got out the firelighters and matches, and Hetty cupped her hands around the firelighter bundle, to shield it from the breeze as Connie struck a match. The firelighters took hold and they placed a corner of the quilt on the flame, but it barely scorched the fabric and quilt backing.

"I think we need to build a good fire first. I will get some sticks," Connie said, and she ran back to the barn, where she knew there was a stack.

Carrying an armful of sticks and peat logs, she made her way back to the front paddock.

"If we light all that, the house might be in danger," Hetty laughed. She held up the quilt to shield the small fire Connie had built. The lower twigs began to crackle, the peat logs taking hold until there was a good, strong fire.

"If anybody asks, we will say we are having a barbecue," Connie said, making Hetty throw her eyes to the sky.

After twenty minutes, they managed to throw the patchwork quilt on the fire. It smoked hard, making them cough as it burned, some of the fabric melting faster than others.

"This memory quilt has set me free," Hetty said quietly.

When they were sure the quilt had burned away black, Connie and Hetty walked back to the house, hand in hand.

23

Connie could not sleep, so she went down to the drawing room, where the patches that were once Molly's clothes were stacked high. Neatly cut into squares of the same size, there were six piles, each one representing a year.

She sat and looked at them. Had it come to this? All the parts that made up Molly, summed up in a few stacks of fabric. A part of her wanted to kick the hills of fabric, yell that life was unfair.

"Here I am. Just love me, Mommy."

The words calmed her down, so she got on her knees, filtering through the patches. Some would have to be lined; others were already ready for placing. She picked up the plain blue patch, a tiny pocket, the shape of a red heart sewed into it in a zigzag stitch. Hetty had a good eye, to pick this little pocket from the overalls Molly wore when she was painting. All the times she had traced that heart, taking off her overalls so she could properly see it.

Behind one of the piles, a T-shirt was neatly folded. Connie picked it up. "Mommy's Little Girl". She knew Hetty had left it there, unsure whether to include it. Connie held the T-shirt close to her face. It was cold from being on the drawing room floor, but she hardly noticed.

They were in the mall one day when Connie saw the T-shirt. Molly pranced about, asking what it said. Connie closed her eyes, feeling the carefree sense of that day, as they wandered hand in hand, making slow progress, but so happy together, Molly sometimes catching on to her leg. Her heart lifted, but as quickly as the memory embraced her, it was gone.

Shivering, she picked up the Disney top. They had such a lovely time. Molly was three years of age and it was their first family holiday, a perfect week. Molly insisted on wearing her Minnie Mouse T-shirt every day. When they got back, there was an offer on the Manhattan apartment Ed had been left by his mother. It would fund the family home she craved for Molly. Ed had promised this time he would ringfence funds for a fine home. Life was good.

Diverting herself away from the next year, when Ed became moody, angry and secretive, she decided to lay out the quilt on the floor, starting with the blue pyjama-top patch at the centre.

Eve had suggested lots of little squares around, radiating out to the first four years, the last year as long strips around the outside. She tried to do this now, putting a variety of colours and tops together from each year. She did not even notice when Eve came in, she was concentrating so hard.

"I would not worry so much on the coordination. The best thing about a memory quilt is the jumble of special moments."

"Hetty colour coordinated her quilt."

"I think Hetty replicated her husband's life: small, petty, perfectly captured in the little squares. Not that anyone will see it now."

"Hetty told you what we did?"

"Do you really think Hetty could keep that to herself? When we came back from Belfast, she was in the door after us, saying she had to talk to me in private."

"Are you upset?"

"I am down a quilt for the festival, but Hetty is happy. What I feel does not come into it. Have you given Bill his answer yet?"

"I told him next weekend is good for a visit."

"That is something. I am glad."

"I wish I was, Eve."

"You both will find a way."

Connie stood up, surveying the quilt. "I just wish things were different."

Eve stood by Connie. "It is going to be a beautiful quilt, Connie. Will you exhibit at the festival?"

"I don't want everybody asking about it, sympathising with me. I don't want that, not again."

"Molly had a full life in her five years. I can see it in the colours and the variety of the fabric. A little girl who was much loved."

Connie sank into the wingback chair. Her stomach felt sick, her mouth dry.

"I failed her, Eve. I failed her."

Eve turned sharply around. "You did not. You are not responsible for the actions of her father. He failed her, not you."

"You don't know all of it, Eve. He knew I was planning to leave, and he knew I could never leave without her. A week earlier I'd told him I needed a break, but he begged me to stay. He knew I was almost afraid to leave. Molly paid the price for my indecision."

"Going back over it will never give a satisfactory answer, only raise ghosts who bring no comfort."

"I was so caught up in myself, I missed the signs. He ploughed all our money into Ludlow Hall without my knowing anything. He knew if I left him and asked for a divorce I would want half our assets. He must have realised if I walked out on him he would be exposed as a conman who had cleaned out our savings."

"Is that why he did this?"

"Who knows how his mind was working?"

"I don't understand these men at all. Why he could not ..." Eve wavered, suddenly realising what she had to say might ignite too much pain.

Connie sighed. "Why he could not have done it to himself and left Molly? I will never know, Eve." She picked up a few squares of fabric. "Maybe he knew that leaving me like this, without Molly, would be far more painful than taking me out too." Connie gulped back the tears, pressing around her eyes to stem the flow. "Will I get a start on the tacking?"

Eve took the hint. "I will get the steam iron and sewing machine set up."

Eve clattered around getting herself organised, while Connie concentrated on her sewing, the patches in her hand from year four, when Molly began to pick her own clothes and opt for trousers more than dresses.

"Life was so simple back then, or maybe that is just the way it looks from this perspective." Suddenly she put down her sewing. "I never asked you about Belfast."

Eve, a smile across her face, held out her hand to show off a solitaire diamond ring.

"Fantastic, are you engaged?"

"We are, but we are not making it public until Michael has told his family."

"I am so happy for you, Eve, for you both, I really am."

When the van from the town florist pulled up on the front driveway, both women were surprised; neither had seen or heard it on the avenue.

Eve stood up. "I will go if you like."

Connie nodded, smiling her appreciation as Eve went to the front door. When she came back, she was carrying a huge bunch of red roses.

"My guess is that these are from that nice young man of yours," she said, presenting the bouquet to Connie, who burst into tears.

"Take them out of my sight, Eve, please."

"What? Why? What is wrong this time? Not again, Connie."

Connie, clenching her fists, walked across the room.

"All right, I will take them out to the yard," Eve said, scurrying off to leave the flowers in the empty water trough outside the barn.

When she came back in, Connie was pacing between the windows in the drawing room.

"I am sorry, Eve, you must think me crazy, but since Molly died, and the funeral, I can't bear cut flowers."

"I brought the card for you to read."

She handed a small red envelope to Connie, who took out the card, reading it aloud.

"Dearest Connie, looking forward to seeing you on Friday. All my love, Bill."

"Just lovely, red roses, the most expensive," Eve said.

"Please, Eve, take them with you."

"That is very kind of you, I am sure, but they are for you. If Bill has any sense, he will say I am more trouble than I am worth."

"I very much doubt that. And what am I going to say to Michael Conway when he comes to the house and sees a beautiful bouquet on the kitchen table?"

"Don't tell him anything. Keep him on his toes."

They both laughed, fiddling with the patchwork.

After a while, Eve raised her head.

"That young man of yours is keen. I don't know him, but I think you should grab the little bit of happiness that is being offered to you."

"Bill is lovely. He deserves a lot better than Connie O'Baggage."

"We all have baggage, whether we know it or not. Look at what Michael Conway took on."

"Yours is such a lovely love story."

Eve blushed pink, making Connie giggle.

"Less of the talk now. There is a fine group of ladies due here any minute."

She had only said it when they saw Kathryn Rodgers leading a convoy of cars up the avenue. Connie made her excuses and disappeared upstairs as Eve opened the front door.

"I have an army with me today, Eve," Kathryn said, directing the women into the drawing room. They set to work straight away, as if they had been briefed on what to do.

Bernie Martin pulled out a plaid skirt.

"It is my old school uniform. Do you think we need to put a square in the Rosdaniel quilt?"

"We can do whatever we like. Were the nuns nice to you?" Dana asked.

Bernie shook her head. "Nice was not part of their language."

"What does the skirt say to you then?" said Dana.

Bernie looked agitated. "That the principal, Sister Margaret, could stop me at any time and run her hands up and down my thighs and legs."

Those who were sewing put down their work and looked at Bernie.

"Are you telling me the head nun went around feeling up everybody?" Dana said.

"It was all pretty stupid. The nuns in the secondary school decided we had to wear white bobby socks, but were afraid because bare skin was visible above the knee, so they decided we had to wear tan tights as well."

"Dreadfully uncomfortable," Marcella interjected.

"A few of us got a bottle of fake tan and lathered it on our legs from the knees up. Sister Margaret was fooled for a few days, but I suppose we gave the game away by suddenly appearing too compliant. Next, she starts doing spot checks, getting down on her knees and feeling around our knees and up under our skirts."

Eithne Hall chuckled. "Remember the day Daisy O'Brien let off a big stinking fart just as Sister was kneeling in front of her?"

"And she got double detention for not wearing her tan tights and fuming up the corridor."

Eve looked from one woman to another. "You are having us on."

"We are not. It only stopped when the bank manager complained his daughter had been indecently assaulted and he threatened to call the Gardaí."

Kathryn took the skirt.

"Jesus Christ, throw the bloody thing out. I am sick and tired of the religious, they only ever had time for those with money and influence." Tossing back her brown hair, she continued. "I know it might appear difficult to understand when you see me now, but when I was growing up we had absolutely nothing. I fought for everything I have achieved."

"So you keep reminding us," Eithne remarked, and everybody busied themselves with their work while Bernie threw the plaid school skirt on the pile for the dump.

Date: May 2, 2013
Subject: THE LUDLOW LADIES' SOCIETY

Ludlow ladies,

Now is the time to work even harder. We are nearly there. It is all go getting the patchwork quilts ready. Eve Brannigan and Hetty Gorman are leading the way when it comes to devoting time and energy to the project. Can we please ask you ladies to continue to attend the weekly meetings of the Ludlow Ladies' Society at Ludlow Hall. Everybody's contribution is vital at this stage to get the project over the line.

The Ludlow Ladies' Society has always prided itself on its exceptional teamwork. Some on the Rosdaniel quilt dropped out once they stitched their patches, but that is hardly fair. We need all hands to the pumps for this last push to get everything finished.

On a different note entirely, I have heard from impeccable sources that Jack Davoren has seen the contents of our emails and is quite exercised by the references to him. This is for you, Jack!

Jack, Jack, get off our backs,
The Ludlow ladies can do more than tack,
Davoren, hide in your den,
The Ludlow ladies are going to win!

Put that in your pipe and smoke it, Jack Davoren.
Kathryn Rodgers,
Chairwoman

24

When Eve and Hetty got a special summons to Ludlow Hall, they rushed, afraid something was wrong.

"Don't tell me she has decided to sell up now that we have all got used to her," Hetty said, after picking up Eve.

"No point getting too excited, we will know soon enough," Eve said, a pang shooting through her that Ludlow might be about to slip away from her again.

The gates were swung back and a big sign advertising the Ludlow Dance School was on the wall beside the stile.

"Oh, lord, the studio must be ready! We must get our dancing shoes on," Hetty said, her voice high-pitched with excitement.

"Do you think she will make a go of it?"

"If there is any justice, she will, after all she has been through."

At the front steps, they were not sure if they should use the key to let themselves in.

"We could do both: knock and then use the key," Hetty said.

Pushing the door open, the music encircled them, loud classical notes travelling through the house, making their ears fizz. Hetty, grabbing Eve's hand, pulled her towards the big room on the left. The door lay open and they could make out the scrape of dancing shoes on the floorboards.

Connie, her body rising and falling, moved with the camber of the music, her feet skipping across the floor like a butterfly dancing between brightly coloured flowers.

Hetty gripped Eve's arm and the two of them stood in awe,

caught up in the emotion of the display, the music raising up their hearts so that a joy welled up in them both.

Eve felt a great sense of happiness that Ludlow Hall was throbbing with life once again.

They watched for several minutes before Connie noticed them. Letting the music continue, she reached them in a few steps, her hands out, pulling them onto the floor.

"Kick off your shoes, join me," she laughed, and they could not protest, seeing her eyes twinkling so bright.

In their stockinged feet, they stood self-consciously as she turned down the volume on the music. Eve made to sit down where some chairs were grouped in the corner.

"No, you don't, Eve. We will just do a few warm-up exercises," Connie said, catching her by the hand.

"I have two left feet. Nothing will get over that."

Connie ignored Eve, pulling her along as she did one, two, three simple steps.

Hetty followed them, trying to keep up. One, two, three, Connie stepping smartly in front, Hetty and Eve almost colliding, collapsing into giggles.

"A superb start. Maybe I can entice the Ludlow Ladies' Society to avail themselves of a free lesson after today's meeting?"

"They will love it, but it is up to you to persuade them to continue."

Hetty pirouetted across the room, almost crashing into Arnold's desk.

"I always wanted to be a dancer. Sign me up for any lessons you like," she said, slightly out of breath.

Eve straightened her clothes. "You have done a fine job, Connie, but for my part, I just wish there were not so many mirrors. Best get the ladies when they arrive, otherwise they will have too much time to think up an excuse."

"You won't notice after a while. Just listen to the music, let your body flow: dancing is food for the soul."

Eve looked around the room. What would Arnold think? It

was as if he had never existed in this room where he had dominated. Mirrors and dance barres where once there were shelves of old books, collected over the years. His desk was the only part of the old room allowed to remain, but was pushed up against the wall and holding a music system.

"Do you approve?" Connie asked.

Eve swung around. "Bar the mirrors, it is fantastic. It is about time there was music and a bit of life around Ludlow Hall. Who would have thought, after all this time, dancing about could breathe life back into the old house?"

Connie reached out and gave Eve a hug, catching her hand and sweeping her along the floor in a type of flowing dance Eve thought was more like a waltz.

"That is what we will do later, just a few simple steps."

Hetty slipped across the floor, taking long, sweeping steps.

"I always wanted to do line dancing. Remember the craze a few years ago? I really wanted to go to the town hall, but Barry said I would only make a show of myself." Her voice trailed off.

Connie, grabbing her under the elbow, led her to the door.

"In time, we will do different classes," Connie said, skipping between the two women as they crossed over to the drawing room. She burst into the centre of the room, swinging around to Eve and Hetty.

"You are probably wondering why I asked you to call in early, but I want Molly's quilt to be on display at the festival."

"This is a bit of a sea change. Are you sure?"

"No, not sure, but I think it could be a step forward."

"What about the quilt's story? Do you want people to know?"

"It might be better to tell everybody at the same time, rather than repeating it over and over."

Hetty, shaking the three-quarters-finished quilt on to the carpet, stopped what she was doing. "There is a certain sense in what you are saying."

"We need not say how it all happened, only that Molly died," Eve said.

Connie put a hand on Eve's shoulder. "I know you are only trying to protect me, but to know me now is to know the loss, the loss compounded by the terrible facts. Not to know that is not to know me."

"If you are sure you can cope."

A car weaving up the avenue brought the three of them to the window. When Hetty spied Rebecca Fleming, she guffawed into her sleeve.

"I am surprised to see her. I don't see why she is coming here, and so early," Eve sniffed, making for the door. She turned back, looking embarrassed. "Look at me, going to answer the door as if I owned the place. I am sorry, Connie."

"Go ahead, I am sure she is looking for you anyway."

Rebecca was shaking with excitement when Eve answered the front door.

"Eve, have you heard about the fire?"

"What fire?"

"It is the town hall: they think it was arson. There was a break-in some time in the early hours, somebody poured petrol over the whole place. It went up in a few minutes."

"Come in," Connie called out from the drawing room.

"Where does that leave us?" Hetty asked.

"It means the town is without a hall, there is no place now for the country market every Saturday, and the Festival is also up in a heap."

Tears glinted in Eve's eyes and she clenched her fists on her lap. "All this work was probably for nothing."

Rebecca sat primly on the edge of the velvet wingback. "I am on the Festival's organising committee. I am also secretary to the Town Hall Committee." She cleared her throat, two fingers nervously tugging at the pointed lapel of her collar. "I am happy I have the authority to ask you, Ms Carter, this question. Is there any chance the Festival could exhibit at

Ludlow Hall? In one of the outhouses, perhaps?"

Connie looked taken back. "I am not sure. Is there even any lighting in the outhouses?"

"The barn has electricity," Eve said quietly.

"Would you mind if the barn was used?" Hetty said, staring pointedly at Eve.

"I am not the owner of Ludlow Hall, and no, I don't mind if you are referring to what happened there."

Rebecca stood up, advancing towards Eve. "Eve, in my rush to find a solution I was insensitive. I am awfully sorry."

"What happened?" Connie asked.

Hetty went puce and looked at Eve.

"The barn is where my husband hanged himself."

"Oh … Oh." Connie was not sure how to answer.

Rebecca Fleming straightened her skirt and scuffed her shoes on the carpet.

"I did not mean to dredge up the memories, Eve—"

Connie broke across her. "Why don't we convert the old stables and yard for the country market, and the exhibition can take place in the drawing room here."

Eve clapped both her hands together, as if calling everybody to attention.

"Connie, you will never get the stables done! There is too much work involved. The barn is the obvious place for the market." Her face flushed pink, Eve looked from one woman to the next. "It is about time I got over my irrational fear of the place. It is quite nice to think Ludlow Hall could become the centre of the community yet again. This room is lovely for the Festival exhibition, and the right size, Connie, as long as you are happy to have the whole of the town traipsing through."

"It seems a way to get to know everybody."

"Are you sure?" Rebecca asked, rubbing her hands in satisfaction that she had solved the problems for both the Town Hall Committee and the Festival in one go.

"We will give it a go, but I think the barn will need a makeover of sorts."

"I will get a team to come around this week. A few days should do it. I will tell them to consult with you."

Eve noticed a new-found confidence in Rebecca, who got up to leave, itching to get back and tell everybody she had saved not only the country market, but had arranged a swish place for the exhibition.

Eve put her hands out to stop her. "Maybe don't say anything until Connie has had a chance for a proper think, a cooling-off period, as it were."

Connie laughed. "Trying to protect me again, Eve. I think I can make my own decisions." Realising she sounded a bit sharp, Connie playfully tapped Eve on the arm. "It is about time I got involved in Rosdaniel: this is a good way to do it."

Relief washed over Rebecca Fleming's face as she hastily walked to the door, promising to be in touch later with times for the workmen.

Connie made sure the front door was firmly shut behind Rebecca before she addressed Eve.

"Are you sure you can handle this?"

"It is only four walls and a roof, why wouldn't I? Haven't I survived this far?"

Eve purposefully picked up her patchwork, Connie and Hetty following her lead, not altogether sure Eve wasn't masking the reawakening of a great pain.

Happy to escape from Eve's insistence that everything was normal, Connie went upstairs to change before the first of her dance classes arrived. A calm quietness blanketed the house. Today Connie's heart was at peace, surrounded by the patchwork colours of Molly. At Ludlow Hall, she felt safe. It was strange that a place she had not even known existed this time last year should now be holding her up, cradling her as she attempted to resurrect a life for herself.

When she heard the first of the mothers come up the avenue,

kids chattering, she stood at the top window, watching them. One woman had her three-year-old girl by the hand, and another had let her boy run on ahead. He was fiercely kicking the grass along the centre of the drive. Connie knew he was the one to watch. The group lingered at the rhododendron, waiting for a woman pushing a double buggy to catch up.

Connie pulled on her new tracksuit and rushed downstairs to open the front door, happy that at least a few mums and kids had turned up.

Eve gave her the thumbs-up as they passed into the dance studio, the children running ahead, jumping and shouting.

"Do you think she will make a go of it?" Eve said.

Hetty looked at her friend. "We will make sure she does. We don't want her to up and leave; she is too good for us for that."

They sat working, smiling as they heard the children, heavy on their feet, the sound of "Nellie the Elephant" making them tap their toes. When the chatter became higher than the music, they knew the class was finished.

"It is show time," Hetty said, tidying away her sewing needle and thread.

Eithne Hall's car pulled up outside, three women squashed into the back and another two sharing the front passenger seat.

Eve walked out to greet them, pulling on Connie's arm as she came out of the studio.

"I think, Connie, spring the dance on them, no touchy-feely, going easy. A bit like you did to Hetty and myself."

Embarrassed, Connie did not know what to say. Hetty bustled forward, her hands out in front of her as if to stop the hordes advancing.

"Ladies, the latest thing is to lose weight through dance exercise, and we are going to lead the way."

"I never said…" Connie started to say, but Eve lightly brushed her ankle to indicate to her to shut up.

"We are nearing the end of the quilts. We thought why not

take a break? Sure, we are making quilts in our dreams. Let's learn to dance," Eve said.

The women stopped in their tracks, bumping up against each other.

"I think we have more than enough work to be getting on with. Maybe another time," Kathryn said.

"Right now?" Dana asked.

"Of course," Eve said, making a feeble attempt to swing her hips.

Hetty clicked her fingers and pointed to the dance studio. Kathryn sighed loudly but followed the others as they trooped in.

"Slip off the shoes at the door, ladies," Hetty said, her voice loud enough to be heard over the gaggle of talk in the hall.

Eithne, a heavy woman around the hips, stood looking from Eve to Hetty to Connie.

"I am not sure anybody wants to see these hips moving."

"Just imagine what you will look like after a few weeks: you will be transformed," Hetty said, leading the way into the dance studio.

"Not that my man would notice anything, but I have an occasion coming up in the next few months," Marcella said, slapping her own hips.

Connie, emboldened by the enthusiasm of the others, slipped ahead and put on jolly, light music.

"Kick off your shoes, ladies. Don't worry how you are dressed, we will be just enjoying ourselves today, see where we are at."

Giggling, the women stepped out of their shoes, lining them in a row down one side of the room. Eithne was the last in line, sheepishly pointing to her odd socks.

"I didn't think the whole world was going to be perusing my toes," she said, jumping from one foot to another, turning, shaking her bottom and making the others guffaw loudly. "I am afraid the only steps any of us know is the Irish dancing," Eithne said, flexing her feet in an Irish reel.

Kathryn Rodgers made a big thing of showing off her pirouettes. Dana Marshall, a little overwhelmed, stood to one side. Connie called the group to attention and, taking Dana by the hand, showed her how to warm up. Soon they were concentrating on their exercises, before she allowed them to attempt a few steps. Slowly the giggles disappeared, each woman focusing on her feet.

"One, two, three, head up, looking in the mirror."

Eve refused to look up. "I know well what I look like, without getting a nasty reminder," she said.

"Ladies, we have to make a pair of curtains to pull over for when the Ludlow Ladies' Society are showing their moves," Hetty said, making everybody chuckle.

"We have to finish our patchwork quilts, that is what we have to do," Kathryn said, a little too sharply.

"Kathryn is right, we can come back to the dancing another day," Eve said, and the other women, though they grumbled, made to get their shoes on, and each promised Connie they would return for more dance lessons another time.

Full of chatter, they crossed to the drawing room, Eithne Hall leading the way. She got the Rosdaniel quilt and pushed it out across the carpet like she was putting a fresh sheet on the bed.

The women stood. It was three-quarters done, colours light and dark, squares of fabric identical in size so that the people of the town could pick out the piece that meant the most to them. The priest's scarf, the apron used by the baker at Connor's Bakery, the green jersey, beside the silks and satins and flowery fabrics the women of the town donated. The schools were represented in plaid; a section of a Garda uniform was beside the lace of a Communion dress. The Town Hall was remembered in detailed embroidery specially done by Rebecca. Ludlow Hall had been given the same treatment.

"We have too much fabric, so we are spoiled for choice for the last quarter," Kathryn said.

Eve picked up a tiny shirt with the sailor collar, navy with a white petersham trim as a border around the square collar.

"Who gave in this?" she asked, a tremor in her voice.

Dana Marshall fidgeted with the lace chairback on the velvet wingback chair.

"I brought it, Eve. It was your boy's, wasn't it? Mammy asked me to bring it, I hope you don't mind."

Kathryn picked it up. "But is there a story attached to it?" she asked.

Dana straightened up. "Well, I think there is, and it is a Rosdaniel story, because there were a lot like us at the time. My father had just lost his job in the local mill when my mother had her first baby: a boy, our Tommy. She said that shirt and the little trousers that went with it meant she could dress her child up going to Mass and walking down the town. 'I could hold my head high I was not letting my baby down,' were her actual words. She said it also gave her hope that they would get through the hard times, as well as a belief in the kindness of others."

"I remember your mother, a lovely woman. She baked some scones and brought them here, something I really appreciated," Eve said quietly.

"She said you invited her in for tea, but she was too scared to go inside Ludlow Hall." Dana faltered.

"In case she met Arnold, I suppose," Eve ventured.

Dana, embarrassed, continued. "Mammy is on the verge of dementia now, forgetting lots, but some things in the past she remembers well, like when she got the sailor suit for Tommy." Dana's eyes welled up. "We would all be very proud if a sailor-shirt patch was included in the quilt."

Eve remembered the little sailor suit well. They had bought it in Brown Thomas, laughing together that it would go to waste if they ended up having a girl. Arnold insisted on forking out for it anyway, sure their child would be a boy.

Shaking her shoulders, she rotated her head to stop the pain sludging her brain. When she spoke, it was softly and firmly.

"It will be lovely to see this included in the Rosdaniel quilt," she said.

Kathryn Rodgers threw the sailor shirt on the to-be-used pile.

Date: May 10, 2013
Subject: THE LUDLOW LADIES' SOCIETY

*****SPECIAL ANNOUNCEMENT*****

Ludlow ladies,

Due to repeated requests, the Ludlow Ladies' Society, with the permission of the owner of Ludlow Hall, Connie Carter, issues this special notice to tell the story of Molly's quilt.

We do this with the kind permission of Connie and we acknowledge the tragedy in her life and the considerable strength and fortitude she has shown. Connie is a shining example to us all that the human spirit is strong.

Molly Carter, age five years, two months and two days, died on July 6, 2011. Molly was suffocated in her bed by her father after her mother, Connie, left early in the morning for work. Mr Ed Carter then left the house and drove his car into a wall and killed himself.

Those are the terrible facts of what happened to little Molly. But the quilt that commemorates her short life is full of happy memories of the good times. She was her mother's pride and joy and much loved. Connie has had to pick up the pieces. Coming to Ludlow Hall has been part of that process.

We in the Ludlow Ladies' Society are honoured to have helped Connie on her journey and pledge to be there for her as she lives with the loss of her beautiful little girl.

Molly's quilt is a stark reminder to all of the fragility of life. Connie Carter and what happened to her beautiful daughter remind us just how precious life is. We hope in the years to come that her patchwork memory quilt – Molly's quilt – can bring some comfort in the face of such a devastating loss.

Thank you, Connie, for sharing your story with us. We want you to know Molly will always have a special place in the hearts of the Ludlow ladies.

Kathryn Rodgers,
Chairwoman

25

Eve touched the soft pile of airmail letters, flimsy, bunched together, hidden away. She could see the address written in a careful hand.

Mr Arnold Brannigan
C/O Rosdaniel Post Office
Co. Wicklow
Ireland

Placing the box on the coffee table, she sat down. Shame flushed through her. Whatever was contained in those letters, he had never intended her to find them. Although the mahogany box belonging to his grandfather was not the safest hiding place, there was no doubt Arnold had tried to conceal something from her.

She sat, her hands tightly gripped on her lap, staring straight ahead.

Shuddering, feeling cold, she knew in her heart that the box contained a ball of trouble which, once released, could never be tidied away. Much the same way as Arnold had hidden the level of their debt to the bank from her, this was just another hurdle he left for her to climb on her own. Her head thumped; a sharp pain was piercing up the back of her neck. Sometimes the dread is worse than the actual, so she reached to take out the bundle of letters, but stopped herself, unable yet to take on board the grief she surely was about to open up.

After his death, she had searched every inch of the library, his desk and even the outside shed where he liked to potter, desperate for clues. One day she went up in the attic and rummaged, not exactly knowing what she was looking for, but wanting to know and understand why her husband had taken his own life, to see if there was a secret she knew nothing of. In the guest room, she looked in various boxes and sorted through a pile of old newspapers in case anything was slipped between the pages, but she never saw the mahogany box, tucked in the corner behind the folds of brocade curtains never pulled across or back.

Arnold had never intended her to find these letters. Maybe she should lock up the box, put the find out of her mind. In the days after his death, she was desperate for answers, any answers, any clues, but now she felt more resentment at the surprise intrusion in her life.

But how could she ignore the letters? Not knowing their contents could lead to hours of dangerous speculation or worry haunting and stalking her. Her fingers extended, she made to reach for the box, but stopped herself, sinking back in the armchair, her breathing heavy.

Connie had brought the box almost immediately after finding it. Nervous, she gave Eve a long-winded explanation. She was clearing out a guest room at Ludlow Hall for Bill and got a lot of empty cardboard boxes from Michael Conway's shop to store all the bits and pieces along with antique boxes in the room. Not sure if she should ask Eve if she wanted anything, Connie decided to put everything in storage until later. She pulled up the windows to air out the room, setting to work, carefully placing ornaments and antiques in the boxes marked Tayto and Flahavan's. It was when she was finished and shutting one of the windows that she saw the dark mahogany box tucked in the corner, a black damp stain around it, the corners of the wood discoloured by condensation.

She shook it, but it gave nothing away. Distracted by the dirty wet patch on the window, she grabbed the spray, wiping stains along with the dirt and water from the glass and windowsill.

Moving next to the bedroom furniture, she polished the solid mahogany until it gleamed in the afternoon light. When she saw the delivery van arrive with the new mattress, she ran downstairs to the front door, scooping up the box as she went. As she waited for the delivery men to struggle upstairs with the mattress, she fiddled with the box, trying to prise it open. Securing a knife from the kitchen, she pushed the steel edge in the small slit of the lock, hoping to click it open, but it did not budge. Putting different pressures on the lock, she had almost given up when she thought of the strange-looking key she had come across in the first few days at Ludlow. It was still in Arnold's desk at the far end of the dance studio.

The key was stiff in the lock, but it fitted. As she turned it, the lid of the box sprung open. Squashed inside were a bundle of airmail envelopes, plain white envelopes underneath. Connie eased out the bundle, turning it over in her hands, before quickly returning it to the box and turning the key to lock it.

She knew she must give this to Eve, but worried what it might do to her friend. However, not to hand over the box would be the worst thing. Once the delivery men left, she snatched up the box and the car keys and left the house, locking the back door behind her. When she got to the car she stopped and took a deep breath, arguing in her head whether she was doing the right thing. But how could she look Eve in the face again if she did not rush the letters to her? Turning on the ignition, she steered down the avenue, still unsure if she was doing the right thing.

Eve had been surprised when she saw Connie at her front door.

"Is there something wrong? You don't look well."

Connie, feeling agitated, stepped into the room, struggling to find the right words.

"I found something. A box. I wasn't sure if I should show it to you, but when I opened it there were letters. I had to come straight over ..."

Eve put her hand out as if to stop the flow of words. "Steady on, Connie, I am only hearing a jumble of words. The last time somebody looked like you do now, it was Arnold telling me that we owed millions to the bank." Her voice was light, and she laughed at her own memory, but she stopped abruptly when she saw Connie's discomfort. Catching Connie by the elbow, she guided her to the armchair by the window.

"Deep breaths, start over," she said kindly.

Connie smiled, outlining in a low, quiet voice how she found the box, before turning the key and showing Eve the contents.

"They are not for me to open," she said. Placing the box in Eve's hands, she got up to go. "Call me if you need me, I will come straight back." She let herself out.

Eve reached in now and took out a bundle of airmail letters, leaving the conventional vellum envelopes at the bottom of the box. Two photographs were stuck against the side of the box. She picked up the colour prints. Her heart tightened: Arnold, holding a baby who was not James. He looked relaxed, smiling, happy, the baby asleep, content in his arms. The other photograph was a typical family pose: man, woman with the child in the middle, except the man who looked like a father was Arnold.

Slowly, she took one of the airmail letters and unfolded it.

San Remo
145 Central Park West
July 30, 1972

My Dearest Arnold,
Now that you are gone, I cannot sleep or settle to anything. Tell me you are coming soon again to be with me. My friend Maryann says I am crazy, but I told her she does not know the love between us.

Hurry back to me, my darling. When I am with you, the whole world is right; when you are away, so many things disturb me.

What I wouldn't give to be able to be at Ludlow Hall with you. What a fine time we would have together. Mr Kalowski says his restaurant is not the same without the two of us sitting at his window seat. He said beautiful lovebirds always bring in good business.

Hurry back, my darling.

All my love,

Ros

xxx

Eve scrunched the letter in her hand. Pain pulsed through her, strangling her brain. She wanted to scream, but there was no sound. She picked up the next letter.

San Remo
145 Central Park West
November 24, 1973

My Dearest Arnold,

Thank you for coming to be with me after the birth of our lovely boy. That you came after suffering such a tragedy shows the sort of man you are, and I am deeply grateful.

I hope Eve likes the dress I picked out for her. I really think it was the nicest of the three sent over by Regina at Bloomingdale's. My wish is that it brings some comfort to Eve at this terrible time for you both.

That you took such joy in the birth of our baby boy and allowed me to call him Arnold Edward fills me with pride. I miss you so, but I promise

I will bring up our son, Arnold Edward Carter,
to be a fine man like his father.

Eve dropped the letter, unable to continue to read the words of love between this woman and her husband. He had left her days after the birth and death of James to celebrate the birth of his American son. In the moment it took her to realise why he had left her so rapidly as she grieved, she hated the man she once called her husband.

That he had conducted an affair, with correspondence routed through the local post office, made shame sweep through her, but that was secondary to the anguished pain she felt on discovering that he had abandoned her for his mistress, so soon after the death of James.

She could never forgive that.

Pain flashed through her; her head was heavy. She was not sure if she was crying, but she must be. She did what she always did when she could not cope: she rang Michael Conway.

"I have to let the evening rush at the shop go before I can lock up. I won't be able to get a stand-in at this short notice."

"Okay."

"You understand, Eve, don't you?"

"I understand," she said, quickly putting down the phone.

Doubling up, she thought the pain now that Michael could not come to her was as bad as Arnold's historic betrayal.

She was lying on the couch when she heard a light tap on the door.

"I had to wait for May Murtagh to pick between Coke and Diet Coke, but I closed up straight after that. I am sorry, Eve, it is only when I put down the phone I realised you didn't sound yourself. What is wrong?"

He reached over with his handkerchief and wiped her face gently. She could only point him to the box, the letters thrown across the floor.

Michael collected up the letters and stuffed them back in the box.

228

After a few minutes, she spoke.

"He had a second family in America. Did you know any of this, Michael?"

He did not answer, but bowed his head.

She jumped up. "You knew and you never told me."

"Eve, I heard a rumour. I had my suspicions. What could I do with that?"

"What are you saying? That everybody was laughing behind my back? You let me carry on like a fool. How long, Michael, how long have I not known?"

"Eve, you are not being fair. How could I tell you what was only a suspicion?"

She stared at him and through him, the pain in her heart so big she thought it would envelop her there and then, choking the life from her.

"It was up to Arnold to tell you," Michael said, his voice trembling.

Eve walked to the front door and opened it wide.

"Get out, get out."

Her voice was low and firm. He knew not to argue with her. As he passed, he reached out to touch her cheek with his hand, but she pushed him away, pulling off her ring and pressing it into his hand.

As soon as he stepped over the threshold, she threw herself at the door, making it bang shut. Tears washed over her, the loss dragging her down. Which was worse, she honestly did not know: the past or present deception, the husband or the lover.

She saw Michael walk down the path, lingering, hunched at the gate. Sitting on the edge of the couch, she was not sure what she should do. There was no need to read the rest of the airmail letters; she had no desire to do so either. Closing the box, she noticed the two plain white envelopes, with Arnold's name and address at Ludlow Hall typed on them.

Slipping one letter from the envelope, she scanned down through it. Her head buzzed with tension as she reached for the second envelope, a few printed paragraphs delivering devastating news. What she would do with this information she was not sure.

Time slipped by. The room became darker. Her mind was blank, her brain numb, the marks of her nails deep in the palm of her hand. A sheet of pain lodged on her chest, and water dripped from her eyes, wetting the soft collar of her blue silk blouse. Curling up into a ball, the last two letters fell to the ground beside her, after floating from her grip.

How long did she stay this way? She only knew the phone rang, the sound of it twirling through the rooms, bouncing off the walls, filling her head. When the doorbell buzzed, she shrank back in the chair, afraid to answer it, worried she would show too much pain of what had befallen her. She was afraid, too, it was one of the women from the Ludlow Ladies' Society. Razor sharp, they would detect immediately her well of pain and create a commotion.

26

Rebecca Fleming sent three men early to clean out the barn and get it ready for the Rosdaniel country market.

"I won't be able to help, I have dance classes back-to-back today," Connie said, a little distracted by the early morning activity in the back yard.

"You carry on, you won't even know we are here," one of the men said, just as another came out of the barn holding a cardboard box.

"Put them in one of the stables please," Connie said.

A blackbird, startled at the activity, flew low as the crows huddling in the high trees at the far end of the barn cawed out in protest at the disturbance. Rebecca Fleming drove her car smartly around the back, disappearing into the barn to give instructions to the three men.

Connie, back in the kitchen, stood at the window by the sink, unsure suddenly of her hasty decision to allow a weekly market in her back yard.

When Rebecca stuck her head around the door, Connie beckoned her inside.

"We have to talk about parking. I would prefer if everybody left their cars somewhere away from the house."

"The only way we are going to be able to do that is if you open up one of the fields."

Connie looked alarmed. "You don't think there will be that many?"

"We don't know. The fact the country market is at Ludlow Hall is quite a draw."

Connie sighed loudly, idly fingering the set of patches on the kitchen table. "I might have made a mistake. I am not sure I want so many people milling around the Hall."

"It is only for a few hours on a Saturday morning. You can't back out now; all the stallholders have been informed."

There was a hint of hysteria in Rebecca's voice. She coughed to try to regain her composure before she spoke again.

"I think we can ask people to enter through the back entrance, and we can cordon off the small field on the right, before we reach the back yard. Would that suit you?" She did not wait for Connie to answer, adding quickly, "Why don't I get the workmen to run a rope across, blocking access to the front of the house, the gardens and the lake from the back yard?" Rebecca, feeling a keen sense of satisfaction at her solution, beamed brightly.

Connie, not wanting to take on the stress of another exchange, nodded.

"Will you join the Ludlow Ladies for a dance class this morning?"

Rebecca scowled. "I have a lot on. Anyway, I can't dance a step."

"Think of it as good exercise. We might even be able to dance a routine at the Festival."

Rebecca sniggered. "Have you said it to any of the ladies yet?"

"Not exactly, the first lesson is today."

"Good luck with that. Do you really think Eve Brannigan will want the whole of Rosdaniel watching her do the foxtrot?" She opened the door to leave. "Connie, you have done me a good turn. I will be back in time for your lesson, but, mark my words, once you mention a performance to the ladies, you might as well forget it."

When she was gone, Connie escaped to the dance studio.

Slowly, she paced across the floor, the music in her head propelling her along, her shoulders loosening, her mind clearing.

Glad she had done her warm-up exercises earlier, she began to dance her favourite ballet solo. It brought her back to when life was uncomplicated, when all she had to do was concentrate on the music and dance.

When she heard a knock on the door, she was ready to meet the Ludlow Ladies' Society for their first official dance class.

Hetty bustled in, wearing a turquoise velour tracksuit and runners.

"You have done something to me, Connie Carter, this is the first time in my life I have worn a tracksuit. Next thing, we will see Eve in leggings."

Eithne Hall and three of the other women arrived, some wearing jeans, Eithne in a long, sweeping skirt.

"Nobody is going to see the width of my ankles, ever," she said, pulling up her skirt only slightly.

As the women kicked off their shoes, Hetty turned to Connie.

"Is Eve not here already?"

"I thought she was coming with you."

"I called in, knocked a few times on the door, even looked in the window, but no Eve."

"We can start. Maybe Michael is dropping her off."

She turned on the music low in the background as the women did their stretching exercises.

"I tried ringing her as well, and no-go. Maybe she really does not want to dance."

Connie frowned. "I will call on her later. It is not like Eve to go back on her word."

She clapped her hands and the women formed a line in front of the mirrors.

"One, two, three, four, turn, five, six, seven, eight."

They followed the beat, their steps so heavy they made the floor bounce.

"More lightness of step! Trust yourselves."

Eithne laughed. "I am a farmer's wife. I have never had to have a light step in my life."

233

"Move from the hips, Eithne."

"Easier said than done: these hips have done too much work over the years," Eithne said, making the others whoop, holler and punch the air. Connie, laughing, threw her hands up, before switching off the music.

"Ladies, I know it is a bit of fun, and believe me, I am enjoying it, but please try and concentrate. You look so good when you get it right."

Contrite, the group shuffled back in line.

"Think you are stepping towards something, turning around, stepping back, now hands out and push it aside. It is heavy. Let me see it."

"What are we pushing away?"

"The problems of life, a heavy tree trunk, anything: now run back, turn and kick out."

Hetty kicked with gusto, almost falling. "I think at our age we should kick low," she laughed.

Eithne, sweating, stopped and bent over, wheezing loudly, her hands on her knees.

Connie said, "For the last fifteen minutes, we will do something different." She reached behind the desk, plucking out several hula hoops. "Great for the hips, Eithne. Let's do it."

Hetty confidently stepped into hers. "I used to be so good at this in my younger days," she said, swinging her hips, the hoop clattering on the floor.

Rebecca Fleming, who had slipped into the house through the back door, took a hula hoop, immediately able to keep it swinging across her hips.

"Ah, Rebecca, is there nothing you can't do," Eithne said, her voice rich with sarcasm.

Hetty let her hoop drop, rattling on to the floor.

"That is enough for today, Connie. Can we have a cuppa before we go?"

"As long as you help yourselves. I have another class next."

Hetty led the women into the kitchen.

"I heard Eve has a sign up, saying the dressmaking business is closed," Eithne said.

Hetty swung around. "That can't be true."

"I saw it with my own eyes, I brought Patricia Fitzpatrick to the house this morning to have a pair of trousers turned up."

"Why would she want to take in work when she is engaged to Michael Conway? He is a good man. He'll take care of her now. He is an awfully good catch."

"I don't think Eve would want to be dependent, after what happened with Arnold."

"Maybe so, but a woman can get used to a bit of luxury, real quick," Eithne said, reaching for the cookie jar and placing it in the middle of the table.

A flurry of happy noise from the hall signalled the arrival of the mothers and toddlers.

"Hasn't Connie made a huge difference to this old place? Arnold Brannigan must be turning in his grave," Eithne said, making the other women snigger.

★

Connie waited until the workmen finished in the barn, before leaving Ludlow Hall to drive to Eve's house. She could have tried phoning, but somehow she suspected Eve was hiding out.

When she pulled up, it looked as if nobody was in. The curtains on the two front windows were drawn across. Still, she walked up the path, the sound of snail shells collapsing under her feet. At the door, a small note – "Eve's Alterations Closed" – was blotted with rainwater.

Connie pressed the bell, the jingle echoing through the house. She pressed harder, as if the extra effort would make the sound stronger. The dog next door snuffled at the dividing fence, growling and whimpering.

She waited, cowering in the doorway as more rain began to fall. Leaning down, she pushed at the letterbox, throwing her voice into the house.

"Eve, it's Connie. I am not going away until you open this door."

She stood waiting, feeling foolish, not sure if Eve was inside, when suddenly the lock was turned and the door opened.

"I am all right, Connie, I just don't feel like visitors at the moment."

Eve's face was blotched red, her eyes swollen from crying.

"Can I come in, Eve?"

"Why, to talk to a woman who has lost everything? Even the memories are gone, Connie."

"What are you talking about?"

"I am not talking at all, Connie. I appreciate you coming, but I can't talk."

She moved to push the door shut, but Connie thrust her foot out. Shoving her way into the house, she reached out to Eve, throwing her arms around her.

"You sat by my bed and brought me back from the dead in my head. I am here for you now."

Eve felt her body lean into Connie, who took her weight.

"Come back to Ludlow Hall, stay as long as you like. If you want to talk, I will listen, I promise," she whispered. Eve gulped her tears.

"What will people think if I move into Ludlow?"

"They can think all they like. Let me bring you home. I don't know why, but I think Ludlow Hall is what you need right now."

Eve nodded, using the sleeve of her cardigan to wipe around her eyes.

"You are good to me, Connie."

"Let's go. I can loan you some clothes for the time being."

Eve gathered up her handbag, the two white envelopes and her keys, making sure to lock the front door behind them. Meekly, she followed Connie to the car. She sat silently, and Connie did not speak either, until they turned right up the avenue to Ludlow Hall.

"You can have the room I have made up for Bill. I have a feeling he won't need to use it anyway."

"I am intruding."

"Nonsense, you are doing no such thing," Connie said, pulling the car up to the kitchen door.

She blathered on as they got into the house, in an effort to cover Eve's discomfort. When she showed her into the guest room, Eve sat on the bed, rubbing the palm of her hand along the top of the duvet.

"You have made it up nice, this room. This was going to be my baby's room."

Connie's cheeks flamed bright red.

"I had no idea. Use my room, I can stay in here."

"This room is perfectly fine for me. If memories were to hold me back, I would not cross the threshold of this house."

Connie fussed about, pulling over the curtains at the window, quietly leaving the room and coming back about fifteen minutes later with folded pyjamas in one hand and a mug of hot chocolate in the other.

"I can go down to your house and pack some stuff for you tomorrow, if you like."

Eve reached out, squeezing Connie's hand.

"It was a good day for Ludlow, and for me, when you came along."

"Get into bed and get some rest. If you feel like talking in the morning, I am always awake early."

Eve did not answer, but pulled back the duvet, so Connie backed out of the room and closed the door. Eve got into bed and must have fallen asleep, because when she woke, it was still dark outside.

Passing lightly along the corridor and down the stairs, she stopped to listen to the grandfather clock at the far end of the hall, ticking down the time, as if it mattered.

The kitchen was cold and damp-smelling. She sneezed, grabbing her coat from the back of a chair, wondering why Connie did not light the Aga every day.

Slumping down beside the table, she was sitting shivering

237

when Connie came in. Draping a blanket over her, Connie got the electric heater, plugging it in, the first puff of heat ponging up the room.

"Are you okay, Eve?" she asked gently.

Eve reached into the pocket at the front of her pyjama top, pulling out the two white envelopes. She handed one to Connie.

"You don't want me to read that, Eve?"

"I do."

"No, I can't, it is private."

Eve snorted loudly, pointing at the envelope. "Connie, please. Just read it."

Gingerly, Connie picked up the letter. Slipping the page free from the envelope, she delicately opened it up and began to read.

Eve sat listening to the sounds of the house, the whirring of the fridge, the wind rattling the old gutter pipe over the kitchen window, whistling around the house, pushing into the cracks and broken seals of the windows. How many times had she sat here, a letter from the bank in her hand, shame flaring through her, sweat prickling at her temples?

Connie, her dressing gown hanging open, leaned over the letter.

Laurel Drive
New Hyde Park
NY 11040
February 2, 2009

Dear Mr Brannigan,
My name is Ed Carter and I understand you are my father. My mother was Rosalyn Carter and when she died I was brought up by my aunt, Kate. Unfortunately, Kate passed away, but she left me details of my birth and the arrangement you had with my mother to finance me until I became an adult. I understand you did that, and I am grateful.

I am married and have a young daughter now. I have lived my

238

life without a father, though I remember you sometimes in my life for short periods, a benevolent and kind family friend. I realise now how important a father is to a child. I realise too how much I lost out on not having you, my father, permanently in my life.

I would love if we could get to know each other now and if there are any other family members I should know. To that end, I would like us to meet, if only to satisfy myself that I look like you. I certainly don't resemble anybody on my mother's side.

My aunt told me the arrangement with my mother included a pledge that neither she nor I would make any demands on your estate. I can assure you again of this. My only interest is to develop a relationship with my father.

I would also dearly love my daughter, Molly, to meet her grandfather.

I realise this may come as a surprise to you, but I hope once you have had time to consider, you will regard this as an opportunity to catch up on lost time.

With that intention, I intend to travel to Ireland and to Ludlow Hall on Saturday, February 21 to visit you.

I very much look forward to meeting you.
Kind regards,
Arnold Edward Carter

Connie was shaking. Trepidation radiated through her, making her read faster When she came to the end, she carefully folded the letter back into the envelope, tossing it onto the table. Nervous, she continued to pick at the corners of the tablecloth before she spoke.

"How weird is this. Edward was my husband's middle name; he hated the name Arnold. He was brought up by his aunt after his mother passed away when he was young."

She flicked her fingers, a nail hitting the envelope, making it move a fraction towards Eve.

"He told me he never knew his father, did not know who he was."

Eve pushed over the second letter. "You had better read this as well. Arnold was a cruel man who rejected his son."

Connie, feeling cold, stretched out and turned up the heater.

Laurel Drive
New Hyde Park
NY 11040
March 17, 2009

Dear Arnold,

You are my father and neither of us can deny that. That you should threaten me and deny me a meeting, even one away from your precious Ludlow Hall, is very upsetting. When I paid a visit to Ludlow Hall, it was locked up and I was not even able to walk up the driveway. Are you so ashamed of me that you will not meet me anywhere and run like a frightened rabbit from looking me in the eye? That I had travelled so far did not bother you either.

I am sorry you think I pile shame on you or that I intend to lay claim to your property. You say you had one son, James, who died soon after birth. I am sad I lost a brother.

I am your son, Arnold Brannigan, and nothing you do now can change that. If I thought you could in time acknowledge me, I would persist, but your anger and shame you have made clear to me in your letter.

Your cruel words will stay with me forever. I return these two photographs to you. My mother gave them to me, I presume so that I would remember you. You say I am not to think of you as a father, and while I cannot do that, I do not want reminders of your pretence of fatherhood.

As I return these two snaps, I want you to know there were times I looked at these photographs and wondered and dreamed of how it would be if this kind, generous man who came to visit was my father.

How wrong I was in my estimation of you. I did not know that under the veneer of a gentleman was a cruel man who won't even go so far as to acknowledge his son.

My hope is that as a father to my daughter I will never be so uncaring. For my part, I have to find a way to be a good father, even though my only example is the worst.

I am your son, Arnold Brannigan. I would give anything to hear you say those words. Without the blood ties to this earth, there is nothing. You have left me dejected, with nothing and worth nothing.

Your son,

Ed Carter

Connie put down the letter, tears streaming down her face.

"What sort of man denies his own son?"

"A cruel man who knew no better than to be looking over his shoulder at how others saw him. He was a fool, but a cruel fool, which makes him infinitely worse," Eve said, her voice flat and cold.

Eve held out the two photographs.

"I presume the baby in the picture with Arnold is Ed."

Connie examined the photos.

"I have never seen either of them before. That is Rosalyn. Ed must have been six or seven years old there. Arnold was a handsome man; Ed looked a lot like him." Suddenly, she banged down the photographs on the table. "What has happened? What has happened to our families, Eve?"

Eve shook her head, unable to answer.

"Ed never let on," said Connie. "I did notice a change in him, but I thought it would pass. I remember after Kate died, he seemed awfully upset for a long time, which I put down to losing the one woman who had been there from the day he was born. I just gave him time to grieve." Wiping away tears, she shook herself. "He must have felt so bad at Arnold's reaction, but I don't understand why, so soon afterwards, he bought Ludlow Hall or why he never tried to persuade Arnold after that brush-off. Why didn't he tell me?"

"Who knows, Connie? He would not have had much time

to persuade my husband: within days, he was dead. The bank came in as soon as it could and put the place up for sale."

"He would not have known any of that, but he did buy Ludlow Hall, sank all our money into it."

"Maybe he wanted his rightful inheritance and that was the only way he could do it."

Connie jumped up, the chair toppling back behind her. "He wanted to knock the place down, after he had covered the land with housing."

"Never."

"He wanted to tear it down, he told the auctioneer."

"Surely not the house, after he'd seen the place."

"He didn't even want to view it properly. He was intent on knocking it down."

Eve pulled her hands along her face. "God, no, because Arnold rejected him?"

Connie paced the kitchen, like a cat circling, waiting to be let out. "Maybe he was hitting back at the hurt Arnold caused. He didn't go through with it, though, when he realised how difficult it would be."

Eve sighed. "Arnold would not have been able to cope with the land ploughed up and concreted over, the house razed to the ground." She looked up at the ceiling. "For the first time in my life, I am glad Arnold decided to leave this world. I know Ed had something to do with it, that the bank bearing down on us had something to do with it, that his feeling of shame had something to do with it but ..." She stopped, choking back the tears. "He left on his own terms. I was left to cope, but he was right to leave at his own bidding."

"Maybe Ed knew Arnold enough, to realise how much Ludlow Hall meant to him."

"Revenge is powerless against death. I don't think Ed knew he was already dead," said Eve.

Connie flopped down at the table. Eve reached over and grabbed Connie's two hands, squeezing them tight.

"This house is rightfully yours. I am happy for you that it may now bring you some peace in your heart. None of this is at your feet. Arnold fell in love with an American woman: that's it, pure and simple."

"Eve, this must be simply terrible for you. It must have been so bad for Ed as well, but no matter how much I try, I don't know if I can understand or forgive."

Eve's head thumped. Her eyes, she knew, were bulging in her head. She was tired and wanted to sleep.

"All the talking in the world won't soften it, Connie, like all the talking in the world won't lighten your great loss."

"Being a good father to Molly meant everything to him …"

Connie dipped her head. Eve, still holding her hands, squeezed tighter.

"There is one more thing, Connie."

Connie pushed Eve's hands away.

"Ed must have tried to persuade Arnold after that; there are bits of torn-up airmail letters and, from what I can gather, one letter opened but resealed. I did not think I should read it."

"What good will it do reading it?"

"Maybe nothing, but not to open it may leave you worse. You don't want it gnawing into you."

Connie took the letter, turning it over in her hands before quickly pushing it back to Eve.

"Will you read it?"

Eve did not argue but got up and, taking a knife from the drawer, carefully slit the sides of the envelope further so she could open it wide. Unfolding it, she scanned it quickly. Plopping down on the chair, she looked directly at Eve.

"I don't know if it will help you, but it does explain the pain Ed felt."

"I can't bear to look at his handwriting again. Can you read it to me please?"

Eve straightened on the chair and cleared her throat before starting to read.

Laurel Drive
New Hyde Park
NY 11040
March 20, 2009

Dear Arnold,

I note you have not answered any of my previous correspondence in which I asked for details about my birth family and particularly a medical history.

I don't intend to make a claim on your extensive property or to burden you with any further visits, but I would like an acknowledgment I am your son and that you have a granddaughter. That you have not even been just a little bit curious about your granddaughter or even enquired as to her name is testament to the man you are.

You leave me fatherless, wondering how can I be a good father to my daughter. It feels as if I was doomed to failure before I even began. That the role model I have aspired to in my mind all these years was a man of noble character would be laughable, were it not so sad.

Your granddaughter's name is Molly. I have nothing to offer her; my love is tainted by my past.

Arnold Brannigan, you have not only turned your back on me, but you have left me gutted, knocked down by your rejection, unable to be confident in my own ability to be a good father.

Life is hard any day of the week, but your anger, rejection and denial of me makes every second and every minute of every hour unbearable.

I shall fight this demon you have placed on my shoulders. I can only hope to God that for my daughter's sake, I win. But if I can't, I hope my past will someday help others understand and maybe forgive.

Don't worry, I will not bother you again.

Your son,

Ed

Eve closed the letter, the rustle of the light paper making a big noise in the still of the room.

"It was probably the last letter Arnold read. Going by the postmark, he received it just before he died," Eve said.

Connie rested her head in her hands.

Eve tidied away the letters in the box. The wind trapped at the top of the chimney wailed, the gutter banged a strange rhythm against the top of the window, the clock loudly ticked down time in the hallway.

27

Hetty, fretting, tried Eve's number several times. In bed, she tossed and turned, worrying Eve was dead or had fallen down the stairs in her little place and was unable to call for help. It was one in the morning when she got into her car and drove to Eve's house, calling in the letterbox, pressing the bell, listening intently in case her friend was inside. When she saw a light come on next door, she scurried down the path, into her car, turning out the road towards Ludlow Hall.

She was not sure why she was here, but resolved to continue slowly up the avenue and to turn for home if there was no sign of anybody up and about.

She prayed Connie was awake, because if she could not talk to somebody about Eve she would surely burst. Rounding the rhododendron, her shoulders slumped when she saw not one flicker of light at the house. Hesitating, she slowed down, intent on turning around, but, afraid the car would get stuck in soft ground, she decided to attempt to drive around the house and out the back lane. At the very least, she would be able to turn the car in the back yard.

As she drove into the yard, Hetty saw the pool of light thrown on to the cobbles from the kitchen. Excited, she stopped the car, rushing across the yard to tap on the back door. Shivering, she waited for Connie to answer, all the time looking over her shoulder, her fear heightened by the knocking of the stable door, which had been left open earlier by the workmen.

When there was no answer, she leaned over on her toes to peep in the window.

Connie and Eve, sitting opposite each other at the kitchen table, did not move. She saw Eve place her head in her hands. A worry went through her that maybe she should not interrupt, that to bear witness was already too much. The stable door slammed louder. Frightened, she rapped hard with her knuckles on the glass.

The two women at the table looked at each other, but neither moved. It was, Hetty thought, as if she was looking at ghosts. Fear surged through her, making her move closer to the window and rap louder with her knuckles.

Connie jumped up and Eve sat up straight, turning towards the door.

"It's me, Hetty," she shouted and she saw the faces of the two women relax.

Connie swung back the door, letting Hetty bustle inside.

"Is there something wrong?" Connie asked.

Slightly embarrassed, Hetty, panic streaked across her face, stuttered her words.

"I was looking for Eve. I was worried."

"What could not wait until daylight hours, Hets?" Eve asked gently.

Hetty flopped down at the table. "I am so worried. What is going on, Eve?"

Eve did not answer, nor did Hetty really expect her to.

"You know she has only left poor Michael devastated: they have split up."

"I know you mean well, Hetty, but this is none of your business and that is that." Eve sounded cross.

Hetty stood up, looking directly at her.

"Somebody has to tell you what an awful fool you are. Mind you, there is nothing new in that. You were married to a philanderer, Eve Brannigan. Most of us who had eyes in our heads knew that, but either you did not know or you ignored that fact.

247

I don't blame you, if you did ignore it. Look at what I lived with for all these years. The day has now come for you to grow up, Eve."

Eve jumped up, the chair screeching across the tiled floor. "You knew? Everyone knew?"

"Knew what? Only that that man in his younger days was gallivanting with any woman he could find. He was free to do what he liked. Weren't you installed here, enthusiastically looking after everything at Ludlow Hall?"

Eve's stomach stirred up sick, her head spinning.

Hetty stopped for a second, but only to take in a deep breath.

"Before you say it, Michael Conway hasn't opened up his heart to me. I have been up all night, thinking why that poor man is so despondent. All he would say was you had split up, you are too upset over Arnold. For God's sake, Eve, don't let your happiness slip away now, because of that philandering no-good fool who cheated on you every week of his life. And he was no different to his father before him."

Connie put a hand on Hetty's shoulders, hoping to restrain her flow. "Maybe Eve has heard enough."

Eve was doubled up at the table, her hands over her ears.

Hetty turned to Connie. "Somebody had to say it. She can't let a good man go. She has to grab this chance of happiness."

"Maybe Eve does not feel that way right now."

Hetty guffawed loudly. "What many of us would not give for a bite of the happiness on offer to her. Wake up, Eve, or that good man will be gone for good."

Eve, trembling all over, stood up and quietly walked out of the kitchen. Hetty and Connie heard her go into the drawing room, closing the door behind her.

"She had to know the truth. She did," Hetty blustered, as if she was trying to convince herself as well as anybody else in the room.

"The truth is complicated and often uncomfortable," Connie said as she stepped out into the hall.

Hetty began to sob, big tears flowing down her face, settling in the thick wrinkles at the base of her neck.

"She is the last person in the world I wanted to hurt. For God's sake, I have wanted those two to get it together for so long."

Connie padded to the drawing room door, knocking gently. When Eve opened it a little, Connie slipped in. Eve went back to the fireplace to study the painting.

"I loved him for so long, but deep down I knew, after the first flurry of love, he did not care one jot about me. Look at that painting. I knew a woman picked that dress for me. He insisted I wear it. I don't bear any ill to that poor woman in America; I imagine he did to her what he did to me. And then he turned his back on his son."

Hetty hovered at the door. Eve swung around to her.

"Hetty, I don't like the way you did it, but I don't hold it against you. Come, join us."

Hetty, wiping her eyes, stepped into the room.

"I never knew how to say it to you, Eve, or maybe I thought you knew, and you were happy enough. I never had the words until now." She stopped. "Maybe my words weren't so good this time either."

Eve walked over and took her hands. "Hets, I am sure you want the best for me."

Hetty began to sob. "I am not a woman for small talking, Eve, not on something like this."

"I know."

The three of them stood awkwardly in the middle of the drawing room.

Eve broke the silence.

"I think it was all right, even good for a while, but Arnold became so distant after our baby died." She pointed at the painting hanging on the chimney breast. "I knew then things would never be the same, and they weren't. Look at the get up of me in a dress he had some floozie pick out for me."

"I was going to ask if you wanted the painting," Connie said.

Eve snorted out a laugh. "If I was strong enough, I would knock it down and burn it."

Hetty took two steps, flinging her arms around Eve.

"There are three of us, and two of us are experts at a bit of arson," she said.

Connie got a chair, climbing up to examine the back of the painting.

"Step far back; I might let it drop," Connie said as the canvas and frame crashed down. A cloud of dust puffed up, the painting bouncing twice on the rug before landing near the bay window. Both Hetty and Eve ran to it as Connie, coughing, came down off the chair.

Eve sat down on the couch, looking at the blank wall, a huge square of dirty green netted with cobwebs. "It makes the room and my heart lighter to have it down."

"Dawn is breaking. If we wait a short while, we can set it alight in the field," Connie said.

Hetty fished in her bag and took out a packet of cigarettes.

"I did not know you smoked, Hetty," Eve said in surprise.

"So?" Hetty answered, and the three of them laughed at the defiant tone of a teenager in her voice.

"I am afraid you will have to smoke outside," Connie said.

"No problem, I am used to the disdain," Hetty said, making for the kitchen and the back door.

Eve walked over, kicking out at the frame of the painting. "How is it, I can do all this now? I was never brave enough to do it before, even when Arnold was gone."

"Time and distance give a certain type of strength," Connie said.

"It will happen for you too, Connie, I know it."

Connie shrugged her shoulders. "I am not so sure about that."

They sat quietly, waiting for Hetty, each absorbed in her own thoughts.

Eve felt an awful pain in her heart for Michael, feeling contrite that she had taken out her own deep hurt on him.

When Hetty came back in, ponging of smoke, she looked at her two friends.

"Have I missed something? What is wrong?"

"Nothing is wrong. We have had enough drama," Eve said.

Weary from being up all night, they went to the painting, grabbing a section each, half carrying it to the front door and down the steps to the field.

Connie climbed the fence first, taking the painting and managing to throw it on to the grass. Eve managed the fence fine, but Hetty, carrying a box of firelighters and two firelogs, called the others to help her out.

"I am going to need a lot more dancing before I am fit for this carry on," she said, slightly out of breath.

Eve patted her on the back. "Come on, Hets, we need your strength."

The three of them dragged the painting, which now had a big tear in the middle, to the scorched spot where Hetty's memory quilt had been set ablaze. They used the painting as a windbreak to light the firelighters and logs, before throwing frame and canvas on top of the fire.

Flames at first licked hesitantly, until the heat, reaching the oil paint, took off in colours of blue, yellow, red and orange. Eve watched the painting crumple and melt, just as her life at Ludlow had done.

Connie and Hetty stood back, the sparks rising high.

"We can leave it here. It is not going to spread anywhere," Hetty said. She turned to Eve. "Will I drop you off at Michael's? You might get him before he goes to the shop."

Eve nodded, and they went inside while she ran upstairs to get her things.

As they waited in the hall, Connie turned to Hetty.

"You are a good friend, Hetty."

"Not very diplomatic."

"But a good friend."

They were on the way down the driveway when Eve asked Hetty to drop her at home instead of Michael's.

"You are not backing out, I hope?" Hetty said, the car swerving on the avenue as she turned to look at Eve.

"I have to do this my own way, Hetty, I am going to have to live with my decision for a very long time."

Hetty, in a huff, did not answer, barely saying goodbye when she dropped off Eve at her terraced house.

28

Eve left the sign on the front door. The last thing she wanted was the likes of Mary McGuane pushing her way in. She could not face the chit-chat of any customers today and particularly the likes of Mary "Tell the World" McGuane.

Settling in the sitting room, Eve reached for the button box. Prising open the lid, she knew the buttons she was looking for: two white pearls left over from when she made her wedding dress. Digging her hands into the box, she shoved the buttons aside impatiently, letting them fall over her hands until she spied the pearl buttons. They were her most treasured buttons at one time, but now she no longer wanted to keep them. How many times had she held them, transported back to the wedding day, when he had danced her across the polished wooden floor of a London hotel as almost one hundred guests looked on.

Pressing the lid back on the box, she snatched the pearl buttons tight. Walking across to the window, she opened it enough so she could throw them out, letting them drop down on the rose bushes to the wet earth below.

There was a new determination in Eve. Having previously baulked at cutting up her wedding dress for the Ludlow memory quilt, she pulled her shears from the drawer. With a whip of her shoulders, she trudged upstairs to where the wedding dress was hanging at the back of the wardrobe, wrapped in an old sheet. She had made it herself from a McCall pattern. Long panels in a soft crepe, it was a snug fit with generous sleeves pulled into a lace cuff, the prim round collar trimmed in lace. The pearl buttons in a row down the bodice glinted in the light; many at the wedding had said it matched the happy sparkle in her eyes. In off-white, the dress skimmed her lovely figure, kicking out in pleats at her knees as she walked, a cape of white lace and a train adding a beautiful flow to the outfit. She loved the dress, remembering she had carried a simple posy of roses to match the rose she had clipped to one side of her head.

Tears streamed down Eve's face as she ran her hands along the crepe, thinking of the way Arnold held her, waltzing her across that floor, calling out to his friends, everybody laughing. Had he ever loved her? She hoped so. Otherwise their whole union was a sham, and she did not want to believe that.

She had loved him for a long time, blaming herself when he became cold and distant after James passed away. She could forgive him for buckling under his bank debts, but to have a second family and not allow his son into his life: how could she ever forgive that?

Draping the dress over her arm, she headed downstairs and laid it carefully on the sitting room couch. So many memories were contained in those crepe folds: the day she picked the pattern and yards of soft crepe. She had spent almost a whole month's wages on it all and the pearl buttons for the bodice, with three on each sleeve, where she had gathered the fabric with a loose machine stitch, so when she raised her hand for Arnold to place the wedding ring on her finger, the buttons glistened in the light. The heavy-duty train, crepe overlaid with Irish lace from her aunt's friends in Cork, was almost a work of art.

Taking her shears, she sliced from the widest point to the waist, where the train was attached with two buttons and loops. The sleeves next: she nicked the cuffs and pulled along the grain, the fabric shrieking as loud as the pain in her heart. Gripping the shears tight, she cut in a straight line from the bottom of the dress through the waistline and bodice to finish at the neck. Flattening out the fabric, out of habit she cut two squares, in case she ever wanted to put the crepe into a patchwork quilt. The rest of the mangled dress she balled up into a bundle, ramming it into the bin.

Not wanting to think how Arnold had flitted from one life to the other, she got her coat. Stopping at the mirror in the hall, she rubbed a little foundation into her face and dabbed on some pink lipstick in an effort to brighten herself up. Afraid she might lose the courage to walk up the street, she stepped quickly out the front door, banging it behind her in her hurry.

It was still early in the morning, so there were few out and about. The butcher looked at her oddly before dipping his head as she came closer, so she did not have to get drawn into a conversation.

Michael Conway's shop was open: there was a delivery of milk not yet taken in and a stack of newspapers still where they had landed when the van slowed down, so they could be thrown from the side door.

Faltering in her resolve, she thought he might not be there. What would she do then?

Her heart skipped when, as she got closer, she saw him in the doorway, bending down to collect the milk and bring it into the shop. He disappeared from view for a few moments and she knew he was placing the milk in the fridge by the door. Her heart thumping, she saw him reappear to pick up the stack of newspapers with his two hands. When he saw Eve, he stopped.

Not sure what to do, Michael did nothing.

She took him in: his face grey, pale and tired-looking, his clothes creased, the pile of newspapers heavy in his hands so that she worried he might keel over. A fear peppered through Eve they wouldn't be able to salvage anything, that she had pushed him too far. When he ducked back into the shop, she wondered whether to turn away.

The postman, about to cross over the street, shoved a letter into her hand, telling her to give it to Michael. She did not let on her discomfort and made her way inside the shop.

Michael, wavering at the counter, pushing newspapers about, saw her come in. He kept his head down, not knowing what to do. He took her in as she fumbled with her handbag. Her face was blotched from crying. She had put on lipstick, but this highlighted the pallor, he thought, the strain around her eyes, the frown lines embedded across her forehead.

"Michael, we need to talk."

"Eve, you don't look well."

"Can you get Richie up to the shop?"

"He is in Dublin today. Maybe Derek can keep an eye. Let me find out."

She stood fiddling with the corner of a magazine on a shelf as she watched him walk across to the butcher's.

When he came back, he stood wringing his hands.

"He has a lad in on work experience: he is trustworthy and Derek will send him over. I will just have to show him how to use my till. Do you want to wait in the back?"

She nodded and he showed her into the small kitchen, where she sat listening to him patiently coach the teenager on the cash till.

When, after ten minutes, Michael came into the kitchen, he looked nervous.

"We might be better getting out of here. Will we go for a drive?" he said.

She stood up and followed him to the car, her head down in case anybody spotted something was wrong.

"Is there anywhere you want to go?" he asked quietly.

"Could we go to Ludlow, walk around the lake? Connie won't mind."

He turned the car, gliding down the hill, turning in at the gates of Ludlow Hall.

"I will park at the hazel trees," he said.

She did not answer, but he got out of the car and opened the passenger door for her.

They started to walk across the grass, their footprints embedded in the sodden ground.

"You have no shoes for this type of terrain. Are you sure you want to continue?" Michael asked.

"Ludlow is the right place to be, for what I have to say."

Not another word was uttered between the two as they walked side by side, sometimes leaning close to each other, each afraid of what was to come.

Crossing in front of the house, they quickened their step, both anxious not to be spotted slipping into the yew walk. Michael, walking two steps ahead, headed for the bench he had put in place almost twenty years before, so she could sit and enjoy the cherry blossom and rhododendron in bloom under the yew trees' arc of shelter. Brushing the bench lightly with his hand to scrape off any loose dirt, along with the brown soupy petals of faded wilted blooms, he motioned to Eve to sit.

"We can talk, if you feel up to it," he said gently.

She sat down and he joined her at the other end of the bench, waiting for her to speak. They listened to the new sounds of Ludlow Hall: men beginning a day at work kitting out the barn, shuffling, coughing, the hammering and pounding of nails, the odd shout, loud music in the air.

"I need to know, Eve, where we are at."

She did not answer immediately, but reached out and took his hand.

"I love you."

She spoke so gently he could barely hear her.

He turned to her, his face puckered in tears.

"There is a 'but', isn't there?"

"I wronged you, I jumped to a conclusion about you, I blamed you, I never gave you a chance to explain. I am sorry."

"Eve, I know it hurts, but I only had suspicions, the rumours of a small town, the habits of the father to go on. I could not risk making you so unhappy when I had no hard facts. All I could do was watch out for you. I have tried my best to do that."

"Do you think Arnold loved me, ever?"

"I am sure he did."

Michael stood up, plodding across the soft, damp ground.

"There is something else I have to tell you, Eve. I am not sure how you are going to take it."

She stiffened, afraid of what he was going to say.

"Is this something I need to know, Michael? There has been so much heartbreak."

She looked old, he thought, shivering even though she was wearing her big coat, tears beginning to inch down her face.

"You are the last person on this earth I want to hurt, but I don't want any more secrets between us. I have to tell you this: it is for you to decide what you want to do with it."

Pain flared through her; she steeled herself for his words. He cleared his throat before continuing.

"Arnold was my half-brother. I don't know if he knew. I never knew it, until my mother died."

He said it in such a rush that the words came jumbling out, so she had to decipher and consider them.

"I am trying to tell you something, but I am doing it so badly."

He stopped, shaking his head. Eve put her hands up to her ears.

"Don't be so stupid, you are talking silly words."

Michael gently removed her hands from her ears. When he spoke again, it was quietly but firmly.

"How do you think we have that shop in the centre of town? Edward moved my mother and I here from Cork when I was just a baby. We were near him, and it was easy to tell everybody the story of a widow left with a baby. I never knew about Edward Brannigan being my father until my mother died. In her will, she also requested that I never let on to Arnold. We never spoke about it, but I always thought Arnold knew something, because I was about the only person from the town he trusted."

"Is that why you love Ludlow so much?"

"I have always loved Ludlow, even when I did not know about Edward."

"You had a right to it, just like Arnold."

"Edward left us well provided for; I have no complaints. I love

258

Ludlow Hall, Eve. If I could have bought the place, I would, but that was not to be."

"How can you not be bitter that Arnold ran it into the ground? Ed Carter was his son and all he wanted to do was destroy Ludlow Hall."

"Connie's husband? The poor man."

"His American mother was well provided for. I have only just found out. Arnold would have nothing to do with his son."

"Eve, all I ever wanted growing up was a father. If I am to be bitter about anything, let it be that. Similar to Ed Carter's case, my mother gave up my right to that for a monthly stipend. The Brannigan men knew how to buy silence."

"Arnold would have liked a brother."

"He had one, he just didn't realise it."

They sat, the breeze ruffling his hair, curling around her ankles, making her shift her feet, because she was cold. A dog ran past, snuffling the ground. They both looked for the owner, but she was far away, crossing the far paddocks, not caring the dog was running loose through the gardens.

"Connie is right: some people have no respect at all," Eve said.

"Why did you give me back the ring, Eve?" The question was asked so gently, but the force of the anguish behind it was powerful.

She followed the dog with her eyes as it scooted across the fields to its owner.

"I felt I was not good enough for you. What am I now? Only a stupid woman who has been duped by her husband." She got up, stamping her feet to get warm. "I allowed myself to be duped. I loved Ludlow Hall so much, I was blind to everything else." She stood directly in front of him. "Michael, at this minute I don't care about anything. I love you. I may not deserve you, but I love you."

He stood in front of her.

"I only want you, Eve. I would live in a makeshift house with a tin roof, if I was with you."

She punched him playfully. "No you wouldn't, you would use your two hands to make it into a mansion. That is the sort of man you are, Michael."

He laughed, enveloping her in a tight hug, kissing the top of her head. "I don't want to spend another day without you at my side, Eve." He pulled out the jeweller's box.

"Put it on my finger, Michael, it can be the engagement and wedding ring. We don't need to stand in front of anyone to declare our love."

He did as she bid, sliding the ring on the second finger of her left hand.

"Hetty will be disappointed to be deprived of a day out." She laughed.

"There will be talk."

"Silly talk in this day and age. What do I care?" She corrected herself. "What do *we* care?"

He laughed and they walked on, their arms wrapped around each other, along the yew walk and across the front paddock to the car. As they passed Ludlow Hall, Eve snuggled closer to Michael.

"Time enough to tell Connie, I think," she said.

Date: May 18, 2013
Subject: THE LUDLOW LADIES' SOCIETY

Ludlow ladies,
   We won all three prizes:

First Prize: Molly's quilt
Second Prize: Ludlow Hall quilt
Third Prize: Rosdaniel quilt

   As you all know, Hetty withdrew her entry before the competition.
   There is a heck of a lot for Davoren to put in his pipe and smoke.
   Seriously, I would at this stage like to extend my commiserations and those of the Ludlow Ladies' Society to Jack Davoren, who came in fourth and runner-up with his beautiful watercolour of Ludlow Hall in the morning light.
   All the entrants, including the winners, will be on display in the drawing room at Ludlow Hall.
   Full steam ahead now for the Obama visit and the opportunity to show off Molly's quilt and the Ludlow Hall quilt. So exciting!
   Kathryn Rodgers,
   Chairwoman

29

Making her way through the hall, Connie checked her appearance in the mirror. Last week she had gone to Arklow on Hetty's insistence and had her hair coloured and cut. Patting her auburn bob, she poked at one stray hair, pushing it into place.

Bill had said to expect him around eleven and it was that now.

Fingering roses in the vase on the hall table, she was almost sick she was so nervous. Connie fumbled, rearranging the flowers, her mind racing that maybe he had decided not to come after all. When she heard a car on the avenue, her heart flipped, but when it went around the back of the house, she knew it was not him.

Rebecca Fleming stuck her head around the kitchen door.

"Just checking, Connie," she said loudly, while stepping into the kitchen, "the men are not disturbing you too much? Wow, you look lovely."

"I am expecting a friend to arrive from the US today."

"Must be some friend. Don't heed us; we will work away in the barn. You don't mind if we paint the walls white to brighten it up?"

"That is fine. Please come in and help yourselves to tea, coffee, cookies."

"Don't worry about those men, they will be fine with a breakfast roll and a takeaway tea from the service station on the Ballyheigue Road," she said, pulling the back door shut before Connie had time to answer.

Connie went into the dance studio. Pacing deliberately across the floor, she waited for him. When they danced the tango, it was only the two of them. They could have been in front of an audience of thousands, but it was only her and him: close, slow, purposeful, deliberate steps, their backs straight, their dance intimate and intense, their passion in the movement.

It was the happiest of times getting to know and love each other, devastating when he said he had a job offer in California.

"Let's start a new life together, just you and me."

He made it sound so easy, but it was terribly complicated. If she could roll back the years, she would tell him she was pregnant, that she did not know if he or Ed was the father. She would tell him of her intention to stay with the father. Ed, she thought, needed her. She wanted a stable home environment for the baby. Her fear that her relationship with Bill might not last made her feel she had no choice but to stay with Ed.

Mindful of Ed, and afraid of the hurt he would suffer, she chose to stay. When Molly was born, it was the happiest time.

If she had a dull ache in her heart, it was the price to pay for giving baby Molly a stable and happy home. Three and a half years later, when Bill returned to Manhattan, he looked her up. It mattered little that it coincided with a time when Ed, under severe financial pressure, was edgy and distant: the minute she saw Bill walking towards her, she knew she loved him. She immediately regretted her decision to stay with her husband. Bill had stepped lightly across the dance studio floor, as if no time had passed. They chatted and laughed, and she felt so alive she did not want it to end. She had to pick Molly up from day care, so they arranged to meet the next day. She told Ed she had to work late, she had to give extra classes ...

Connie shook herself and went back to the drawing room window. The room was bright, the windows gleaming, the chairs and couches gone, the arts and crafts exhibition ready for the weekend opening, Molly's quilt hanging on the chimney piece. Connie looked out at the fields and driveway that were home to her now. Somehow, she did not know how Bill fitted in here, fitted into her life here.

When she saw the strange car make its way slowly up the avenue, she shrank back, mindful that the bare windows left her exposed. Part of her wanted to hide, a bigger part of her wanted to run to him, but she stayed where she was, a trepidation feeding through her as she waited for the first glimpse of him in too many years.

After Molly died, something happened and nothing happened. She slept and ate, existing, locked in guilt and grief. She knew he spoke to Amy, but she couldn't bear to be near him or even see him. It was not that she blamed him; she blamed herself too much.

Peering hard from her hiding place, she smiled as he came closer. His broad frame appeared uncomfortably cramped in the economy car. When he pulled up at the front, she watched him unfurling from the car like a cat stretching after a long nap. He gave a low whistle as he took in the big house. She watched him skip up the stone steps, tripping along, eager to get inside. As he stamped his feet at the front door to dislodge some dirt, she felt fixed to the spot, tense, waiting for the doorbell to ring. Even so, when the sound twirled across the hall, bouncing through the rooms, she jumped, pain coursing through her, her head thumping. Would he understand and forgive? She did not know.

Sluggishly, she made her way to the front door, faltering when the bell sounded again. Glancing in the mirror, she flicked a thread from her shoulder before pulling back the door.

"Sorry, Bill, I was at the top of the house."

"Connie, it is nice to see you."

She did not know what to do. The formality between them was strangely upsetting. She could smell the musky aftershave he always wore. His black hair still flopped over his forehead, almost in his eyes, and the trousers he was wearing were just a little too short, because he could never get a pair long enough to fit his big frame.

"Can I come in, Connie?"

"Yes, of course, I am sorry."

She stepped back to allow him in, feeling the warmth of his body as he brushed past her into the hall.

"You got the flowers?"

"They are beautiful, thank you."

He walked further down the hall, turning right into the drawing room.

"Everybody in the town, when I mentioned Ludlow Hall, told me I had to see this exhibition when it opens."

She followed him, not sure how to answer. He stood, gazing at Molly's quilt.

"A fitting tribute. I salute you."

She twiddled with her hair, unsure of what to say. He turned, letting his hand brush her cheek gently.

"I love you, Connie. I wish you would have let me be there for you."

"I am sorry."

"Don't be sorry, just tell me why."

It all happened on a Wednesday; she had planned to leave Ed on the Friday with Molly. In her head, she had composed a note, talking reasonably about separation and access to Molly. Bill, who was in Boston for that week, had given her a key to his place. When Bill came back, she had planned to completely open up, tell him everything.

Now, all these years later, after so much heartache, she still had to find the words to tell him.

He pointed to the quilt. "Thank you for including the pyjama top I bought Molly. She loved it, didn't she?"

"She loved trains. Just like her dad."

Bill swung round. She clenched her fists by her side, the tension rising in her.

"What are you saying, Connie?"

Her heart was racing; pains were shooting across her head. Her brain was fogged over, her anxiety pinching her so she could only blurt it out.

"You are Molly's father, Bill. I got a DNA test back before Ed... before it happened. I was going to tell you ..."

He stepped towards her. "What do you mean?"

"I was going to tell you when you came back from Boston. I found out on the Wednesday, I planned to come to you on Friday with Molly. I'd already told Ed I needed a break. Maybe he suspected about Molly, I don't know."

She put her hand out to steady herself, but Bill did not move to help her.

"Molly is my daughter?"

"Yes."

"Why didn't you tell me?"

"I was going to—"

"How could you do this to me?"

"After she died, I could not even think—"

"I had a right to know."

"I am sorry."

"I had a right to grieve her, to be at her funeral."

"I know."

"I had a right to say goodbye."

"I know."

Connie's voice was croaky dry, tears pushing on to her face.

"Connie, in the months I knew her, I loved her. You know that. I had a right to grieve as her father."

"I can't explain it, only the pain and heartbreak were too much. I did not know what I was doing. I did not want to live. I was only existing. I had a breakdown, Bill. I couldn't even think. I don't remember much of the last two years, a black fog of grief."

She made to move to him, but he put his hands up.

"You shut me out. You should not have done that."

He paced the length of the room.

266

"Connie, I have to take it in. This is huge, I need time."

His face contorted, his fists clenched, he pushed past her to the hall. He wavered for a moment, but he did not turn back. Next thing, she heard the front door bang and the car start up. He took off too quickly, crunching the gears in his rush. She watched Bill's car bump down the avenue towards the rhododendron bush and around the bend out of sight. It was then she allowed herself to collapse on the floor, crying bitter tears.

She was still there when the Ludlow ladies came in for their dance class.

"Jesus, what has happened, Connie?" Hetty shouted, running to her.

Eve, seeing her friend's stricken face, ushered the other women into the dance studio, telling them Connie was feeling a little unwell and would be with them shortly.

"But I thought we were going to be able to see the exhibition, a proper preview before everybody else," Eithne Hall piped up. Eve threw her a fierce look.

"In good time, Eithne. Now please, ladies, go into the dance studio. Start with the warm-up exercises. The class will begin shortly."

Grumbling, the small group made their way into the dance studio, as Eve helped Hetty bring Connie to the kitchen.

"What happened?" Eve asked gently.

Connie did not answer. Hetty scurried off to get the whiskey. She placed a generous measure in front of Connie, who downed it in one go.

"Bill is not coming back. I don't blame him."

"Give him a bit of space. He did not come all the way here to storm off during a row. He will be back," Eve said.

"I told him he was Molly's dad. I got the DNA test results just two days before Ed killed her."

Hetty sat down at the table. "The poor man."

Connie looked at her. "It is terrible news for him. I was wrong,

267

I know that now, but I was not thinking straight. He surely can see that."

"Give him time," Eve said quietly. She looked at Connie. "Do you think Ed suspected?"

Connie let her head drop into her hands, afraid to answer that possibility.

"I can't take the dance lesson, not now."

"Not a bother, we can manage on our own. Hetty, you set up the music and what have you, I will be along in a few minutes to help whip the women into shape," Eve said.

Hetty, slightly miffed Eve was trying to get rid of her, nevertheless did as she was bid.

Eve reached out, holding Connie lightly across the shoulders.

"You have come so far. This is just another hurdle. Bill's true colours will shine through. Give him time. Only you know the pain he is feeling right now."

"He hates me, for sure."

"He shouldn't. There will be outrage, huge pain and, hopefully too, the realisation you did what you had to do at the time, good or bad."

"I hope you are right, Eve."

Eve smiled, silently saying a prayer she was right and this poor woman could somehow grab a chance of happiness with the man she clearly loved.

"I had better get into the dance studio. I hope it is still standing with that lot horsing about unsupervised," she said, leaving Connie sitting tracing the contours of a pink flower on the oilcloth, so deep in thought that she did not even hear Eve leave.

The Ludlow ladies in the dance studio had a lot of ideas about what was wrong with Connie Carter, but neither Eve nor Hetty would be drawn on it.

Kicking off her shoes and walking to the top of the class, Eve clapped her hands to grab the group's attention.

"Ladies, the best we can do at this stage is get on with it

268

for Connie's sake. She is under the weather, but we enjoy the dancing so much we will carry on regardless."

"Are you going to show us your fancy footwork, Eve?" Eithne called out, to the sniggers of the others.

"I am going to do my best," Eve said, motioning Hetty to switch on the music. "One, two, three, turn." Eve tried to avoid looking in the mirror. Not all the women joined in, until Hetty had her say.

"Eve, we are mightily sick of these meek steps. Could we not change the tempo? I was going to ask Connie anyway." Hetty ran to her handbag, pulling out a CD. "Anyone for line dancing?"

A chorus of approval ran through the group, making Eve laugh.

"All very well, but do any of us know line dancing?"

Hetty stepped to the front of the group. "I have been teaching myself at home, following a video. I could show everybody." Hetty gave the CD to Eithne to put on. "It is the Cowgirl's Twist, but it will do fine for us today," she said, making the others snigger. Hetty, ignoring the excitement, got in front of the group. "I will teach a few basic steps. Let's have fun! Follow me," she said, turning her back to them.

Eve turned the music down a little, so they could properly hear Hetty.

Hetty, her hands down by her sides, called out loud as she moved across the floor.

"Follow me, right foot, left behind, right again and bring the left to meet the right."

She did not wait for them.

"Change to the left. Left foot, right behind, left again, bring the right to meet the left foot."

Not able to keep up, some got their sides wrong, bumping against each other, collapsing giggling when they shuffled the wrong way.

"Hetty, I think we will do it one leg at a time," Eithne quipped, and the others laughed loudly.

Hetty persisted until each woman concentrated on her steps. The mood lightened and there was the odd happy giggle.

When the doorbell rang, they ignored it, forgetting about it when there was not a persistent follow-up.

"I think we may have found our dance. Connie will kill us," Marcella said, as they gathered up their things and moved to the exhibition in the drawing room.

"I have to say I am not surprised Molly's quilt has been picked for the Obama tour: head and shoulders above the rest," Eithne Hall announced, as they moved along examining in detail each item on display.

When the time came to leave, it was Hetty and Eve who let out the Ludlow ladies.

"Do you think we should stick around and see how Connie is?" Hetty asked.

"I think maybe she wants to be on her own. We can check later or tomorrow," Eve said, smiling when she saw Hetty's face fall.

Date: May 20, 2013
Subject: THE LUDLOW LADIES' SOCIETY

Ludlow ladies,

We have to pick a representative to travel to Glendalough and be on hand in case Michelle Obama has any questions regarding our memory quilts.

While I was willing to put myself forward and endure the security red tape that surrounds a US president, it has been pointed out by a number of you that Eve Brannigan might be the best person for the job.

Never one to push myself forward, and mindful of the high stakes, I am going to withdraw my name. We cannot afford, ladies, to be bogged down by petty rivalry at such an important time for the Society.

It seems fitting that Eve Brannigan should represent this society at the Obama exhibition. Eve has been the backbone of the Ludlow Ladies' Society for decades now and we all love her so. If anyone represents all that is good about a Ludlow lady, it is Eve, who in her own life has triumphed over adversary. This too is the woman who gave a lifeline to our society, when we needed it most. Eve is a beautiful, kind person and an excellent representative for the Ludlow Ladies' Society. We are so proud of her and of the quilt completed by Connie, with the help of both Hetty and Eve, which will go on display at the Obama exhibition.

The Ludlow Ladies' Society has been propelled into the limelight and we will not be found lacking at this auspicious time.

Kathryn Rodgers
Chairwoman

30

Eve arrived early at Ludlow Hall. She was already busy tidying up the fabric left over after the memory quilts, when Hetty came along.

"I thought you could do with a bit of help, can't have you overdoing it, considering you are meeting the First Lady later in the week."

"Are you jealous?" Eve laughed.

"Damn right I am, you will be plastered over the *Wicklow People* as well."

"I was thinking more of an interview on *Good Morning America*."

Hetty dropped the patches from her hand. "Are you serious?"

"No," giggled Eve. Hetty made to swipe at her with a long panel of purple lace fabric.

"You had me going there for a while," Hetty said, her face betraying that she was still slightly miffed. Looking out the window, she saw Connie.

"I am surprised to see Connie giving a class."

"She is made of steel sometimes, said she could not let her business go down or Ed Carter would have won out."

"I would have buckled a long time ago."

"Somehow, I don't think you would."

Hetty went to the far end of the room, where a pile of fabric was stashed in the corner.

"Are you making your outfit for meeting Michelle Obama?"

Eve straightened up. "I am not. Don't you think I have scrimped and scraped long enough? Michael is bringing me up to Arnotts in Dublin tomorrow, I am sure I will find something."

"Don't go for green, too obvious. Blue would be lovely on you."

Hetty looked around when Eve did not answer.

Eve was folding Molly's little clothes left over after making the quilt, carefully putting them in a special pink box Connie had bought in Arklow. She pulled a blue fleece jacket from inside a red jacket to fold it separately. Catching it up, folding it in half, she felt the crumple of something balled into the pocket. Sticking her hand in, she picked out a piece of paper.

Bright blue paper from a child's notebook, with butterflies across the top, it was never intended to carry heavy thoughts. The writing was adult and rushed. Casting her eye over it, Eve felt a weakness pass over her, a piercing cry emanating from inside her.

Hetty rushed to her.

"What is wrong? Has something happened?"

Eve, buckling over, held the note out to Hetty.

"From the child's pocket."

Hetty flattened it out, before reading it slowly and carefully.

"Jesus Christ, does Connie know about this?"

"I wouldn't say so."

"Does she have to know? It will kill her."

"We have to tell her."

They walked over to the window together, to watch Connie in the field with the mother and toddler group dancing with big bouncy balls.

"I hate to shake her world up again," Hetty said.

"She is strong."

Hetty shivered. "That will take more than strength."

"We will wait until her classes are over. You may have to teach line dancing again to the Ludlow ladies," Eve said, and Hetty, though she tried not to, giggled.

Eve folded the note along the worn lines of the paper.

"I will put it back in the pocket. She will want it like that."

They worked quietly, gathering up the last bits of fabric and placing them in boxes, brushing up stray threads still left on the rug.

"Michael can put them up in the attic for her another time. Just now we can push the boxes into the kitchen," Eve said.

When they heard Connie waving goodbye to her class, they waited nervously, standing in the middle of the kitchen. Connie came in, a big smile on her face.

"Those kids are such darlings. I feel better from just being with them." She stopped, looking from Eve to Hetty. "What's up?"

Eve held out the blue fleece.

Connie gasped.

"Where did you get that? Molly wore it the day before she died. I looked for it, could never find it."

"It was caught inside a jacket. They must have been taken off together."

Connie's heart skipped. She could see Molly in her rush at the door, pulling the two of them off, shouting when she got stuck, so that Connie had to help her. They were both laughing, Connie throwing the red jacket on the shelf beside the shoes, not bothering to pick it up when it fell down the back.

"There is something in the pocket."

"What?"

Eve pushed the fleece into Connie's hands.

"We are going back in to do the final bits in the drawing room. We will be there if you need us."

Hetty, passing Connie, gave her a quick hug.

"Stay strong, sweetheart."

Connie, her hands shaking, opened out the fleece. Clasping it to her face, she felt the softness, feeling Molly, smelling her, running with her in the woods that day, laughing over food at the local diner.

Gingerly, she put her hand in the pocket, caressing the crumple of paper. Gently pulling it out, she unfolded it carefully.

My lovely Molly,
   Come dance with me. Trust me, little one, and we will dance all day every day.
   I love you so completely.
   Mommy is going to leave. I know she is going to take you away from me.
   I can't let that happen, we must be together always.
   I have found a way. Mommy is strong. She can be on her own.
   I want to take you to another place where we can play every day.
   Come dance with me. Trust me, little one, and we will dance all day every day.
   Daddy

Her heart thumped. Anger tore through her. She had never thought of that fleece until the boxes arrived, but she did not see it. Ed had run and jumped in the woods with them, making mountains of leaves. He had stood watching Molly laugh, screech and play. How could he do that, and then what followed? The note might have been written to Molly, but Connie was sure Ed meant it for her. It was a cruel act carefully thought out and designed to torment her.

Suddenly, she crushed the note tight in the grip of her hand. Reaching for a saucepan, she fired it in. Quickly, before she had time to change her mind, she struck a match, holding it to a bright blue corner. The blue of the note changed to purple and black, and the butterflies were obliterated one by one as the heat of the fire took hold. The inside of the saucepan blackened. Connie waited until every fragment of the note had disappeared, before throwing the pot into the sink and turning on the tap.

His words no longer had power, melted to blackness, flaky first, then sodden, washed away down the drain.

Connie called out to Eve and Hetty that she was going down by the yew walk. She left the house, Molly's voice in her head.

"Here I am. Just love me, Mommy."

"Do you think we should go after her?" Hetty asked.

Eve, walking to the kitchen to throw a few last threads she had found in the corner of the drawing room in the bin, saw wisps of smoke in the air, the blackened pan in the kitchen sink.

"Somehow, I think she is fine. We will get a start on tidying up the Hall. She wants it looking right for the exhibition's official opening tomorrow."

★

Connie sat on the bench at the yew walk. People were trooping into Ludlow Hall, walking around to the back to the country market. The gardens, yew walk and lake were cordoned off. She hoped the visitors would respect the blue rope, the small signs saying "no entry".

Ludlow Hall was a hive of activity. Rebecca Fleming's laugh penetrated through, the outside generator for the industrial-type fridges hummed loudly and there were the cries of children playing in the front paddock while their mothers bought food at the market.

There were times when she had found some comfort in the thought that Ed must have been out of his mind, deluded, or that he had killed himself in despair after suffocating Molly. The note put all that to nought.

This was the second note of his she had set alight. She had burned the note he had tossed on the kitchen counter and was found by police. It was a different time, the burning offering no reprieve from the words, which haunted her every waking minute.

All I ask is that you understand and forgive, Connie, and bury us together.

She refused to comply with his request, standing firm that her daughter would not be interred with her killer. Unable to vent her anger on Ed, she blocked Bill from her life when she should have taken him in. She pushed him away, instead of inviting him to share together their enormous grief.

A small child came toddling down the yew walk, skipping, sometimes falling and picking himself up. Connie looked to see if there was a parent hovering nearby. The three-year-old catapulted past her, making towards the jetty and the lake.

When nobody appeared to follow, Connie ran after him. Catching his hand, she turned him around, enjoying the feel of his little hand in hers, his innocent trust in the direction she was taking him. They were nearly back at the house when a young woman, her face blotted with worry, tore into the yew walk shouting, "Colm. Colm."

The boy answered, pulling his hand from Connie, pelting towards his mother. She scooped him up, laughing and crying at the same time, pirouetting across the ground like it was a stage. When she saw Connie, she stopped abruptly.

"I thought he was gone to the lake," she said, tears of relief flowing down her face. "You are her, aren't you, Molly's mum?"

"Yes."

"I am sorry about what happened to Molly."

Connie nodded, tears gurgling, rising inside her.

The young woman, mindful she had raised ghosts, said she had better go.

Understand. Forgive.

Connie was walking back to her seat when she heard a step fast behind her.

"Connie, can we talk?"

Bill looked like he had not slept, his clothes crumpled, his hair tousled.

"I came back yesterday, rang the bell ..."

"I didn't hear. The Ludlow Ladies' Society had their line dancing music blaring loud."

"I want to apologise, to say I understand everything. For my part, I found Molly and I lost her in the same few minutes."

Connie sat down, silently crying, tears pouring out of her. He knelt beside her, looking into her face.

"I was outraged in my grief. I was only thinking of myself." He cupped her face. "I understand. You did what you did, to survive."

She made to pull from him, but he would not let her.

"I love you, Connie. Can we have a second chance?"

"Do you really understand?"

"I am in pain, I am angry, but not at you. I am grieving, but I understand. We can make it work."

A breeze swirled the light cherry blossom leaves around them. He gently picked two out of her hair.

"Can you forgive me?" she asked.

"There is nothing to forgive."

She leaned into him and he held her, like a father holds a tired child on his shoulder. After a while, he eased gently away. Taking her hand, he pulled her to her feet.

They walked together along the yew walk, the sun shining across the paddocks, the daffodils swaying in the light breeze, three children playing hide and seek among the flower beds, Hetty busy cleaning the brass on the front door, Ludlow Hall busy on market day.

Date: June 20, 2013
Subject: THE LUDLOW LADIES' SOCIETY

Ludlow ladies,

We are beyond thrilled to report on the huge success of the visit of the First Lady of the United States to Glendalough, Co. Wicklow.

We are so proud of our small part in that success and beyond proud to have represented our community there.

We are very happy to report that not only did Michelle Obama stop off at the exhibit stand of the Ludlow Ladies' Society, but she chatted to our representative Eve Brannigan about Molly's quilt and the delight of patchwork.

Such an honour, and the occasion will go down as exceedingly important in the history of our humble society. It is the highlight of the year for us Ludlow ladies.

For my own part, I had the honour of receiving an invitation to a private meeting with Mrs Obama and her two beautiful daughters. It was all hush-hush, but wonderful when one's connections can produce the goods! It was quite bizarre: we talked about the nasty midges at Glendalough, which had no respect for the presidential party. I gave them the name of my favourite perfume, which I find to be a wonderful insect repellent, and they thanked me for the tip.

Ludlow ladies, let us pledge all this new-found fame will not go to our heads and we will continue to serve our community, just as before.

We are asking, please, for a very good turnout for the next meeting of the Ludlow Ladies' Society at Ludlow Hall next Tuesday night. We are so looking forward to Eve giving us a detailed account of her wonderful adventure and tête-à-tête with the First Lady.

As a sidenote, Jack Davoren has offered us space in the new Town Hall when it is rebuilt, but I, as chairwoman, turned him down. How a little bit of fame can lead to a major change of heart.

Ludlow Hall has been good to us, and particularly in our hour of need. The Ludlow Ladies' Society is not going to abandon Ludlow Hall now.

Jack Davoren, in fairness, took the rejection well and said he would just have to put it in his pipe and smoke it.

Indeed.

Kathryn Rodgers,
Chairwoman